IGNITE

IGNITE

THE TERRIBLE LOVE MEMOIRS: BOOK ONE

MARIE A. WISHERT

atmosphere press

Published by Atmosphere Press

Ignite
2021, Marie A. Wishert

atmospherepress.com

In loving memory of Shane Allen Burton. The day I reached out to celebrate the publishing of this book was the day you left this earth. Thank you for bringing my writer's voice to life. You were a brilliant and thought-provoking editor, and you saw me through the craziest of times. I know you are somewhere dancing in the purple rain my friend.

CONTENTS

It stands to good reason I am crazy, but imagine for *one second,* that I'm not. What if everything I'm doing is calculated? Would you stick around for the end?

There are days in our winters where the temperatures drop to dangerously low levels, despite the sun shining like flames burning up the sky. On these days, the sun's rays reach forth and penetrate prisms of diamond dust scattered at low levels in the atmosphere, melting and deflecting instead of penetrating earth and life. They refract horizontally and project arcs of brilliant light known as "sun dogs," reminiscent of two rainbows, with one bright red beam initiating the pattern then convalescing outwardly through the established spectrum of change,

Red

Orange

Yellow

Green

Blue

Indigo

Violet

But these arcs are not rainbows; they are much denser in form, so individual colors are never seen. The arcs span broad widths and possess a center white flare, as if they themselves are capable of luminescence.

The effect is positively ethereal.

On these phantom days, the presence of the sun does not prophesize warmth and life and all of the things associated with properly projected sun's rays; rather, it prophesizes something frigid and maleficent is in the air.

On these perfectly clear days, when sun rays pass

through ice crystals and warp—reconstructing in a panoramic fresco hung in the sky—I am acutely aware that it is fucking cold. But, on these days, I am also reminded of another truth: even though life is suspended and everything is crystallized, and it is fucking cold, there can still be transcendental beauty and wonder and awe.

I find peace in that.

CHAPTER 1

It was on one of those surreal and frozen days that I found myself positioned at an unfamiliar table, nursing a mocha to avoid the books stacked in front of me. Instead of the books, I was studying the walls. *These walls are similar. Maybe I can get used to this place. There's some kind of potential here.* I thought optimistically, as though solidifying commonality would recreate the ambiance I sought from my regular college study space, a space mysteriously closed that morning.

The brick walls of this nouveau coffee shop intrigued me. The design was haphazard and chaotic, with mortar so thick the full tip of my finger traced its path with free space on either side. Its pattern was impossible to predict—in obvious disarray, so much so it had to be intentional. The walls of my coffee shop were brick as well, only they were structured and tight and uniform, with layers of mortar barely visible between the dense stacks.

But there was something unique about the mortar I hadn't seen at first glance—tiny holes bored out; little caves hidden amongst the grainy labyrinth. As I traced my finger along, I was pleased to find inside of some were hidden notes. Sacred thoughts strangers tucked away, and I became eager to discover what kind of wisdom they held. Optimistic I could locate a note capable of smoothing over my discontented mood, I selected the first one I saw, flattened it, and read:

"There's no better job than a blow job."

I blinked slowly at it, wishing my stare the power to engulf the thing in flames.

Goodness sakes, thoughts from a high school genius. Dejectedly, I crumpled it up to a cavern shaped size then shoved it back into its hole. *There's got to be something better here.*

Grasping the next eye-catching one, I unrolled it with cautious skepticism.

"My brother is a tool," it read, in meticulous penmanship reminding me of the effort I put forth when I was a ten-year-old girl.

Wow. Nice handwriting. Thanks for the insider info on your brother. I gently rolled the paper back to its form and situated it back in its hole. *One more and then I give up.*

My hand drifted slowly across a higher line mortar, outside the reach of little arms, seeking out another. Once I located one, I held onto the promising charm of the third time. Focusing my gaze upon the paper while unrolling it timidly, I pressed the edges down with pointed fingers and read:

"Take every chance you get in life because some things only happen once."

Well now, here's something. . . Squinting my eyes shut, I tried to imagine embracing all the opportunities I'd seen. How different would my life be had I gone to the art school I'd been accepted to in California? What if I hadn't backed out because my parents didn't support me?

It didn't matter . . . those lives were for other people, not me. It wasn't just art school I'd skipped out on; I had passed on several adventures citing that I didn't have time or money. Not that I didn't intend to venture out someday, it's just, I couldn't allow myself until I earned it properly.

As a child of divorce who spent her formative years living in low-income housing, eating welfare subsidized meals, and wearing thrift store clothes, I was intimately aware of the oppressive nature of poverty. My primary objective was to break out of the mold of my youth and create financial independence prior to adventuring. Financial security first meant freedom, freedom to live however I pleased. And my vow was to be entirely independent—prosperity would arise by my volition because, if I earned it, no one could take it away. Anything perceived as outside the confines of my narrow path to a healthy career trajectory set me off track, potentially perpetuating the cycle. It was crucial I keep my head in the game.

My flip phone rang in the middle of this quixotic thinking, with my best friend Katie on the line.

"Sweetieee," I said as I answered the phone.

"Daahhrrling," she replied in a perfect British drawl, sending us both into giggles.

Sensing my volume may be disruptive, I did a quick sweep of the room to see if anyone could overhear. The coffee shop, despite being sparsely dotted with patrons, was packed with sound. A coffee roaster was churning behind the bar, cracking and humming and buzzing contentedly, a fitting din overlaid by the sounds of Snow Patrol. Despite the ambient music, the barista donned large headphones and sat poised on the edge of a barstool, hovering over a book. The coast was clear.

"You won't believe this, but I'm studying at Lena's." I paused there, waiting for the reaction I knew was coming.

"Have you lost your mind? Do you need me to come take you somewhere for therapy?"

"Yes. Yes, darling, I believe I have," I laughed. "Seriously though, I feel so out of place."

"Yes, well, you should have called me. I would have talked you out of going."

Our coffee shop, the Trentino, was a diamond-in-the-rough, and its appeal, to us, was centering. Stepping into its smoke-infused sphere instantly set my mind at ease. Every crucial dive requirement box was checked. Sandwiched between a Moose Lodge and a downtown high-rise slum residence, it was a hipster's paradise hole-in-the-wall outlined with brick and dressed in drab folding tables and chairs. Touring artists, one man shows, and open mic's animated almost every night, but even on the ones where no one was performing, the patrons were all enigmatic and their dialog was priceless entertainment.

Ironically, the first time I went there I was out with a preppy friend who was allergic to smoke and allergic to hipster intellectuals. "This place is horrible!" he declared, directing us right back out the door and driving straight to Lena's. "This is the perfect place to study," he exclaimed, swiftly ushering me inside. I had agreed, but secretly, I knew we uncovered a place where I would be completely at home. The next night, I went back to the Trentino alone, with my books and my Newport's and my secret binder of poetry, and studied the night away. I'd been showing up daily since. I repressed the panic that came when I considered I may have spent the previous day there not knowing it was my last, and carried on explaining.

"Honestly though, I'm a bit concerned. I went to The Trentino and it was closed."

"That's strange."

"I know, right? I went there at nine, right when they open, and the doors were locked and the lights were off..."

"...It's probably this atrocious cold. Or, whoever's opening stayed out all night drinking and couldn't get their car to start from wherever they found themselves this morning," she said, finishing with her signature low pitched laugh.

Her scenario was highly likely; yet, though The Trentino didn't abide by commercial grade rules, enough people held keys that someone should have stepped up to get the doors open on time.

"Let's go with that," I said, though my heart wasn't buying it. "In any event, I'm trying to forget about that right now so I can focus . . . not going so hot. Anyway, listen to me blathering. What's up?"

"Oh, ya know, just getting fabulous for the party tonight, darling," she said.

"Of course, of course. I'd expect nothing less. You always do start early."

"I'll be starving myself all day in anticipation of the brat we'll be splitting."

"That's my Patsy. Well done," I laughed. Splitting a brat was her way of jabbing at my lunacy. On one of our first outings together, we biked from Fargo to my parent's place in Detroit Lake, about a forty-five mile trip. Then, at dinner, when my mom asked how many brat's we'd each like, I spoke up and said she'd split one with me. "You force me to bike all over the world and then suggest my dinner be half a brat?" she had said. "Don't listen to her, I'll take five."

I had to admit she was right, but honestly, I hadn't

thought it strange until she'd called me out. Now, she called me out all the time.

"How 'bout you call me back in thirty? I've gotta at least try to study."

"You got it Eddie."

After closing the cover of my phone, I returned to surveying the space. The smell of roasted coffee lingered in the air, but the usually sweet aroma hit me as pungent. The scent was disquieting. Being there felt empty and hollow and foreign. And something else new, something else about my senses was off. Foggy seemed like an appropriate descriptor, which, in frozen weather, could be plausible. My body could be converting to a hibernation-like state, which may account for the sluggishness weighing down my limbs that felt nearly insurmountable. Yet, my instincts kept trying to point at something else. Something I wasn't emotionally prepared to feel.

As much as I wanted to believe I was calculated and in control, I was also human. For me, the emotional effects of birth control hormones were devastating, so I relied on a natural method. I maintained a tidy logbook of dates, analysis, and projections, and found the prediction of my cycles came easily. I followed that calendar like a bible. It was fool proof, I believed. I had it down to an art, I believed. Utterly pleased with my cleverness, I claimed to be unfailingly in tune with my female "equilibrium of normal." In hindsight, I should have taken my ultra-confidence for smugness and been less cavalier.

Something must have been calculated wrong because my body wasn't right. The delay heightened my senses, and I felt as though there was an increase in the density of my blood, lagging its pace through my vessels. This awareness, coupled with an unfamiliar sluggishness I couldn't shake, was indisputably outside the equilibrium of normal.

The previous month there had been one night I assumed was safe to have sex, but there was a solid chance it was not. Over Christmas break I had my wisdom teeth removed and ended up with a dry socket, so I spent a week mixing Vicodin and alcohol like only college kids on holiday break can, rendering my body and judgment clouded. The potential uncertainty was more pressing than my studies. I switched to circling days on the previous month's calendar and counting back and forth, checking and rechecking.

It was in the middle of this activity Katie rang again.

"Darrrrling, what are you doing?"

"Does pain medication delay someone's ovulation?" I blurted out, unthinkingly.

"Good lord, why would you ask such a thing?"

"It's a sample question on a practice test for physiology," I lied.

"Well, if I were blindly guessing, I'd say yes. But you need to finish up there and start studying real life. Rudolph's party is less than two hours away. We need to get our drink on beforehand. I can't walk into that environment both sober and starving. What do you think this is?"

"Okay, okay. I'll wrap up and head home. Studying in this place isn't possible anyway. Let's meet at my place in thirty, take three shots of tequila rose, split a brat, and then head over," I said, my mouth forming the stream of words in automation while my head formulated an entirely different action plan.

"Fabulous," Katie threw in for her signature closing.

I flipped the phone shut and looked at the mess on my table. A purple binder decorated with mandala type curlicues and dots sat closed next to a small stack of text books. Shaking my head at the wasted effort, I cleared the table and shoved the books into my bag. While lifting my mocha to toss back the dregs, the napkin stuck to the bottom of the cup. I peeled it away and rubbed it between my fingers, sliding the front and back layers together, seeking to determine its quality. It felt sturdy. Sturdy like it would hold ink and not bleed. I ripped off a little corner piece to compose a note of my own. With trembling fingers, I allowed the fear jabbing at the corners of my psyche to take shape–*I think I might be pregnant,* I wrote, then rolled it up and slipped it into a vacant hollow among the cavernous mortar.

CHAPTER 2

The engine of my Taurus protested in soft murmurs, slowly drawing out the process of turning over. *We've got this,* I spoke, rubbing the dashboard in consolation, though my chattering jaw was so spastic my teeth risked cracking and my body was so stiff I wasn't sure I should drive. Letting out a scream, I pressed my foot hard on the gas, revving the engine until it settled into a throaty purr. Once the car and I achieved safe driving temperatures, I shifted out of park and traveled one block down the street, stopping in front of a CVS pharmacy.

Once inside, I bee lined for the family planning aisle. Almost as if on purpose, the fluorescent light overhead flickered in short bursts and long spans, with chaotic flurries in between. It wasn't an environment fit for meandering, so despite a veritable buffet of test offerings, I had to just decide. The single test pack Clear Blue Easy was the first to catch my eye. It was simple. Clear. Blue. Easy. What's not to love about each of those three things? I snatched it from the shelf and tucked in under my jacket sleeve, grabbing a red Powerade and Snickers as I made my way to the counter.

Intermingling the items and approaching the register with the confidence of a woman collecting her afternoon needs, I smiled at the youthful cashier. His face was so smooth he appeared younger than sixteen, but I knew in his case looks were deceiving. CVS cashiers in my town had to be at least eighteen.

"Hi! Did you find everything okay?" he asked.

"Yep," I said, in the polite yet closed off sort of way one does when trying to shut down conversation.

"It's a cold one, huh?" he carried on, missing my cue and scanning the test like it was an innocuous thing, tossing it in the bag hanging next to him.

"Yeah, sure is," I replied, wondering if he was so young and innocent that he had no idea what he'd been handling.

"The bank clock display was negative 15 degrees this morning. Isn't that amazing?"

"Amazing," I agreed, twirling my credit card while watching him scan and toss the other two items into the bag.

"Can't beat these winters," he smiled broadly. "Braving this cold makes us a special breed."

"Special breed indeed," I agreed, trying to return the smile sincerely, though the overwhelming anxiety from purchasing a pregnancy test squashed the effort and resulted in a grimace at best.

"That'll be $18.27."

I passed over the card and held my face in the same pose while shifting weight from foot to foot, eager for him to complete the exchange.

"Enjoy! Have a great night!" he said cheerily, extending the bag toward me.

I clasped it and rushed away quickly, unable to match his enthusiasm to tender a fitting farewell. Shaking my head at the whole ridiculousness of the day, I muttered to myself while passing through the front door in haste.

Did he see what I just bought? Who sells someone a

pregnancy test and then says "Enjoy!" Enjoy!?! How did he expect me to respond? "Thanks! Here's to the hope this thing comes out negative. And also a great night to you!" Goodness' sakes–

As soon as I stepped outside, my silent muttering got cut off by a blast in the face with icy air. There was a futile attempt to shield it by turning my head as far as I could sideways, which resulted in only half a cheek lighting up in pain from the impact of high velocity frozen crystals. I stood statue still while the wind blasted past, and through squinted eyes, I looked upon luminous arcs circling a blazing sun on the backdrop of a pale blue sky. *Sundogs, ugh.*

Sundogs–my mom always said–meant the day was going to get colder, which, to me, was just bad manners. Sundogs only came out when it was deathly cold, like rainbows to a sun shower. And they were an awe-inspiring sight. But for something so magnificent to mean something so unpleasant: that bitter freezing cold was a precursor to even more bitter freezing cold–was all too much to accept. Looking at the sky right then, some more beautiful reason seemed necessary. Perhaps, the striking imagery was trying to thaw my frozen core? And, maybe, even though the air was menacing, beautiful transformation was on the horizon. That was a forecast I could get behind. Soothed by the striking beauty of a sky bursting into flames, I trained my eyes back to my vehicle and got moving.

* * *

Back home, I clutched the newly acquired pregnancy

test with shaky fingers. Pulling open the edges of the box, I first came across a complexly folded manual of a thin, gossamer type paper. I spread it carefully across the table and stared down the plethora of minuscule words dancing across it, convincing myself this was schoolwork. It wasn't hard to think that way, as the chemical reaction had recently been a lesson in my biochemistry class.

I already knew the results came from invisible lines inside two ovals, lines that would pick up stain after coming into contact with urine. One oval contained a reactive line detecting the hallmark pregnancy hormone, hCG. If present, the hormone became bound by an initiator, kicking off a cascade of activity ending in a colored line. The other oval's line picked up color regardless—serving as the control.

Clear Blue Easy had two clearly blue lines in the event of a pregnancy, which, as the manual disclaimer said, was never a one-hundred percent certainty. Yet, given that ninety-eight percent accuracy was touted on the box, those things held some sway.

Comprehending the science was easy, the hard thing was moving forward with the test. I focused on the miraculous product of applied biochemistry, pounded a water, and waited for the urge to pee. When it came, I followed the directions to a T. The test, once complete, required five uninterrupted minutes on a flat surface while the chemical reactions took place. So, as soon as it was secure and stable on the floor, I turned my back to the thing and walked away. Then, I anxiously phoned the other person who would be affected by the result, Logan, to kill the allotted five minutes of eternity.

"Hey Ruby," he answered.

"Hey," I began, then paused, unsure how this was supposed to go.

"What's up?"

"Ummm. I thought you should know," I began with feeble confidence, "that I am taking a pregnancy test before heading to Rudolph's with Katie."

Silence filled his end of the line.

"It's nothing. I'm sure I'm fine. I'm exercising caution because . . . well . . . obviously. And I don't want to do anything harmful if there's a chance."

His breath wasn't even audible.

"I'm sure it's fine. I'm going to check it right now," I said as I re-entered the bathroom.

There, upon my cream linoleum, rested the little test, centered perfectly in a square outlined by lines mimicking grout. The two matching ovals were split at their center, each possessing a thick dark blue line, as plain as day and as bold as the arcs in the sky. Two clearly extraordinary blue lines, suggesting, with ninety-eight percent accuracy, that I was pregnant.

A shock wave radiated through my body—everything flickered and dimmed. The entire world as I knew it pulsed and mutated. I felt it. I felt the atmosphere in my immediate presence warp, thick and menacing, densely compacting its elements. I opened my mouth, but words would not form, my mind was too black to translate its confusion to vocalizations. There was only one thing I was capable of blurting out after a solid minute of silent mouthing, perceived mentally as a whisper but delivered as a scream.

"FUCK!" I yelled, hanging up and tossing my phone at the test.

I ran through the hall and bounded down the stairs, bursting out the front door without a winter coat, too fazed to realize death from cold still applied. Fortunately for me, Katie was just pulling up.

"What are you doing?" she said, assessing my status with squinted eyes as I bounded into the passenger seat.

"I just took a pregnancy test, and it came out positive," I said.

Her usually pale Swedish skin flushed, then drained of color. Her grey-blue eyes seemed almost to vibrate as she studied me, but her thin rouged lips stayed uncharacteristically pursed. I locked eyes with her in an attempt to bring calm to the surroundings and confidently carried on.

"Take me to the nearest grocery store; we need to buy more tests. Maybe it was wrong? I don't know. I need more tests," I said, convinced the test was the problem, not me.

By the end of our excursion, we had bought multiple tests, which we brought back to my place for further experimentation. Unfortunately, each and every one I took came out positive. As a control, Katie also took one, but her result was clearly negative. As a last resort, I saved one test to try the following week.

At that point, we decided to go to the party anyway. My world may have been rocked, but until I could make up the two-percent difference, I needed to keep moving forward like it hadn't. And I dreadfully needed a night out, though I promised I would only pretend to drink.

The perplexing closure of our beloved coffee shop was the main topic of conversation, providing an elegant theme around which to wrap my mind. No one had a proper answer, but the consensus was that the owner had financial trouble. But then, in the midst of our conversation, one loose end was teased out. A truly awful thing I'd done earlier that entirely slipped my mind: Logan never heard back from me.

Logan was among the Trentino's regulars who, along with Katie, I considered a best friend. Yet, because Logan was a guy, our relationship fell into a more "it's complicated" category. He was a man who, despite my overtly expressed desire to never settle down, spent all his time with me like a committed boyfriend. When we first met, I'd thought nothing of him, but after meeting up at the Trentino every day for a week, he became this inviting and friendly face, present everywhere I was. He bummed me his Newport's, invited me to house parties, and always had Dr. Pepper and vanilla vodka on hand because he knew the mixture was my favorite.

Logan won me over slowly. He was a man unaffected by the contemporary world which was something I'd never before seen. He had crystal blue eyes that were nearly translucent and wild, curly hair that parted in strange ways. He was bespectacled in defunct glasses and wore baggy, beaten clothes, and didn't belong to any group. Yet, none of that phased me because he was welcoming and compassionate. He didn't stir up any emotions inside me, and I adored that. Around him, I was comfortable enough to relax and simply be me.

With Logan, everything came easily. I was warmed by his presence and loved how he seemed incapable of arrogant opinion—like that brush stroke never hit his canvas. He never challenged or questioned or tried to change who I was, he knew. And he hung around me because he liked me. I'd never met anyone else who wasn't chasing their own agenda and needing me to change to align, and I found that character trait his most attractive. But our relationship was never something I planned on extending past college. He was my friend and we had fun, yet our level of intimacy for other people progressed toward something, and I knew I was leading him on.

Then, to top it all off, I had hung up on him after screaming "FUCK!" and he hadn't heard from me since. Katie and I were so wrapped up in testing and then going to the party that I never even considered he may still be petrified in the center of his couch clutching his phone in silence. No one considered a best friend ought to be treated like that. I dismissed myself from the conversation to give him a ring.

"Hey," I said when he answered the phone.

"Hey," he said, with such strained effort he appeared to be breaking through the silence like it was an invincible enemy.

"I took a lot of tests and they all came out positive, but its fine. I'm fine. I'm at Rudolph's with Katie."

"Do you want me to come join you guys?"

"Might as well. Life goes on, right? We'll be fine. We can figure this all out later," I said, with such assured bravado he knew no more words were necessary.

"Sounds good, see ya soon," he said, and the line went dead.

I stashed my phone back in my bag and returned to the party, projecting a hazy smile. Logan joined us up shortly, and together, we played out in a state as though nothing in our world had changed. We resumed our place with those around us, determined to move forward with routine.

CHAPTER 3

It turned out that ninety-eight percent was one-hundred percent.

"Your test came back positive," said the doctor at my college health clinic. I should have been focusing on what she was saying, but all I could see was her soft brown hair and her soft brown eyes contrasting her long, thick fingers, cracked from the dry winter air. Her fingers were turning the dial of a gadget labeled "pregnancy wheel," while she was saying other things I didn't want to be hearing. After a few stops, she set the wheel atop a manila chart I assumed contained my results and held me in a not-trying-to-pass-judgment gaze.

"By plotting out your history, it looks like you are seven weeks pregnant."

What? That piece of data jarred my brain and brought my focus back to the hard topic. *How the heck did that happen?*

"Oh, no, that's wrong," I insisted. "I just found out. Literally just took the test yesterday because my period was due a few days ago." She started me in a panic, but I knew I must be right.

"It may feel that way," she said, "but the time of conception is not based off missed periods. It's based off of what came previously."

Holding up her pregnancy wheel like a flight attendant

with a seat belt, she reviewed her calculations.

"First, you go back from the first day of your last period and count the weeks forward from there," she said while first setting the window, then rotating along as she spoke. "If everything lines up, you likely conceived on this date," setting another window over the same date circled in my logbook. "Given that, you should be due on October 2nd." She pointed to the output window on the dial. "Now, we work back." She said, rotating an inner dial. "Counting the weeks back from today puts us at seven weeks."

I watched in amazement as she demonstrated, unquestionably, that seven weeks was a reality I had to own. Her calculations aligned perfectly with my logbook, only, I had never looked at the data that way.

"Okay," I said, exhaling slowly.

"You have plenty of time to decide what's right, honey," the doctor said, resting her hands in her lap and tilting her head with a sigh. "There are many ways to proceed from here. I'm going to give you some pamphlets to review. Give yourself a few days to do some research and don't make a decision too hastily."

Reaching out to take the offered items, I thanked her and turned to walk away. But then, I thought of something she was well suited to answer for me.

"I am supposed to become a dentist. Do you think I can still go to dental school if I have a baby?" I said, turning back and looking at her squarely.

"Of course, you can," she said softly. "I had both of my boys during medical school, and I wouldn't ask for things to be any other way."

"Thanks," I said and walked out the door.

Unplanned pregnancy is not something to throw into

casual conversation lightly. In fact, I'm pretty convinced that's how you kill every interaction you ever want to end, so hammering this dilemma out with friends or family was out of the question. I needed to act independently. When I returned home, I set an intention to force a course of action. According to the doctor, there was plenty of time, but I didn't feel like I could waste one second. Shakily, I pulled out a phone book and lowered myself into a chair, seeking to locate numbers for two places. The first was the abortion clinic I used to protest outside downtown and the second was the obstetrics department at the hospital my mother used to work at. It was already pretty obvious from my history with the two places where my heart was leaning, but I couldn't make a decision hastily. I wanted to make both appointments and survey my emotional state surrounding each. Once I analyzed both gut reactions, I vowed to keep whichever felt best.

The abortion clinic's number was listed first, so that was where I started.

"Hello," answered a woman's voice, delivered with such acrimony it seemed as though my call single handedly ruined her day.

"Hello," I said in matched harsh tones, the initial interaction already short-circuiting my mind.

"What can I help you with?"

"I need to make an appointment for an abortion," I said—the words leaving my mouth, but my mind feeling as though another person was saying them.

"How far along are you?"

"Seven weeks."

"Well, we don't have openings for at least another two weeks, so by the time you come in that will make you nine weeks pregnant. I need to inform you that we will be doing an ultrasound as part of this process, and you will hear the baby's heartbeat."

This information was delivered so robotically it seemed as though it was coming from a script. Though void of emotion and tone, the news stunned me. I wasn't prepared to hear a heartbeat. A heartbeat meant this baby was real, which would certainly heighten my guilt. It was all I could do to bark a reply.

"Ok, whatever," I said, trying to reclaim composure. "I'll take your next available."

She set me up for an appointment for a Friday two weeks away. While my fingers struggled to transcribe the appointment to paper, my stomach felt vile and my vision swayed. It was blatantly obvious abortion was not sitting well.

Next, I called the obstetrics department of St Mary's Clinic and connected with a welcoming voice, the polar opposite of the last receptionist. Immediately, her calm demeanor washed the sickness away. That appointment was made contentedly, but I couldn't get in for four weeks due to the doctor's busy schedule. I penciled it in on my calendar and then flipped from one appointment day to the other. My task was complete—I had arranged two future action plans, and their timing was perfect. Two weeks out and two weeks apart. Two weeks, either way, to decide.

Looking at the appointment coming up in two weeks, I closed my eyes and pictured walking out of the clinic, going home to recover, and having to pretend like I was sick for a couple of days. Having to pretend like I just lost that money. Pretending like nothing happened. For the rest of my life, I'd be pretending, and every time I looked people in the eye and lied, a little voice in my head would remind me I killed my child. I had to stop thinking.

Rising from my chair, I paced the room and contemplated. Could I push back the negative stigma my upbringing planted in me surrounding abortion? Having been raised in an extremist religious background—one preaching that abortion resulted in lifelong, life-altering shell-shocked tragedy—I had been fervently anti-abortion through high school. It was only since I started college and started seeing the world through a new lens that I flipped-flopped, becoming an overnight opposite side extremist.

I thought I had converted thought processes entirely, and going through with an abortion would seem normal and logical, but it didn't. Assessing my emotions surrounding the abortion appointment, it was clear I felt it sentenced me to a life mired in sadness and regret. It was not a weight I envisioned myself able to bear. But then, if I kept this child, the dream of becoming an independent woman vanished. Neither Logan nor motherhood had been part of the plan, and I didn't see single parenthood conducive to it either. How the hell does one create financial freedom through a career in dentistry so they can live the life of someone untethered while another being is tethered to them? Neither option logically panned out.

A third option existed that was undeniably hard and equally crushing but did satisfy my needs. Adoption. It was a way. I could give life to this being I created, but not give up mine in the process. Nothing convincing promised I wouldn't unravel in that process either, but it was the only option where my soul sensed peace.

CHAPTER 4

Eight hard months passed. Eight hard months of talking and soul searching, of rifling through pristine scrapbooks compiled by loving couples desperately trying to look attractive on paper. Eight months of doctors' appointments and ultrasounds and maternity clothes. Eight months of questioning this little person—five with him touching me from inside. Eight months of confusion and eight months of torture. Eight months of crying myself to sleep. And then, eight months turned into one single moment that altered the trajectory of my life.

On a Saturday morning, three weeks out from my due date, I reported to my waitressing job at a local wine bar with a pretentious head chef who had all the makings of a reality TV dick. Part of my morning routine was to review the specials with him, and on that particular day, he was feeling feisty.

"Sea bass with fennel salad, parsnip puree, and orange beurre blanc. And beurre blanc has two r's and no k," he said, jabbing at my pad where I'd finished writing.

"Got it," I said, inserting an r and crossing of the k sloppily.

"Also, we have three side options - roasted broccolini, creamed spinach, and haricot verts with almonds and caramelized shallots."

"Sounds good. Thanks."

"Do you even know what a 'haricot vert' is?" he asked, scrunching his face in a cold look reserved for people who matter less than dirt.

I searched my mind for a proper answer, but nothing rightly applied. I had no clue what a "haricot vert" was, and I couldn't have cared less. I looked down at my pad and prayed for the strength to answer kindly.

"No," I muttered quietly, my eyes trained on the ground.

"Maybe you need to go look it up before you try and sell it."

"Why don't you spare me the effort and just tell me?" I replied. More boldly than one should, but I was unable to mask my contempt.

"Because that would make things too easy," he said with a huff, sauntering toward the kitchen.

As soon as his form disappeared into the galley, I bolted for the bathroom, locked up inside the largest stall, and lost my shit completely. Muffling heavy sobs with wadded up tissue held to my face, I cried it out. It was a solid ten minutes before I could unlock the door and wander around to the mirror to gain composure. When I did, the woman gazing back threw me. Something was off. Emotional outbursts were distinctly out of character, and flushed, shiny cheeks looked foreign on me. *That asshole just pushed you too hard. Go out there and show him you're amazing.* I splashed cool water on my face, gave my hair a fluff, and returned as though nothing fazed me.

After discovering from the bartender haricot vert is French for 'green bean,' I hit the floor, worked through lunch, and then turned the restaurant over for dinner. At the end of my shift, when I sat down with the last lunch special and a cup of soup, it was my first time to sit all day. As I settled into the heavy wooden bar stool, I became aware of a familiar sensation. Familiar, though not applicable. What I knew that sensation to mean was currently impossible. If anyone would have asked, "What just happened?" I would have answered, "I got my period," but that would not be right.

In movies and TV when a woman's water breaks, it is this monumental event that leaves people in panicked hysteria. Couples abandoning half-full shopping carts in grocery stores, or rushing out of buildings in haste, but Lamaze class preaches the truth—this is not the case; seventy-five percent of the time, many women just develop a slow leak. The trick is to know when this slow leak has started. My Lamaze class taught a surefire way to test for it.

"You sit on the toilet with a wadded up dry tissue held against your vagina and cough," the Lamaze coach was explaining, while I sat next to a serious faced Logan giving me the eye as I choked on another laugh.

"She wants me to do what?" I asked him under my breath.

"Shhhhh," he said, a grin trying to sneak out from behind his scowl. "You have to take this seriously."

"Surely you can't be serious," I said sarcastically, shaking my head, giving a quick eye roll.

Logan whacked my leg playfully and pointed to the front of the room, nodding his head with a grimace. "Pay attention."

"Okay," I conceded with a frown before turning back to the woman at the front of the room.

"I would recommend trying this at least five times. If

the tissue comes out wet every time, you can be sure your water is broken."

"Well shit, hope I don't have to do that," I whispered to Logan.

It was a good thing I'd paid attention. Excusing myself from the bar, I prepared for another deeply personal session in the bathroom's largest stall, only this time, I wasn't holding wadded up tissue to my face. And low and behold, when I coughed, the tissue got wet. All five times. I decided it was time to call the nurse.

"How far apart are your contractions?" she asked after I'd filled her in on the testing story.

"I'm not having contractions," I answered clearly.

"Are you sure your water broke?" she asked, like it was absurd someone's water could break while they weren't having contractions.

"Positive," I said, "I coughed, and the paper was wet, multiple times. Promise. I'm sure of this."

"And you are certain you aren't having contractions?" she asked.

To be fair, I wasn't certain. With her prompting, I closed my eyes and focused inward, trying to feel if anything was going on in my abdomen. I could sense that maybe the tiniest flurry of activity was starting, like the muscles were slowly waving in sequence, but I had no pain, and I had no discomfort, just the inciting of a premonition that maybe something was happening. It carried little weight.

I said as much in a statement to her.

"Well, if your water broke, you'll be admitted, but you should also be prepared to be sent home if it's not. From everything you've said, it sounds like it's worth a look. Go ahead and grab your hospital bag and head over. I'll let the urgent care staff know you are on your way."

The drive to the hospital was a blur. Somehow Logan wound up there with me. I remember a lady taking me into an urgent care examination room and completing my intake paperwork. I remember being escorted to a labor and delivery room. I remember by the time I crawled up on the bed I knew I wasn't going home because it was obvious I was in hard labor. I didn't even progress through the sixteen hours of easy stuff they had prepared me for. One minute I was unaware anything was going on and the next minute my abdomen was on fire, with razor sharp, undulating currents starting out small and punctuating in a zenith of such intense pain my brain gave out. The pain would hover briefly there before receding.

I endured alternating bouts of relaxation and psyche-altering pain for one hour before breaking down and asking for an epidural. I don't remember why I hadn't asked until then, but at that point I knew there was no way I could suffer the physical pain of giving birth and the emotional pain of giving my child up and survive.

It took less than four hours, and my son was born—the most beautiful child in the world. The nurses whisked him away because everyone knew I was not keeping him, so they avoided measures that would foster a bond. Instead, they carried him straight to a bin and bathed him and fawned over him loudly. His skin was perfect, his black hair thick and amazing. He was the most beautiful baby they had ever seen. They kept counting the vessels in his umbilical cord, again and again, marveling at the fact there were only two. Only two.

Two vessels when there should have been three—one

vein and two arteries. Two vessels that made my first ultrasound so lengthy, the one where I found out it was a boy. Two vessels that my doctor assured me would nourish him fine as I cried hysterically in her office. Not because of the possible deformities to the organs developing concurrently with the vessels, but because it was a *boy*. Two vessels that made it so I had ultrasounds every few weeks and a complete workup on his heart to ensure he was okay. Two vessels that ensured I was acutely aware of the child inside me, so much so we had actual dates marking the progress of our relationship and allowing me to watch him grow and change on a screen. Two vessels, joining two hearts. United inside of me.

I anxiously listened as they worked over my child, but the incessant counting drove me over the edge. "Let me see him!" I cried out. So, the ladies quickened their pace, finished their task, and my delivery nurse brought over a tiny bundle.

"Here you go," she said, beaming as she passed him to me.

"Thank you," I said, accepting my little child wrapped up as tight as a taco.

I traced my finger along his angelic face and saw he was, indeed, perfect. Absolutely perfect. I was not fond of babies, but this one was perfect. He was mine, and I loved him instantly. I didn't just love him—he was connected to me. Like he had been this presence throughout my whole life, and it was only up until that moment he wasn't physically there. But now, he was. He was my child. The most beautiful thing in the world. The effect was positively ethereal.

I could never let this child go.

CHAPTER 5

The summer before leaving for dental school, Logan and I exchanged vows in a Presbyterian Church, chosen for its downtown location and Romanesque portico. The gothic architectural style suited us, though everything else surrounding the occasion did not. To me, the ideology of marriage was antiquated. However, when pressed by life's commitments and traditions, we felt we had to. Moments before walking down the aisle, a panic settled in me so deeply I nearly dropped to the floor under its weight. "Pre-wedding jitters," was the label I deemed appropriate, bolstering my confidence enough to see the ceremony through.

And just like that, the three of us became a family. *I* became part of a *we*. No longer the single, independent woman I wanted to be . . . which was okay. It was who I had to become to keep our little man in my world. Logan was comfortable and okay. Admittedly, I wasn't in love, but it would all be okay because he let me be me. So we were, and to that end, I settled.

But then, I carried on settling. I attended dental school at the University of Minnesota because it was convenient to stay close to home. I've always been told "it takes a village to raise a child," and our village was Logan's and my family. While my classmates partied at exclusive clubs, traveled to exotic places, and entertained romantic entanglements, Logan and I sung karaoke on a Walmart Singing Machine, dug trenches in my parent's lakeside beach, and clinked plastic champagne glasses to sippy cups. Hardly the trajectory I'd plotted in college, but when I beheld my beautiful son, my heart was content. Motherhood has mystical effects.

When dental school ended, I was eight months pregnant with our second son, and we moved back home to plant roots and fasten a stable life. Definitively settling, we bought our forever home: a standard architectural Tuscany planted amongst kitschy cabin ramblers all a half-story shorter. Its design assured it didn't dissolve into obscurity, but also wasn't so bold it broke any major molds. The classic Midwestern way.

For us, the selling feature was a breathtaking view of a pond out back. It was a picturesque mirror of the ever-changing landscape painting the wide-open sky. Glancing out at it put things into perspective and always made me smile.

No Midwestern home is complete without a three-stall garage, and ours was attached properly to the front—the epitome of what we had set out not to buy. In private, Logan and I referred to it as our "front-facing-three stall garage," taking a jab at how easily we compromised.

Yet, it hadn't felt like a compromise. Our world was the product of the woman I became so my children could have a sturdy foundation surrounded by loving grandparents. It was a way of life Logan and I thrived in and excelled at. We were considered amongst our friends as the perfect couple. We never fought, collaborated on everything, communicated open and honestly, and trusted each other absolutely. We lived in balanced harmony.

However, eight more years passed in weighty blinks of a sleepy child's eyes, and with each fresh opening, the greater picture changed from grainy lines to dull forms, until everything hit a precision lens, projecting onto my brain in crystal clear focus. Eight years later, I looked around at the life we built compared to the life I set out to build and gawked at the dichotomy. All the while Logan and I were married, we prioritized family without an iota of regret. One could theorize that I had matured, yet the greater truth was the old me inside the new me had been slumbering.

CHAPTER 6

Winter storms in my region usually produce snow, but the first night in that December was exceptional. The confluence of a gentle rain with air temperatures hovering just above freezing produced a drastic front of glacial winds that crystallized everything in its wake. The valley was coated in a pristine glaze, as though hovering in suspended animation, encased by a sheet of black ice.

At the onset, it felt like a perfectly routine day. I was headed off to the gym, the thing I did every Monday. By December, the sky is nearly always painted black, so on that morning, like all winter mornings, when I glanced out my bedroom window to see what the weather was offering, I saw only scattered beams of street lights amid shadows. But something was off. The shadows cast over the valley wrinkled in a way that seemed eerie. Everything carried a luster and ripple and bent in interesting ways.

I pulled away from my house at 5:15 a.m. in my white Ford Fusion via my attached garage. As I pulled out of my neighborhood and onto the streets, I immediately discovered the cause. There was no traction. I revved the engine to speed onto the main road and my wheels spun around uselessly. Determined to not let the weather get in my way, I adjusted speed and negotiated the empty skating rink posing as a street to arrive at my destination on time.

Unfortunately, my first step out of the car was a disaster. I swung open the door and planted my foot on ground coated in black ice, with all the force required to propel one up and out from a seated position. Only, that was not what happened. In one blinding flash my foot slipped, and I landed flat on my back. Fortunately, after laying there for a moment contemplating the lights dancing at the backs of my eyes, everything seemed okay. Shaking off the crash, I rose, entered the gym, and carried on with the business of the day.

There are others though, who—when faced with this exact same sequence of events—would suffer devastating and life altering injuries. My mother is one of those people.

5:30 a.m. - I meant to call her, I thought about it as soon as I fell, but no one welcomes phone calls at so ungodly an hour.

6:15 a.m. - Workout complete, I navigated the black ice rink home. Still too early to call.

7:15 a.m. – Back on the streets and off to work. Perfect time to call. However, while negotiating an ice skating rink in heavy morning traffic, it is ill-fated not to be paying full attention. When the weather in large cities mirrors these conditions, travel routes lock down for days. Not the case in my home, where winter reigns supreme and our ability to conquer it defines us. Proper Midwesterners drive in that shit.

7:45 a.m. - Arriving just shy of late to my office. We laughed our way through the morning huddle then I danced unceremoniously through my parking lot with a giant can of ice melt, sprinkling its contents like fairy dust. In true Midwestern fashion, despite the inclement weather and treacherous driving conditions, every single patient, plus a few add-ins, showed up. Any intention of warning my mother slipped from my conscious mind.

8:30 a.m. - My mother arrived bright and early at her chiropractor's office, assured the weather shouldn't break her routine. She swung open her car door and planted one foot down on ground coated in black ice with all the force required to propel up and out from a seated position.

Only, that was not what happened.

My mother fell and fractured her patella, half pulled into her shin, half tucked into her quad. It was a clean break, but either shard carried the potential to puncture through her skin. In order to prevent this, doctors advised emergency surgery.

During the preceding summer, she had hip surgery in St. Paul, where she didn't come out of an anesthetic-induced stupor for a week. Immediately post-op, I expected her to be confused, one day out should be better. Two days post-op and she should have recovered clarity, but instead, she hovered in full disillusion. Our conversations were one-sided—me trying to get details and her zoning in and out of consciousness—unable to produce a lucid thought, unable to end a sentence.

On rare occasions she would become clear, stammering, "Oh Ruby, help me!" before retreating into obscurity. In those moments, my heart wanted to howl in pain. It killed me that I could not sweep in and fix the madness. It killed me that, instead, I had to come to terms with the fact that protecting her was an impossible goal.

After her spell in St. Paul, she had a full workup at Mayo in Rochester, and they advised her to hold off on all surgeries for one year. Because of this, I begged my parents to get to Mayo immediately and have the doctors there create a plan for her, but my mom refused to take the time. In the end, my persuasive efforts didn't make a blind bit of difference.

Her local orthopedic surgeon heard "difficult" and his god complex puffed up, promising her there were no foreseeable issues and insisting she proceed immediately. So, after one day of deliberation, my mother entered into surgery.

During this time, my step-father Tom stayed with us. Tom had recently retired from dentistry, and ever since, subtle cues suggested his memory was lagging. He was always losing his keys. He would ask where we were going for dinner repeatedly. He didn't remember which day of the week it was. But "newly retired" was a logical excuse to explain it away with grace. However, our new proximity made it clear that he was suffering from something other than retirement brain. Tom, a man I revered for mental acuity, was confused and forgetful to an inexplicable degree. His behavior was pathognomonic of Alzheimer's disease.

Logan and I took turns visiting my mom and helping Tom, while occasionally bringing up the boys upon my mom's insistence, but mostly keeping them away because she wasn't herself. She had the same level of confusion for the same amount of time, only, by then, I lost faith. It was obvious no one could keep her safe.

When she was finally released from the hospital five days later, we set her up with us, alongside Tom, promising to keep them through Christmas. As the eve of the first night approached, my mother became determined to shower without her brace, despite explicit instructions for constant immobilization of the joint. I tried to convince her to proceed with a sponge bath, but in matters of discretion, one must defer to their elder.

"Oh Ruby," she said, a childlike expression dancing across her face, "it's fine. I can do this. I can't stand to feel dirty. It's more important to clean up, plus, it's normal if it bends a little," she said, smiling with a quick wink. "Doctors' recommendations are always overly cautious." My mother prides herself on successful disregard for instructions.

I set up my shower and positioned her into the nook on the side. Next, I readied a towel to prop up her leg and readied myself to help her undress. Her body contorted in awkward shapes, and menial tasks I take for granted daily became perplexing with her form. We fought with her shirt because of her shoulder and fought with her pants because of her knee. Finally, we fought with each other over her brace, which I reluctantly removed rather than physically restrain her from shedding, enabling her self-destructive pattern.

Her current state disturbed Tom, and it was apparent this inconsistent schedule was not conducive to his well-being. The general stress of it all weighed heavily upon him; you could see it like a physical object resting on his shoulders. Logan and I didn't know what to do; his ailments were beyond our control. We only knew he needed to get home–routine and familiarity were his drugs.

As the bustle of the holiday quieted down and New Year's Eve crept in, I paused and took stock of my emotional health. My stability quivered like a precariously taut thread, and I felt at any moment I could snap.

"I am done with Christmas," I informed Logan the

morning of New Year's Eve. "Each year gets harder. And each year, we spend our time trying to make everyone else happy just to wind up exhausted and miserable. We cannot go through that again. This is not fun for anybody. I want to enjoy the boys. I want to enjoy our time. I want to start living our lives."

He contemplated my face with his warm blue eyes and blinked slowly. "Why don't we just start with a weekend off?"

"Absolutely. Done. Please. Anything. Just get me away!"

"How 'bout we enlist my parents to look after yours while we take the boys on a ski vacation?"

"Love it! I don't care what it costs; if you can find something, make it happen. I'd hit the road as soon as tonight."

-Vvvvvrrrrrrrrrrrrrrrr

The vibration of a phone on the table pulled us away from plotting. We both glanced around to locate the source and saw it was mine. The screen was lit up with a photo of my mom, and it was creeping toward the edge from the oscillations.

"Yours," Logan called. "You should take this. Everyone knows you never answer the phone; if she's calling, it's probably serious."

Rolling my eyes with a dramatic flair, I grabbed the vibrating phone and answered in a firm tone.

"Hello?"

"Where are you?" my mom said, her voice breaking apart as she spoke.

"We are just about to plan an impromptu mini-vacation," I replied matter-of-factly, hopeful this information would deter her from asking something of me.

"Tom and I are at the eye doctor—"

"—How did you get to the eye doctor?" I asked, articulating clearly so Logan could hear while squinting my eyes at him.

"Tom drove."

"And how did he get you along with him?" I pressed, throwing up my free hand in an exasperated display.

"Ruby, will you stop cutting me off and listen. Tom has a detached retina. He has to have surgery immediately. I need you guys to come over here right now," she said, her voice echoing strangely through my mind, as though ricocheting off the walls of a cave.

Detached retina? My mind hitched on her words. I couldn't immediately recall what that entailed, but I knew it was something dire. Reflexively, I grabbed up Logan's iPhone and googled the condition. The top result registered this:

"A disorder of the eye in which the retina peels away from its underlying layer of support . . . without rapid treatment the entire retina may detach, leading to vision loss and blindness. It is almost always classified as a medical emergency. Permanent damage may occur if the detachment is not repaired within 24-72 hours."

It was not time to take a weekend off. So, instead of negotiating heavy traffic toward Minneapolis on I-94, we found ourselves meandering desolate Highway 10, into the chaos we intended to escape. I cried the whole way and failed miserably at consoling my boys who were crying along with me in the back seat.

We tried to make light of the evening by taking them

to our favorite local restaurant to ring in the New Year, but when I look back on photos from that night, I see only strain on our faces. The restaurant had a pile of New Year's themed regalia which the kids raided like pirates. We decked ourselves out in sparkling party favors and ordered up crafty New Year's themed drinks, but no outward projection could adequately veil the glaringly obvious mood. The general takeaway was the upcoming year was shaping up to be one to forget.

After the surgery, Tom and my mom came back home with us. I carried on the duties for my mom and piled on new ones pertaining to the care of Tom's eye. I survived by convincing myself it was all temporary. I could operate on adrenaline from heightened pressure; transitory distress is surmountable. I was sprinting for the end of the tunnel. There had to be a light at the end of the tunnel. Only, there was no light at the end of the tunnel.

Instead of getting better, things got worse. One tragedy after another befell them, and a downward spiral of my parents' health took shape. First, my mom's knee surgery failed and was infected, then Tom's surgery failed, and then my mom's surgery failed, again, and was still infected. Then Tom's eye, again. They were advised to rest, but ignored post-op instructions required to heal and overextended themselves trying to tend to the other. Instead of two people lifting one another up, their combination was toxic.

It was horrifying to watch and impossible to control. I wanted to care for them, but I felt like I was running around a leaking water tank bursting with new holes. I kept patching and patching, but as hard as I tried, they spouted anew again.

My parents' health crisis was a dismal situation that made me acutely aware of how little time people get to enjoy the fruits of this life. Tom lived modestly, choosing to invest and wait for retirement, assured those years would be his glory days. An avid fisherman, he was nicknamed "Lucky" for his ability to always land the biggest fish. After retirement, the world should have been his oyster, only, his health declined immediately thereafter. Like an Olympic cross-country skier passing out on the ground at the finish, he hit his end and collapsed. Only, Olympic skiers recover. They get back up after resting a few minutes, collect themselves, and move on. Tom was not so lucky. He was only sixty-three years old.

My mom had always been one misstep away from complete incapacitation, a state which was now as impending as the wind. She was only fifty-five years old. They were too young for this new state of decrepitude—they had an abundance of life left to live, and yet, there they were, actively dying. The existence they were relinquished to was a fate worse than death in my mind; a fate from which death would be perceived as mercy.

None of it felt right, and the whole situation threw me. Caring for them left me incapable of caring for anyone else. My village became my private hell, and I found myself forced to choose between the lesser of two atrocities. It was time. I had been gaping for too long, wide-eyed and horrified, from a front row seat to their demise. In the absence of a way to shield my eyes, I opted to abandon the show.

CHAPTER 7

Follow the white line, follow the white line, follow the white line . . . I chanted internally, driving into a screen of black obliterated by streaks of white tufts. The patterns cast by the blustery snow were mesmerizing, but it was the center line I forced my eyes to hold focus to. It was Sunday night, I had returned my parents to their lake home, and I was returning to mine. Through the month of January, they stayed in our home, but when the added duties became too much, I asked them to turn for others for a while. I had become acutely aware of a hairline fracture propagating through my body; this step I took to decelerate its effect. An Armageddon-style blizzard wouldn't have stopped me.

I was optimistic, feeling as though some of the stress attached to caring for my parents was laid to rest. Plus, the weekend ahead kicked off an implant symposium I was psyched to be attending. A gnawing inside my belly had begun a few months prior, hinting at me to change something. Expansion into a new professional arena had felt like a safe, logical choice. My goal after dental school graduation had been to master implantology. It called to me the way something does when you know the difference between a job and a passion. It was an ever-changing frontier and, in my opinion, the future of dentistry.

Unfortunately, implants were not a core part of my

school's curriculum. I sought out as much education as I could from any professor who would teach me, but it was well understood that, before broadening my scope of practice to include implant surgery, I needed to take some type of mini-residency.

"The first thing I'm going to do is take an implant residency," I expressed to my fellow classmates at dental school graduation.

I was so sure I was saying something I'd be seeing to immediate fruition, but then, reality intervened. Practicing dentistry was nothing of what I had imagined. I hoped to be traveling, to be learning new things, to be in control of my life and master of my domain, only, none of these things were true until I became a solo practice owner five years after my grandiose decree. Owning a practice makes continuing education a business expense, which is a wildly attractive feature. Education is costly, and intelligent doctors build empires centered around their philosophy. Many doctors create their own training courses and facilities, and the stratification of offerings is as varied as lodgings, from Super 8 to the Hyatt. To find a legit one, you have to sift through a compendium of bullshit. Multiple options existed, but I never felt inspired by or attracted to any particular one. They were always too inconvenient, too expensive, too comprehensive, or not comprehensive enough. I felt like Goldilocks in the *Three Little Bears* of continuing education perusal, wobbling in between this one being too long and that one being too short. Then one magical day, I had two encounters that illuminated my exact path of just right.

First, I posted a question on a dental forum about proper closure for bone graft sites and received an outrageous mixed bag of responses. From, "the only way to ensure clinical success is to obtain primary closure over a pericardial membrane," to "just stuff a CollaPlug in it." One month later, I encountered a former classmate who recently completed a weekend seminar on implant dentistry. She detailed how the lecturer used my question to kick off the day and then read a few choice responses from the mix. In summary, he said: "With such a heinous array of contradicting replies, I would be shocked if she ever places a graft." Then, he taught them his simple technique, which she graciously shared.

Second, the week following that encounter, I received an email from the coordinators of that specific seminar, offering discounted tuition to the Chicago winter session. I checked the dates against my routinely overbooked calendar, and miraculously, all of them were free.

With Chicago only an hour away via direct flight, I could attend the seminars while detracting less than forty-eight hours from my life. Plus, the series kicked off in a little over two months. For me—being a hallmarked impetuous personality—expedience was the tipping factor.

The month flew by in a tornado of family crisis, and the next thing I knew, the seminar start date was less than a week away. Certainly, things were taking a turn for the better, I believed. However . . .

On Monday: my mother discovered her most recent surgery failed. So much for healing; she was back at square one.

On Tuesday: I punctured my hand with a dirty knife. In true dense headed, nitwit fashion, I scrubbed rubbing alcohol into it and declared "looks good!" Shockingly, that was ineffective. By evening, the backside of my hand was swollen as if it had a baseball inset in it.

On Wednesday: my associate resigned. He was poised to be the business partner with whom I developed my practice. I had brought him on to grow our patient base so by the time we moved that summer—to a space doubling our size—he and I could have full-time schedules. In the interim, he was splitting time between two clinics. Then suddenly, he was offered a full-time job at a local hospital starting immediately, brandishing benefits I could not match. It was impossible for him to say no.

He had been my impeccable match. Finding a partner with whom you see eye to eye is akin to winning the lottery, and with him, I had tapped into something amazing. But then, like lightning, he was gone. I could have tried to counter with an attractive response, but I didn't have the drive. Sadly, with the timing as it was, the blow hit the hard wall of a numb mind. I accepted given circumstances and moved on. It could have crushed me, but all it did was make me harder.

And then, my hand. It was hideous. Everyone around me decided a trip to a doctor was in order, claiming no one should board a plane looking like that. My fantastic team of ladies coordinated an exam, and during a sliver of downtime, I rushed to the clinic.

My first exam was with a youthful physician assistant, vibrantly bedecked in golf regalia that could easily double as hunting garb. "Have you had any recent encounters with MRSA?" he asked, methodically inspecting my baseball. I shrugged and looked past his gaze

"Um, well, my mom has an infected surgical wound she's on intravenous antibiotics for right now," I said, "but I haven't had direct contact with her since my injury," delivering my response with false confidence.

He looked at my face and back down to my hand. "Well, if that's the case, you should proceed to the nearest ER for immediate incision and drainage," he said with a firm gaze.

"But what if I can't do that?" I replied, assuredly matching his face.

I had left my clinic unattended in the hopes I would be given an antibiotic and dismissed. The physician assistant called upon his elder doctor, whose crisp white lab coat was emblazoned with robust black font. He graciously conceded such impulsive treatment was aggressive, but in consolation, he inscribed a very large circle on the back of my hand, delineating the borders of the infection. As he passed over a prescription and dismissal forms, the elder doctor said, "Make sure you make your follow-up visit first thing tomorrow morning. We need to make sure you are progressing on the right path."

"But what if I can't do that?" I replied, my eyes trained down at the forms he handed over to me.

These gentlemen were united on the front that I should not be headed to Chicago, as my twenty-four hour follow-up visit was crucial. I was adamant, though, that I had no other choice. Instead, I pledged to discontinue food and colored beverages and proceed straight to the nearest ER if the swelling made its way outside the bold circle sketched around my baseball, and to return for a follow-up next week.

Amid all the chaos, the simmering excitement for advancing professionally crackled and flickered and died. As far as satisfying a sinking mind goes, I dropped to full on clinging-to-the-earth-to-survive.

However, if I knew then what I know now, I would have been petrified. If I glimpsed into the future and saw this kicked off unimaginable shit—sirens whose enticing songs were impervious to my greatest silencing efforts—I would have run screaming for the hills. If Doc Brown were to appear to me in a flux capacitor-equipped DeLorean to alter one crucial moment in my life, I would consider that day. But realistically, what transpired was simply the match. I was destined to ignite.

CHAPTER 8

Thursday morning: officially the beginning of the end.

That morning marked the first of many mornings of preparing myself and packing up my beautification essentials in a flurry before racing to the airport, arriving twenty to thirty minutes before my plane's departure. Amateurishly, I fumbled through the process, but I was putting extra effort into achieving a unique look. My day-to-day life was quite ordinary and called for routine attire. But I had a squandered penchant for eccentric fashion, so when traveling, I tended to go a little overboard.

On that morning, I was hoping to recreate a Pinterest look: a demure gray sweater dress glamorously accessorized for fresh, adorable street style. The night before, I laid all my pieces out on the floor like a child preparing for the first day of school. I compiled all the necessities, down to the infinity scarf, tights, ankle boots, and to-go coffee cup—all integral to the completion of the look. I added one accouterment that was solely my own—fingerless gloves with fur trim. Always a must on winter days where both hand coverage and iPhone screen manipulation are mandatory. Bonus—they provided camouflage for the bold map scrawled on the back of my hand.

My flight path set me at the Chicago O'Hare airport at 7:40 a.m., and the conference hotel was a swift ten-minute shuttle ride away. Assuming a void of glaring errors, I calculated my arrival should be well cushioned for the 8:30 a.m. class. Unfortunately, I was overly confident in my ability to schedule this all so seamlessly.

The panic accompanying the descent through thick layers of clouds started me off on the wrong foot. I was baffled that the covert experts in the cockpit were able to land this thing successfully when the ground wasn't even visible until the final seconds before touchdown—it was all I could do to stifle my screams. Descent into Chicago in the wee morning hours is a positively harrowing experience.

While exiting the plane, I passed through a familiar stream of frigid outdoor air escaping the seal of the jet bridge. I had banked on Chicago providing some type of reprieve from my intractably frozen state, but this unfriendly wind tendered me a deflating reality—Chicago was going to be as insanely cold as my home.

Also, as I walked briskly up the jet bridge and entered into the wide open expanse of the airport terminal, I realized I had no clue where I was going. I knew there was a shuttle, which was about it. I had failed to do any premeditated recon, assuming one always finds their way. In these situations, I abide by one simple rule— act as though you know precisely where you are going. When properly enacted, this rule produces my desired result—avoidance. If you get it wrong, people are liable to think you are lost, or worse, an outsider, and target you for unwanted bullshit. So, with that mindset in place, I pressed on, discretely trying to collect the specifics from my surroundings, all the while projecting *I am a girl walking confidently.*

Chicago O'Hare is an orbicular labyrinth outside the

baggage claim's sliding glass doors. I passed through them and walked at great length on a route I believed would deliver me to the shuttle bus area, taking cues from an errant sign. I continued, brisk and confident, until I came to an end that was, by all measure, a hard stop. At that point, I circled one time to take stock of my surroundings and found nothing monumental to convince me to turn elsewhere. I continued along spinning another 180 degrees and found myself back from where I came.

In that direction, I noticed that, no matter where I went, everything appeared the same. I was, for all intents and purposes, abysmally lost. But I wasn't going to give up my charade. I pressed assuredly on. After ten more minutes in that direction, I swear I ended up in the same place. By then, I decided to call the hotel.

The receptionist with whom I connected relayed one mildly beneficial tidbit of information, "Once you reach the area, proceed to gate one. That is where our bus picks up."

"Excellent!" I exclaimed. "That data will be of great use to me once I actually locate the shuttle bus area," I said with a fake laugh into the phone. I was the only one laughing; I don't think she found it amusing.

Finally, after a few more probing attempts at somber confusion, I must have given off an air of desperation, which was an utter fail, but worked wonders in my present circumstance. A gentleman approached and inquired where it was I was so obviously seeking. After delivering my exasperated tale, he pointed me off in some arbitrary direction, along winding sidewalks and beneath suspended rail lines, relevant to nothing, supposedly capable of landing me at my shuttle bus pickup destination.

I began to head off in the way I believed he was motioning, but instantly he flagged me down. "No, ma'am," he bellowed after me, "you go this way," gesturing his hand in the opposite direction from where I began. *I am a complete idiot.*

I gathered up my things and the vestiges of my confidence and crossed over the sidewalk, over to *there,* and started venturing off again toward the elusive shuttle bus stop, which I am now convinced appears only in your most desperate hour.

If you are ever in Chicago O'Hare and need to find the shuttle bus terminal to get you to one of the airport hotels within the ten-mile radius of the area, here are my directions for you:

Wander to and fro, pondering desperately your need to escape the purgatory of this terminal. When you want it badly enough—when you have frozen your limbs to the point of dull numbness edging on searing hot pain—when you have given up all hope of ever escaping this place, a blissful walkway across the boulevard magically appears. It only presents itself in your most desperate hour.

For me, when I found it, I was elated to a degree unfit the accomplishment. But my smugness was short-lived. As soon as I settled in on the shuttle and checked the time, it became obvious that my wandering set me back significantly. Despite all my preplanning and confidence in timing, I was now running fashionably late. The first day starting off a four-month-long educational journey and I already placed my worst foot forward.

I entered the hotel through the large revolving door and rode up the tall escalator to the lobby level where the check-in counters lined the far left wall and a large open restaurant formed the back. I wandered about and discovered the class was one floor down. I entered one of the four ornate glass elevators, framing an eloquent belvedere, and depressed the smooth round button to carry me to my correct floor.

Once there, I easily located the seminar group in the hallway to my right. The check-in table was a bustle of activity, attended by a throng of dark-skinned beauties that all looked like they walked straight off the dance floor of a Miami club. Each lady was squeezed into what I can only describe as a mini dress, blurring into their actual selves, so as to leave observers questioning whether or not the garment was painted on. Their shoes were beyond impractical, heels of five inches tall or more, and they all had mid-back length sleek black hair and perfectly bronzed skin with just the right amount of too much make-up to match. I wanted to turn around and walk away.

Maybe I should act confused and flee. I thought. This was all a big mistake. I really didn't want to be here anyway, and these ladies confirmed my worst nightmare—this was all a cheesy sales pitch, and I had been swindled. To frame it appropriately, I was fucking annoyed.

As I stood motionless, surveying the table and contemplating my exit strategy, one of the ladies loudly called me out, and I was forced into interactions. They retrieved my name and overenthusiastically complimented my street style. I did my best to reciprocate. I've been told I suffer from resting bitch face (RBF), and it's doubtful I pulled off a genuine compliment. "You look interesting," was the only thought I could muster, which I said silently instead of aloud.

They ushered me to an open chair in the back and secured my bag with them at the front. The seat to my immediate left housed an older gentleman donning a kippah, and the seat to my immediate right remained empty. Two seats to the right sat a former classmate, whom I never befriended, as dental school felt worse than high school for me. Here I was, married with a child, and there they were, single and experiencing life to the fullest. Take that and combine it with an introvert, and you have yourself a girl who felt like she never fit in.

It was apparent that my present surroundings would procure no fast friends, but that really came as no surprise. At CE conferences I retreated inward. I shied away, hid out, avoided everyone's eyes. I was the girl wandering the floor with headphones securely in place—the bigger, the better—so as to give off the air of "leave me alone." That combined with my classic RBF, I got accommodated ninety-nine percent of the time.

I took out my binder and my iPad and set my mind to the task of learning. My fingerless gloves achieved a second functionality I took advantage of that day—providing warmth in lecture halls kept the right temperature required by men to not sweat, which is usually just barely above the temperature that turns me into an icicle.

I tried my best to be a studious professional, but my note-taking was interrupted with my usual doodles and scrawling, as my mind constantly zones in and out of focus. The material held my attention mildly at best. Mostly, I concentrated on mastering how to write with my finger on an iPad screen while contemplating the eccentricities of our lecturer.

He had been heralded a genius, a guru. I had read multiple dental threads declaring this guy was legit, but so far, I was not picking up on any of it. The most I could tell was that the man delivering the content was very proud of his past and qualifications yet lacked the ability to lecture with any extemporaneous delivery. I wondered if the amazing guy everyone raved about was sick, and maybe the gentleman at the podium was filling in.

During the lunch break, I returned to the lobby in the giant glass elevators and checked into my suite on the eleventh floor. I found it easily and fell into the bed, grasping the TV remote for comfort. When I decided to open my eyes and explore my surroundings, I was pleased to discover that my room was exceptionally inviting. The design of the hotel was bookended by two large circular towers, interconnected by a lower atrium. My room was housed in one of those circular towers, and the walls were wavy and friendly. The heat was set to fantastically warm, and I was wrapped in comfort the moment I entered.

My window overlooked the airport, and I had a constant view of planes ascending and descending, along with the welcome white noise that entails. It was peaceful there, an unadulterated retreat—a prime environment for my insulant soul, so I stayed. Lifting the remote in the air, I turned on the TV and explored the menu. I was pleased to discover that I could have lunch delivered to me for a small fee, and I wouldn't have to return to that shit show for another solid hour. I pushed the button that sealed the deal and drifted off to sleep.

In the span of an instant, I was jolted awake by a rap at the door, quickly drawing me back to my surroundings. Surveying the clock, I noticed that the lunch hour was waning—I had less than ten minutes before class picked back up. I choked down my food, gulped a glass of water, and flew out the door in haste.

Back down the glass elevator and back down the hall, I found the table of ladies crowded with men, each being held by the arm or touched along the side; all engaging in serious sales pitches, and these guys were eating it up. They were like pigs being brought to slaughter. I bolted past them, evading their eyes, and resituated tensely in my back row seat, next to my Jewish companion. I glanced his way and caught his expression, and we shared one brief moment of incredulity. I was reassured by him; at least one other person seemed as annoyed by their tactics as I was.

Around 2:00 p.m., I excused myself for a break and wandered the halls for air. Upon my return, all the ladies were drinking glasses of white wine, so I joked with them that I wanted in. Not actually thinking they would oblige, I entered the class and resumed my perch, to find only that, moments later, a full glass appeared at my space, which they continued to refill for the remainder of the day. I didn't mind; the sweet white liquid took the edge off, and I found myself despising them slightly less. When the class wrapped up for the day, my wine consumption had me feeling confident enough to engage in conversation with my former classmate two to my right, Gregg.

As it turns out, he was nearly as unsettled as I was, and equally disenchanted with day one's offerings. Then, a third companion joined in our conversation. His name was Ty, and he also attended school with us and had been out with me on numerous conference travels over that time. He had been sitting front and center, enrapt and being most professional, so I hadn't been aware of him until then.

It was decided that our little party of three would head out and dine together, so we chose to meet up an hour and a half later and then parted ways to kill time. Despite the fact that I had been drinking for three hours already, I went to the gym and hit the treadmill, droning away six miles. Then I went to my room, showered, and readied myself in casual attire before meandering out to meet my classmates.

We alternately walked and ran the four short blocks over to a restaurant called Gibson's, in the frigid January air. It was a lively, pretentious steakhouse, where the wait staff don tuxedos and present trays of raw cuts of meat while describing how the marbling affects the flavor, the inclusion of bone softens the texture, blah, blah, blah, more details in which I didn't have a modicum of interest. I ordered the salmon.

During the wait, Gregg and Ty droned on about premium steaks while I hunched in my corner, wishing I was wearing ear muffs, occasionally nodding to pretend like I cared. After the boys had exhausted their meat topic, Ty moved onto a speech about how particularly awesome his life was, bludgeoning us with the minutia of his amazing travels, the great success of his practice, the big-name lecturers he counted as close friends, and how he was going to be the new face of some product line that I could give zero fucks about.

When Gregg got his turn, the conversation flipped to hockey and small town politics, and again, I stayed silent, fascinated by his ability to put down one Bud Light after another, like an Ironman competitor seeking water. They were on such different tracks in their lives that I felt entirely outside of my comfort zone; being a discontented interloper among them sent my skin crawling. I felt like I had nothing of value to offer conversationally, and there was no mental energy in my reserve to pull out something forced. All I craved was an end so I could fall back into the arms of my cozy warm suite on the eleventh floor to decompress.

When our food arrived, I reveled in the forced silence that proper good manners like "don't eat with your mouth full" produce–I ate in haste. When we were all done, I could no longer contain my discomfort and insisted that I was exhausted, requesting we head straight back. Once inside the large revolving door, I proceeded up the long escalator, onto the glass elevator, and straight into the warmth of my bed with the perfect white noise lulling me. That night, I slept like a baby.

The second day passed quickly, and I spent break times on the phone with the nice people from United trying desperately to change my itinerary. I knew they had a flight out that night at 7:30 p.m. with seats still available for purchase. If I was on the flight leaving the next day at 7:00 a.m. but arrived at the airport twelve hours earlier, it made sense to me that I could sit standby.

Irrespective of my sound logic, each person I spoke with unconditionally assured me there was no way to do this without paying a sick fee. I still didn't believe them. I proceeded to the airport immediately following the lecture and tried out my reasoning in person. Face to face, no one could turn down this sad girl and force me to stay one more night in this hellhole, right? Spoiler Alert–*they can.*

Dejected, I found myself in the hotel bar around 7:00

p.m., consuming a modest supper and an un-celebratory beer, with my winter gear taking up seats at my table like companions, definitively implying I'm alone. My adorable fingerless gloves were positioned in a neat heap alongside my beer, and I was toying with my phone doing some mindless task to calm the flurry of angst that settled thickly in my mind.

In this moment of weakness, I must have lowered my wall, because a stranger with bright, friendly eyes approached. He had a smile that couldn't come from anywhere but the truth, and showed no sign of fear.

"Hi! You were in the implant class today, right?" he asked.

"Yes," was all my surprised voice could muster.

"I recognized your gloves and the back of your hand, so I figured it was safe to come over and talk to you," he said with a laugh.

I smiled at this and was put to ease by his demeanor. He was the picture of non-threatening.

"Is it alright if I come and join you?" he asked, as if he did this kind of thing all the time, joined tables with strangers and kicked around conversation like it was effortless. Fun. Not exhausting and terrifying. Dumbfounded, I assented, sweeping away my things to clear space.

His name was Chad, and he was from Iowa. He was married and had three boys around the same ages as mine. His flight home was in a couple of hours, so he was hanging there killing time. I rattled off my story of the standby that *wasn't*, and in no time at all I found myself engaged in a lovely and real conversation. Nothing felt forced, no one was projecting. We had a connection and went with it.

His practice background and philosophy were comparable to mine, so we immediately found common ground. Peeling back the layers, I discovered that his middle child is his tenacious genetic blueprint, much like my eldest is mine. I always felt relieved to hear other people admit to parenting challenges. Most people beam about how perfect their parenting life is, and I always end up feeling like a leper. Parenting has always been hard for me.

Whenever I try to be authentic and detail my pitfalls, people will tell me, all matter-of-fact like, that my struggles can easily be corrected by using their methods or some book that they've read. Like I should be able to snap my fingers and everything will be all right. I try to explain that my troubles go beyond that, but it only confuses them more.

But Chad got *me*. His past mimicked mine eerily well, and I found him reassuring. He made me feel confident that what I dealt with was real, not a figment of my imagination or a problem I created for myself. Our conversation likely saved me hundreds of dollars of therapy. He reaffirmed my practice trajectory and buoyed my soul that day.

Most doctors are cautiously friendly, projecting a shield and masking their true personality, lest their fallibility be discovered. As medical professionals, it is an unspoken rule that we are all perfect, healthy, and stable. But the truth is, we're human. We all have blemishes, we're just not free to express them. As soon as our faults are exposed, anyone can wield them insurgently, like paparazzi with a million dollar shot. Your most trusted friend in possession of that information will still curate your demise. We've been ingrained since dental school to safeguard ruthlessly.

But Chad was different; he had no walls. He treated me like an equal, and for the first time in forever, I felt like I was on an even playing field with another doctor. Most of the time, I feel like I'm pretending, a faux-doctor, fraudulent somehow. There is no real grounding for my paranoia, but I think I've never been good at the game.

My weekend started out in a chaotic flurry and concluded in considerable peace, but I was still not completely sold. On CE trips I was also looking to find adventure—a big city with novel running routes and scenery, foreign terrain to conquer and explore, challenges to transfix my mind. The version of "Chicago" these conferences offered was an underwhelming airport hotel, too far from the city to make trips viable, and too suburban to lay out adventurous running routes.

The classes were held on Thursday and Friday in Chicago and Saturday and Sunday in Washington, D.C. The February trip was still covered by my associate, but once he was gone, the next two months presented complications. Closing a clinic is no simple task, and patients are never pleased. So, I decided to switch my last two sessions. The dates didn't line up perfectly, and the change would push my third weekend out one extra month, but to that end, I did not care. It freed my office to function without interruption, and I positively love D.C.

I jostled my work schedule, modified my itineraries, and in one frenetic burst of activity, changed my third and fourth seminars to Washington D.C. Of particular significance was the fact that these weekends spanned cherry blossom season, one of my favorite events in our nation.

CHAPTER 9

The four weeks between my January and February seminars passed in an opaque fog. The rarely blue sky tendered the standard fare for Upper Midwestern winters—snow painted the landscape and below-freezing winds whipped across the valley, keeping people in their homes and making all trips outdoors short-lived and purpose-driven.

I completed a marathon in early January and was hoping to use this interstitial period to rest briefly then ramp back up for another. Amid the insanity of daily life, running had become essential to my stability. I needed my feet to connect with the ground, to remind me that it was still there. However, the bitter cold days were not conducive. People who stay out too long in that type of cold risk death—that's a thing!

My back-to-back marathon dream had to be crushed, and my running became restricted to treadmills, frigid tracks circling ice rinks, and from one protective warm shelter to the next. I would run out to the car, run into the store, run into my practice, protecting myself from the cold. I was growing weary of running from the cold. Habitually, I tallied the days until I returned to the air.

That morning marked the second occurrence of my ritual of hurriedly preparing myself and my bags, rushing off to the airport, and arriving fashionably late.

Regrettably, it was worse than the one prior. I awoke late and dallied. Eventually, Logan entered into our bathroom, took in the scene of unfortunate clutter, and said, "I think it's time we get going." His tone was casual, maybe a slight hint of coercion.

"I'm just finishing up," I said, checking the mirror one last time before zipping up my make-up case and stashing it in my carry-on. Nothing was going to phase me. Only, one hurried glance at the bathroom clock was capable of provoking alarm. It's neon green blocky numbers strikingly displayed 4:30 a.m. My plane departed at 5:00 a.m.

I sat in a daze while Logan sped through the sleepy lanes of the dimly lit interstate. About five minutes in, he broke the silence.

"I usually let you get away with these things, but this morning you are pushing your luck," he said, with no visible change in expression as he kept his eyes fixed on the road.

"I know," I said. "I'm pushing it, I know. I'm sorry."

And I was. It was the least prepared I had been for any trip, but admittedly, I couldn't find it within me to care. If I missed my flight, I was fine. If I missed my class, I was fine. All I wanted was to be dropped off at the airport so I could finally be alone. For the incapability of shaking that mentality, I was truly sorry.

We pulled up to the airport at 4:50 a.m. Now, given it was the Fargo airport, it's not unheard of to arrive twenty minutes early and make a flight, but ten minutes before is a mess. I flew through the sliding doors, scaled the escalator two steps at a time, and nervously took my place at the back of the TSA queue in an obvious state of panic.

As soon as I settled into the back of the line, a clear voice announced over the loud speaker, "Ruby Carlson, please come to gate four. Ruby Carlson, please report to gate four, for departure."

I waved my hand and alerted an agent, "That's me! I need to get on that flight."

The agent glared my way, "You need to ask each person ahead of you if they are okay with you cutting before I will allow you through," she said through pursed lips.

The waiting passengers looked as dumbfounded by her statement as I was, and each met my concerned gaze with allying eyes. I took their silent gesture to imply consensus, and hurried to the head of the checkpoint, taking measures to be efficiently processed.

That morning I chose to dress in a way that rendered a real jacket superfluous, so I had many layers to shed. I started with a long sleeve dress boldly striped with horizontal layers of black, tan, and gold, alternating each plain stripe with one embossed in metallic accent thread. Then, I added thick black tights and gray sweater leggings, peeking up strategically beneath black leather boots. I accessorized further with a chunky, black sequined scarf to match flair and thickness for utility, and a perfect puffy black vest that provided just the right element of central body warmth, but also charming style to complete a polished look.

After all the accessorizing, I managed to walk briefly outside and not cower at the threat of the cold, briefly being key–it was enough to get from the car to a door, much beyond that wasn't practical. I had to tear off eighty percent of my outfit to get through the scanner, which I did in a flash, and then rushed inside the tall tube, placing both feet on the mat and my arms in the air, surrendering to the TSA gods, praying nothing would trip the system.

While waiting for the agent to dismiss me, I trained all focus on occupying the carpet foot outlines perfectly. Only, dismissing was not what happened.

“Don’t move,” he barked, blocking my forward path with his hand.

“I didn't,” I said back defensively. Probably the wrong reaction, but it was instinctual. I’m not really sure what other option I had.

He waved over his female agent counterpart and motioned to me to go with her. Before doing so, I turned back to the screen to see where on the body they’d be searching. The diagramed figure made me laugh for the first time that morning.

The body outline lit up the scanner in alternating rows of Xs. Apparently, the metallic thread of my dress was not OK. A female agent escorted me to the side and methodically patted me down while “tsking-tsking” the fiasco, wasting precious minutes while enhancing the dramatic flair of my lateness.

Let’s be honest—this process could be more efficient and less embarrassing if everyone just had to strip naked. And right then and there, I would have. Fortunately, I passed her screening, and the gate agent collected my bag while I re-established my attire. She whisked me away from the security checkpoint and onto the plane in a flash.

Logan would comment six months later, “I wonder if our lives would be drastically different if you had just missed your flight.” I assured him things would not. My kerosene-covered heart had long been soaking. All I was waiting for was a match.

The Delta flight had me laying over in Minneapolis, and then on to Chicago, arriving moments before the start of class. It was a risky move and a ridiculous flight path, but I saved four hundred dollars over my United itinerary. One thing I hadn't taken into account, though, was direct flights are less likely to be impeded by weather challenges in the dead of winter—one unassuming stop can wreck a well-laid plan.

Chicago was under snow, so at MSP we spent an hour nestled in the crook of the apron. In Chicago, we were postponed another hour, idle in the taxiway, waiting for an open gate to deplane. These situations tip Type A travelers into maniacal panic states, but that day, I was not in it for the destination. Stress would have deflated my contented mood, so even though I was sitting on planes amongst travelers whose angst bogged down the filtered cabin air to a thick and muggy consistency, I remained calm.

Eventually, we were cleared to make way for a gate, and all the cramped travelers spilled out, skittering to their next destinations. After some ill-thought-out maneuvering through the magical strip outside the glass doors, I found myself crossing the street. Next to the suspended rail lines and unidentifiable crosswalks, relevant to nothing, stumbling fortuitously upon a path that led me to the shuttle bus pickup at gate one. This time, I approached it from the back side.

I nearly froze waiting for the bus and cursed myself for thinking it smart to dress adorably warm but not intelligently covered. The weather was severe, and I was getting wet from blustery melting snow. My black leather boots were distressed from the messy salted sidewalks, and my feet were on fire in that transient state that hovers briefly before total numbness sets in.

When the shuttle arrived, I was a freezing cold, wet disaster. Then, I boarded and transformed into a burning hot, wet disaster because they had the heat blasted. By the end of it all, I arrived at the Hilton three hours late, with matted down hair and splotchy eye make-up, in a sweaty dress and black leather boots streaked white, a wayworn sight to behold. And, after setting a new record of lateness, I must have also appeared to be completely lacking judgment.

As I was getting a coffee before walking into class, a tall, middle-aged guy wearing skinny jeans, converse sneakers, and a hoodie, approached. "That's definitely an outfit fit for this cold," he said with a chuckle.

I matched his laugh to be polite, but honestly, I wasn't interested in conversation. I had been through enough of a morning, and there were no reserves for anybody. Squinting my eyes in protest, I made a display of measuring up his outfit in return. "Yes, these leggings and boots and tights are all necessary," I said, flicking the edge of my coffee lid loudly.

"I'm from California, so I'm not used to this cold either," he said, in a manner seeming to imply I should know what that means. As it stood, perpetual bitter cold was my reality, and in that exasperated state, he poked a sleeping beast.

So, he thinks boasting about being from a fanciful yuppie land where the weather is perfect and culture is such that it's acceptable for middle-aged guys to dress like teenagers will impress me in some way?

I pursed my lips and said, "I'm from up here. It's unbearably cold five months out of the year, and I always dress like this."

This cocky California jackass with the perfect weather and casual street attire, he has no idea what it's like to suffer!

I was not interested in cluing him in. I gave him a dismissive look, implying I was done with our interaction, then turned awkwardly on my heels in retreat. Inwardly, I chastised myself.

Ugh, I definitely failed that interaction.

CHAPTER 10

I nabbed the only open seat properly hidden in the back row of the conference room, next to an unfamiliar gentleman with wild sandy blond hair and strikingly bold blue eyes. I strategically aligned my notebook and iPad, then gathered myself to start paying attention. Unfortunately, I forgot how bizarre it was that our lecturer relied on incongruent stutter phrases like *and so on, if you'd like, all right now,* and the most popular, variants of *but*. Fifty percent of his lecture was *but-ahhh, but-ummm, but-but,* filling what should be reserved for silent pauses.

The previous month his stutter was noteworthy, but that day, my brain was not equipped to listen for content. The snubbed idle space was more attention-grabbing than the subject matter of his lecture. I spent ten minutes trying to be studious, but eventually, I found myself also jotting down his habit words and, at the end of each page, tallying them up.

The activity was fascinating to a degree unfitting the task, so I decided to turn it into a game. I wrote each word down and then checked against the time, to calculate a stutter-word-to-minute ratio (SW/M). Pages filled up quickly, and after ten minutes, I calculated thirty-five to one—it was shocking he got in functional words at all!

I recognized this to be counterproductive, so I picked up notetaking again, making tick marks for each word. It was a studious compromise—note taking combined with data collection—thereby allowing me to recalculate the SW/M ratio over a greater span of time.

The young gentleman next to me noticed what I was doing and leaned over my shoulder, "Are you counting the times he says 'but?'" he whispered.

Stifling a laugh, I turned toward him, "He's said it thirty times in the past ten minutes!" I whispered, widening my eyes and rolling them for effect. Tearing a sheet from the hotel notepad, I diagrammed the game and wrote a short summary, then set it between us. I offered my pen and gestured for him to partake. With him weighing in, the remainder of the morning passed quickly.

During the break, we wandered the sales tables and got acquainted. Jack, I learned, was a recent grad who bought an elderly gentleman's practice in Indianapolis. He was working hard to bring it up to the current era, and implants, as he said, "were the next big thing." Jack and another attendee had driven to Chicago the night prior, and the same blizzard delaying my flights had doubled their three hour drive.

Jack was young and confident, smooth, and flirtatious, the embodiment of "that guy" all girls can name. I watched in shock as he fondled the tawdry sales girls without a hint of restraint, draping his arm across their waist or laying his hand on top of their arm, as they led him through the process of purchasing their overpriced crap. They adored him. I sat silent in awe.

Throughout life I had avoided guys like him on principle. Normally, I wouldn't have given him the time of day, but for some reason, that day, I didn't mind. He was making me laugh, and in my present state, distraction was welcome. I stayed out of the way and observed his actions as we worked through the throngs of sales ladies.

When we hit the end of the line, we returned to our seats. Just as we were settling back in, one of the seminar ladies approached us, holding a full glass of wine.

"Dr. Carlson," said the cleavage in a sequined mini dress, "you prefer red, if I recall?"

Taking the glass from her outstretched hand, I forced a broad smile. "Oh my gosh, I can't believe you remembered! First rate service. Thank you."

"My pleasure," she said with a wink. Motioning to her table along the backdoor, she added, "you know where to find me if you need more."

I set the wine on the table in front of me, secured the base with my fingers, and swirled the wine until the dark red liquid reached the rim of the glass. Then, I picked it up cautiously and brought it to my lips, taking a long, slow sip. I swallowed with closed eyes, then popped them open wide. Setting the glass down, I turned toward where she had been standing and addressed the open air, "I'll be there in about thirty minutes."

I returned to a forward gaze and feigned exasperation.

"How did you get so lucky?" Jack said, lifting the lonely glass of water at his place and nodding his eyes toward my wine.

"This is the oldest sales trick in the book!" I said. "Look at these women, I mean . . . obviously you are, but like – that shit doesn't work on me. I'm straight. How else are they going to loosen me up enough to buy in?"

Sure, I may have been a little blunt right then, but it was so pathetically obvious. This man's sycophantic posse seduced men and plastered women with wine. My disgust was next level.

"These ladies actually know their stuff, Ruby," Jack said, his slate grey eyes lighting up as he ran his fingers through his hair, "I'm getting their whole set up—it makes total sense. They're gonna come to Indianapolis to help set it up, and they're guaranteeing it all for twelve months—"

"Hey, that's great," I said, twirling the red wine and watching the legs trickle down, "I'm not dissing the product. It's just, personally, I can't buy anything when people act like this. His whole circus makes me non-functional. They got my tuition dollars, that's enough."

Jack shrugged and began thumbing through the papers in front of him.

"Free wine is a nice touch though; at least it gets me talking," I said, clinking my wine glass against his water, "Cheers!"

"Cheers indeed," he said with a laugh.

A low buzz live microphone feed cut through the air, silencing the room quickly. "All right. Ummm . . . I hope you've all had enough of a break, we have one more hour to get through. I'm going to talk now about air purifiers I use to maintain a sterile operatory, but, but but . . . ah . . . before we go there, any questions on the morning's material?"

Jack tapped the paper with our game notes and winked. "I think it's time we get back to business."

For the remaining hour, the wine and the game kept my mind occupied, and I was feeling quite giddy when everything began wrapping up.

"Ruby," Jack said, pulling on my arm after the lecturer vacated his post. "This is Craig, the guy I drove here with last night." He was motioning to the gentleman on his left, a man I hadn't noticed until then. After one glance, it was surprising I had entirely missed him. His cleft chin was a razor precision cut and his dark brown hair was so perfectly styled I had to suppress the urge to reach over and mangle it. He was the poster child for "All-American guy."

"Craig, this is Ruby. She practices in Fargo, like the movie!"

"Thanks for the reminder," I said, hitting him playfully on the arm.

"No way," said Craig, "Do you all really talk like that?"

"Yeh, sure you betcha we do," I said, gesturing with an up-swing of my fist in front of my chest and widening my eyes into a salt-of-the-Earth kind of face.

"Hey, nothing wrong with it. We're from Indianapolis." Jack said, motioning between Craig and himself and raising his eyebrows in contempt.

"The Indy 500 at least doesn't provoke strangers to ask if you've ever thrown someone into a woodchipper."

"Classic move," said Craig.

"Baller status," Jack agreed.

"But seriously, have you?" Craig asked, narrowing his eyes and cocking his head sideways.

"In any event," Jack cut in, "Ruby and I met after she rolled into lecture about three hours late—"

"Oh man, don't get me started," I said, "I mean, I tried, I really tried you guys."

"Oh sure, we get it," Jack said. "You wanted the market share on fashionably late."

"I thought that was our thing?" Craig chimed in. "We barely made it here through that shit storm."

"Oh, come on, man. Let the lady have it."

"Now, now, gentleman," I said waving my arms, "I'm willing to share the glory."

"How 'bout you just join us for dinner?" Jack said. "Craig and I are going to Gibson's, along with another guy we met last time."

His invite caught me off guard. I had not packed for extracurricular activity and was not prepared for a social anything. But we were having fun. What harm was there in showing up and making the most of one evening? I pulled out my phone and pretended to check my schedule. "Looks like I'm free," I said, pointing to an empty screen.

* * *

We weren't scheduled to meet up for a couple of hours, so again, I hit the gym beforehand. This time, the wine and excitement of going out were too much for six straight miles of monotonous treadmill running, so I opted for a mixed bag of activity. I started with a treadmill high-intensity interval and then transferred to a stationary bike for twenty minutes of sustained cardio, taking advantage of the burn I initiated. After that, I moved onto the floor for stretching and core to complete the circuit.

As I moved into that space, I noted the presence of California Guy from earlier. I watched his movements in the mirror facing me and noticed he kept glancing my way. It felt odd, knowing he was watching, and I wondered what was running through his mind. I considered smiling and making friends, but when I finally caught his attention, his expression was uninviting. He made no note of recognition, so I assumed my social awkwardness from earlier killed any future interactions.

Back in my room, I scoured the contents of my luggage to piece together an outfit, hoping I could find something I could pull off for an evening out. I had boldly patterned, form-fitting yoga tights I could pair this with my boots and vest from earlier, which could potentially be conveyed as "pulling it off," but it was a far cry from *appropriate*. It was barely fit for a sixteen-year-old. Yet, my options were that, back into my sweaty dress from earlier, or into my outfit for the following day. After contemplating far too long, I settled on leggings as pants, believing I would never see these guys again.

I styled my hair and makeup into that of an acceptable professional heading out for dinner among colleagues, then dressed in my "sixteen-year-old" gear. Before leaving, I checked the full-length mirror for appropriateness. One glance at my ridiculously dichotomous appearance and it was apparent I was not pulling it off; I looked like a desperate housewife. But, if I wanted to go, I had to accept it was what it was.

I plastered on a self-assured face and ventured to the lobby, feeling half confident and half terrified as to how they would receive me. Uneasy about where this night could end. As I exited the open glass elevator and spotted Jack near the concierge desk, I immediately recognized their other friend - California Guy.

Ugh, figures.

CHAPTER 11

"I swear - look it up yourselves. We had both a Dr. Toothaker and a Dr. Payne. And if that wasn't enough, Dr. Toothaker just got arrested for stealing scrap gold or some shit like that. Obviously, he's a real stand up guy," Nick said, throwing his head back and laughing out loud.

"No way. Some shit is just too good to be true," said Craig, stabbing an asparagus spear and eating the whole thing as one bite.

"I'd buy it," I said. "We had a Dr. Molar doing an oral surgery residency. Every time a patient checked in it was: 'Dr. Molar, your two o'clock patient is ready.' I mean, really, did that guy have another career choice?"

"Chemist . . ." Nick offered.

"Oh, you would!" I said, shaking my head and throwing my hands up in defeat. "Okay, well, I don't have a great name to attach to this," I continued, "but, our old bench instructors circulated a story of some Delta Sig guy in the sixties who was kicked out of school for etherizing his roommate, doing lord knows what to him when he was out!"

"Aw heeaaalll nahh," said Jack, scrunching up all the muscles in his face. "They just say that shit to make people uneasy. And scare us away from the ether. Oh – by the way . . ." Jack set his iPhone face-up on the table and slid it across to Craig, "See for yourself. This man speaks the truth."

Craig picked up the phone and started to read out loud while scrolling down the screen, "Dr. Toothaker, a dentist in Omaha, now faces a federal theft charge for stealing from his employer almost a year ago . . . stole more than $16,000 of VA precious metals . . . police found them in his gym bag . . .he said he had no idea how it got there." Craig tossed the phone back to Jack, "Are you kidding me? No idea?"

-SHCHING!!

The sound of a knife running along a plate pulled my mind from the conversation. Reflexively, my head jolted to the right, where the sound appeared to originate. I expected to see people responding to the ear-splitting sound, only, no chaotic reaction was seen. A woman in a thick wool dress was sipping a cucumber martini, her cheekbones cradling squinted eyes, giving credence to the intent gaze she held on her companion. His eyes were alight as he animatedly detailed something she found amusing. Pieces of flatware were being moved around the white linen cloth like figures, mapping out a scene for effect. He seemed to be feeding off her gaze, as though it gave breath to his lungs and elevated his monolog.

Fearing one of them would see me gawking, I turned back to face our group. While my attention was away, the boys had moved onto a new topic. Accepting an elegant excuse to mentally pause, I gave my thoughts freedom to wander.

The short four-block walk to Gibson's Steakhouse had been a flurry of activity, with our crew taking the cordial measures to break the ice. Each of these guys was an enigma, and I found myself in novel terrain—me, a solitary girl amongst three guys, each uniquely handsome and interesting, being genuinely nice to me. It should have scared the hell out of me, but it didn't. Something was happening. My defenses were starting to weaken.

We were dining at Gibson's, despite the fact the previous month I couldn't stand the place. The pretentious restaurant aura was exactly the same. The tuxedo wearing waiters looked exactly the same. My salmon order was exactly the same. But, because of the company, my experience was a one-eighty.

California Guy, Nick, after opening up and resolving my failed interaction from earlier, turned out to be the most irreverent and magnetic personality I'd ever met. We were on the same wavelength, and within this newly formed quartet, the two of us instinctually formed a pair.

I threw a piece of food Nick's way to catch his attention, then motioned toward the couple next to me, "Check these two out. What on earth could he be saying that's so captivating?"

He glanced their way, studied them for a moment, and then looked back at me with a smoldering gaze. "I find nothing more relaxing than a good round of bowling," he said, mimicking the man's facial expressions.

"How fascinating!" I played in, putting off my best sultry voice while trying to hold a serious face. We held each other in feigned adoration for a long, silent pause, our breathing audible as we waited to see who would break character first. For one, flickering moment, the adoration felt deceptively real. When I did break character, his angular jawline softened as he flashed a boyish grin.

"What the hell you two? Are you even paying attention?" Jack's voice carried through the air, pulling me out of the trance. He motioned to waiters who were standing at our sides, trying to deliver our plates.

"Oh, yeah. Sorry 'bout that," I laughed, sitting back and clearing space.

The remainder of our dinner passed blissfully. Nothing crass was taboo and I laughed like I hadn't in years. We honed our impressions of the lecturer and his colloquial mannerisms and cracked jokes about mishaps that I have never heard other doctors admit to in my life.

Most CE gatherings left me feeling suffocated. I had resorted to stifling my authentic self on the professional level to act the proper part. But these guys were legit, and with them, I took down my walls and was *me*. It felt liberating. The honesty in our conversation was assuredly the product of Nick's ice-breaking abandon; he was the catalyst that made our group thrive. He opened the floor for anything and everything, and we ran with it. The night passed in a whirlwind of amusement, and I secretly wished the dinner would never end.

Nick insisted the boys split my bill, and then we retraced the four-block span back to the hotel, paired two-by-two on a sidewalk under constant threat from heavy traffic. I found myself conveniently matched with Nick, who had guided me onto the inner half while he occupied the outside, freely spilling confessions about my discontented life.

"I think I had more fun tonight than I did in all of dental school," I said, shaking my head in annoyance. "I anticipated it to be the best time of my life, but as a new mom, I was not at the same phase as everyone else. No one could relate."

"Actually, I interviewed and toured where you went to

school, but nothing presented a significant pull. I opted for Minnesota for convenience," I said, keeping my eyes focused on the curb and trying extra hard to walk the straight line along it without brushing against his arm.

"You would have gone there if you had met me on that tour," he said with confidence.

"Is that so?" I pressed, squinting back at him, assessing the veracity of such a bold statement.

His deep brown eyes relayed genuine sincerity, and in their trance, I felt something inexplicable, like my soul recognizing kin. Being there next to him was like we were the only two people in the whole wide world. The atmosphere surrounding us was so enthralling I could have stood blissfully in that spot all night.

I retrained my eyes to the flying lights ahead and tried to play off his comment like an insignificant thing, though gauging my gut reaction to it, I had to agree wordlessly. His brazen sentiment was correct.

"Hey Ruby, where exactly is Fargo?" Jack's half turned head shouted back our direction, snapping me back to the present.

"Smack dab in the middle of nowhere!" I answered, "Maybe eight-hundred or so miles northwest of here. It's a picturesque black hole in a valley that sucks all the bad weather in." I carried on with a laugh, then trailed. I continued more solemnly. "A black hole from which there is no escape. I've tried many times to leave," I disclosed with less confidence, "but no door has ever opened up for me."

"Where would you go if you could anywhere?" Jack said, stretching his arms wide to convey the limitless sea of possibilities.

"Anywhere other than there," Nick answered for me, turning my way again and nodding approvingly at the look on my face. My head bowed back in silent assent.

"Sounds good to me," Jack hooted, then commenced motioning wildly with his arms, trying to dissuade us from returning to the hotel so early on in the night. The rest of us were not so enlivened, but a compromise was made that the four of us would have one quick stop at the hotel bar before officially calling it a night.

Nick was the first to abandon our group, and secretly, I wanted to leave when he did, but I thought that would seem forward, so I stayed. Craig was the next to head off to his room, and again I stayed, assuming I too should take an individual leave.

What I didn't consider was that my inaction now made it the two of us, Jack and me, alone in the dark of the hotel bar, which appeared most forward in hindsight. I should have realized his invitation to dinner held ulterior motives. Unfortunately, giddiness had skewed my usual good judgment. Upon illumination of his intent, claustrophobia descended.

CHAPTER 12

Jack ordered one more beer for me and struck a deal—I would hang out with him for one last drink. As soon as I was aware of his motivations, I regretted agreeing to this deal, but it was where I ended up. I started this night anxious things might end poorly. I accepted my fate, and I paid.

"Ask me anything, I'll tell you anything," he began, staring me down hard with his slate blue eyes. I had zero interest in knowing about him, but my beer just arrived, and I pride myself on being a woman of my word.

"Why did you invite me out tonight?" I said, uncomfortably shifting my weight.

"I don't know. You seemed like a cool girl," He said, while starting to rub my thigh. Instinctually, I moved it out of reach.

"So, what is your practice like?" I asked, trying to steer the conversation in another direction.

"I only bought it a year ago," he said. "It's small, and I'm working on building it up. The owner-doctor was getting dementia, so there is a lot of work to be done."

That hit home a little too hard.

"My stepdad was a dentist. He just retired and already has dementia. He's only sixty-three years old. I'm terrified of ending up like him," I confessed, spilling this intimate detail like he was a trusted friend. Then I looked up, and his eyes met mine. They were piercing. Like they could penetrate the most solid of defenses.

"I'm sorry to hear that," he said kindly. Then he started rubbing my leg again.

"You have the most beautiful eyes," he said.

"You know I'm married," I told him sternly.

"And I have a girlfriend. I'm not trying to hit on you," he said with his mouth, while his hand said the opposite thing to my thigh. I repositioned myself further away.

"So, your girlfriend," I asked, "is she a legit thing?" again trying to deviate from where this interaction was so curiously heading.

"You are not like any other girl I've ever met," he said, skirting my inquiry. "The way you talk and the way you act, it's so different from other girls."

I recognized this remark as a token dick line and nearly yelled: "I'm not *that girl.*" I was wild with frustration. "I don't do this kind of thing," I firmly imposed, making my move to leave.

"I'll stop," he promised. "Just stay, please," he said, working me over with his eyes.

"Okay," I agreed, "but you need to behave," I asserted, trying to establish control.

We began bonding over mutual insomnia struggles and other things dental-related, but again, after ten minutes had passed, he resumed his antics.

"Just give me one kiss," he said. "Please, just one," he begged, reaching up to touch the side of my face.

"I can't do this!" I yelled at him irritably, standing up to take my leave. He stood as well, sweeping in for my mouth, but I maneuvered a near miss and kissed him instead on the cheek. I wished him a good night and then turned briskly in retreat.

What the hell just happened? How I even got to that point was utterly perplexing—I knew I didn't want anything with him, why couldn't I just be more frank?

With the briskness of a shopping mall speed walker, I made my way toward the elevators. While doing so, I aligned my steps with the herringbone pattern inset in the hardwood floor, getting lost in the rhythm. Skip two lines, place my foot center on the third, and repeat. The pattern was soothingly familiar, my mom and Tom's kitchen floor had the same design, so stepping in sync felt natural. I counted and stepped and counted and stepped, inhaled and exhaled, and ruminated.

It wasn't supposed to be like this.

When I became a dentist, I assumed I'd start my career beneath the caring wings of Tom. Long ago, that dream died for reasons unrelated to now, yet I'd veered so far from where I believed I was going I couldn't recount how it all got lost. All I knew was who I'd become felt immovable. And Tom was never going to be the same; Alzheimer's is an irreversible degenerative disease, to hope for a return to normal was delusional. Jack's story churned up the heartrending reality our family was facing, and as much as I wanted to run from the truth, it was in relentless pursuit.

The elevator doors were open when I reached the atrium. I stepped inside, depressed the number, and, as I sank into memory, I watched the heavy doors close.

* * *

"They are dying in front of my eyes!" I sobbed into the

phone to my sister Krista, pacing from my bed to the window as we spoke.

"They were just here in Phoenix for Thanksgiving and seemed fine," she said rationally. Which, to her credit, made sense. It had only been a couple of months since my mom's fall. But I needed her to understand the severity wasn't as overhyped as she thought I was making it.

"They are not fine! You aren't here seeing them day after day," I explained. While holding to my line and focusing on heel to toe contact with each step, I divulged their plight in gross detail. I explained that the depth perception required to tie fishing line wasn't going to return to Tom, that mom wasn't ever going to walk with a normal gait again. That the ailments plaguing their health before these incidents seemed manageable, right up until these factors spiraled everything out of control. "I don't believe the mess they are in now is recoverable! I can't fix this. I can't help," I sobbed, desperate for her to catch on.

Only, she didn't catch on. She had a counter argument for everything, reminding me I wasn't their doctor and I wasn't God. She stressed how banal the belief anything could be inside my control was, with intonation as vapid as an automated voice mail.

"It can't be that bad Ruby. Come on," she admonished me, which made me stomp and pace furiously.

"It's that bad! Please, believe me," I pleaded through pursed lips, repressing the urge to scream at the top of my lungs.

"Uff-da," she said, in on point reproduction of our mom's intonation right before exclaiming "you're making a mountain out of a molehill." Her sarcastic application of mom's signature idiom was a trump card for perspective. It was obvious Krista wasn't budging, there was nowhere else for this argument to go.

"–I know, I know," I said, exhaling a long, slow sigh. But I had one more point to make.

"Look at it this way. I'm thirty-four years old and Mom is fifty-five. There's twenty-one years until I'm possibly at that same point. What if I'm doomed to repeat their fate? Twenty-one years is the blink of an eye!"

The magnitude of this truth had been oscillating in my head for some time, yet in vocalizing it to her, the ugly truth was a backhanded slap to the jawline. I staggered and mis-stepped, tripping over a claw foot jutting out from my bed frame. Stopping at the footboard, I gripped its rolled sleigh curve for stability. The cool, smooth mahogany surface shifted my thinking, and suddenly, I was pissed beyond reason that this furniture was obstructing my path.

Our bedroom set was gaudy and gargantuan and entirely unfit for our taste. Covertly, I hated it, but I couldn't say so because it came from my parents. It was a Thomasville set they had bought only a few years prior, yet my mom insisted was an "heirloom."

"It's tradition for it to pass onto you," she had said when they were permanently moving to their lake home. From a practical standpoint, Logan and I had just moved into a consciously empty house; free furniture was a blessing. However, the greater truth was that, when it came to my mom, I simply couldn't say no. I had never been able to. All my life I'd been who she said I had to be and done what she said I had to do, without question.

It was as though I was waiting for some mystical rite

of passage, a handing-over-of-reigns type of ceremony, finally legitimizing my independence. Was that time ever going to come? Or was I destined to spend the last twenty-one years of my life in the shadow of my parents?

"What if in twenty-one years I die never having gotten to live my life?" I cried. "Everything I've done is for mom."

How I switched topics so drastically was beyond comprehension. One minute I wanted her to understand our parents' health crisis was real, the next I wanted to explain I felt trapped by everything under the sun. I'm sure to her I was no longer coherent, but what I knew then was there was no holding back, I'd given permission to the thoughts flying off my lips. There was an abrupt shift from talking about our parents to me carrying on in hysterics about how miserable I was.

Krista cut me off after a couple minutes, "Ruby, stop. Your life is amazing."

"You say that, but you moved away! If you thought this would be so amazing, why didn't you stay to do it?" I challenged back. The accusation was a low blow indeed and entirely uncalled for, but the bitterness was acid on my tongue. Silence on her end of the line let me know she wasn't going to give a response.

"I stayed home and now I'm stuck in this godawful mess!" I howled, in an irrational argumentative tone, as though pleading for the right to reclaim my life.

By this time, Krista was done entertaining my diatribe, and rightfully moved to end our call, but not before reminding me that it was all going to be fine and implying I was simply overtired.

I threw the phone onto my bed and crossed to the armchair overlooking our pond, slumping into it and unfocusing my eyes on the reflection of a cloudless sky. The blurry landscape was a fitting accompaniment to the current state of events. Everything was out of focus. Krista was wrong, yet there was nothing I could do to change her mind.

When Logan came home, I complained to him how Krista didn't believe me. He listened patiently and spoke reassuring words, calming me down finally. Logan, the only other person privy to the truth—the man in the midst of the eddy with me—only he was steadying me also.

"Ruby, you need a break," he said, tilting his chin down to deliver a concerned look over the rim of his glasses. "Go to Chicago tomorrow and shut down. I've got things covered here. Don't think about anything going on back home. Relax and disengage for a while."

His suggestion caught me off guard. Clearly the immensity of this fight proved beyond my skill level, but what good-hearted person allows themselves to walk away for a while?

One who is on the brink herself.

Logan was the wisest, most rational man I knew. And he was right. Assessing my current state, no other options seemed viable.

* * *

Well, the evening of calamity with Jack had been a complete and utter fail. All I'd done was propagate a hysteria I had been hoping to hold back from resurgence, compiling refuse in a psyche on its way to a full-blown meltdown. Hardly what was needed.

I fell back into the wavy comfort of my hotel room,

brushed my teeth, washed off my make-up, and considered the face that considered me back along the wall. *Stupid girl.* I was hardly recognizable in the macabre ambiance of the fluorescent gleam, and the superimposed figure staring me down was fundamentally disconcerting.

Sleepless nights were the defining characteristic of the previous three years of my life. As anyone similarly afflicted can confirm, unchecked insomnia is an evil bitch capable of vexing your mind. The havoc will often loosen the reigns, and that night, as I fought for sleep, I instead commenced ruminating and obsessing, fretting and worrying—not over logical fears to the lucid day's mind, but in my twisted state, they were concrete.

I felt guilty. My dismissal tactics were severe by the end, and it was obvious Jack was not in a safe place. I was concerned about his well-being. He'd had so much to drink. I feared he wouldn't make it back to his room alive. I couldn't focus until I resolved the issue, so like a massive idiot, I texted him. I was hoping to quiet my anxiety with confirmation of vitality. However, my desperate act fired up a text flirtation that carried us through the next hour with him coaxing me to his room, and me articulately refusing.

It was a continuation of the stupid conversation from the bar, and eventually, I messaged him: "You are asking me to put my entire life at stake. Walking to your room will never happen because I couldn't complete all those steps knowing what I was sacrificing."

"Then let me come to your room. Just so we could be next to each other, so we don't have to be alone," he replied.

And like a moron, I considered it.

I was lonely and incapable of sleep. Maybe having someone near who felt the same might ease my suffering? After a few more cryptic messages, I caved and gave him my room number. Then I lay there horrified.

Fortunately for me, he changed his mind, and interrupted my petrified contemplation with more messages. I was tiring of the game, and eventually, my phone fell from my fingertips and I passed into something like sleep. Several unanswered messages graced my screen the next morning.

I'm uncertain what would have transpired had he appeared at my door. I didn't want *him*, but assessing my behavior enlightened me to the reality that I was in bizarre territory where affairs were readily available.

CHAPTER 13

The click and hum of the heater kicking on drew me out of sleep. In my twilight phase of alertness, the late-night bar scene and future string of texts felt like elements of a dream. A dream untethered to real life in any way—fanciful—such that it was only due to a deep sleep trance my mind generated it. This delusion was a feather floating off in the wind—a decadent notion. Sure, I'd returned to my room and dressed in comfies and settled into a spot so deeply my body impressed. None of that other stuff happened.

As I was resting in that comfortable delusion, chasing the feather with my mind, a sharp calf twinge forced my leg to jolt up—rapid and stiff and automatic—hurling me back to reality. My brain shuddered as I drew in a deep breath, rolling my head side to side. *No no no no no no.*

I slid my fingers across the smooth covers until I located the cold case of my phone. In defiance of the voice inside urging me to stay ignorant, I drew it close for inspection. Sure enough, the screen was littered with evidence. Meaningless messages that felt significantly more meaningless in the somber light of day. How could I carry on so long with such a stupid, stupid thing?

In the heat of the moment, I cited the need to ensure he was okay as motivation, and right then, that need felt genuine. It felt like I couldn't go to sleep without satisfying it. What was this compulsion to take care of him? Maybe it was because he was drunk . . . a stranger in need? Or maybe because he was a young man, boyish even, and taking care of him was a motherly instinct? If that were true, I'd really have a conundrum because letting him in was a complete threat to my position, how would a maternal subconscious push me to take care of someone when doing so was in direct contrast to the stability of it?

I chased the igniting branches until it hurt to think. I needed to accept a solid answer wasn't coming. It was time to drop it. Plus, there were other pressing, less existential matters I needed to tend to with that mental energy.

Day two of the conference began in one hour, and it went on with or without me. I needed to get up and face the guys. First things first though, I needed to double the efforts of my previous night's beautification protocol. It was of paramount importance I show up looking fresh, as though I had an unquestionably solo evening.

Once downstairs, it became clear no one else executed their morning routine with the same exacting degree to detail. Craig and Jack were the first I laid eyes on, and both were dressed in worn jeans and T-shirts, still standing out among the nerdier doctors wearing scrubs because we were doing a hands-on lab that morning.

An anxious twinge piqued my stomach. *Now I'm the oddball who's dolled up; the only other women putting forth this much effort are the sales hussies!* My eyes scanned from Jack and Craig, resting against the wall nursing coffee, to the bevy of women lounging around booths set up on either side of the lecture hall entrance. It's hard to not gawk when your brain is pondering— *does the way I look hit other people as off putting as the way this woman is affecting me?*—which was what I'm sure I looked like I was doing when the head hussy waved at me enthusiastically.

"Dr. Carlson," she crooned, shuffling over in that awkward manner a Barbie doll in a mini dress walks in heels. She was accompanied by a chunky male with wavy brown hair, her heels so high he was an inch or two below her height. "You must meet Dr. Blankenshine; he's the head of our teaching clinic in Cuba," she said, her glamorous smile extending to her eyes as they drifted back and forth between us.

He extended his hand firmly and clasped mine with the degree of certainty guys who know their place in this world employ. But I wasn't buying. Though he didn't look a day over thirty, his lips appeared to be injected with that shit pushed upon aging women. No man assured of himself would do something so silly. I gripped his warm hand a little too tight, trying to send out a silent message of my own

"Pleasure to meet you," I said with a false smile.

"They're here this weekend to answer any questions you have about our hands-on program," she said, passing over a brochure with our instructor's portrait on the cover. The same portrait that had been popping up all over my browsers ever since I started these classes.

"Clinical practice in a teaching environment is the fastest way to master surgery," she said, jabbing at my arm in a playful way and squinting like a girl selling age-defying makeup.

"—Really the fastest and the best," her counterpart added, "Everyone is guaranteed hands on placement of at least fifty fixtures. No other seminar offers that."

"Sounds amazing," I said, cutting him off abruptly. "I'll definitely put some thought into it." Turning to rummage through my bag rather than meet their faces, I add, "Right now though, please, you'll have to excuse me. I just realized I forgot my loupes and I have to grab them before class gets started." I mustered up a distressed expression and flashed it politely before turning to walk away.

Successful ending of that interaction, check.

As I darted down the hall congratulating myself smugly, I nearly crashed into Craig, who was racing toward the bathroom with the same level of enthusiasm I was channeling. "Whoa there, girl," he said, laughing with the boyish charm that draws girls to Tom Cruise even when he's fumbling through life as Jerry Maguire.

"Holy shit Craig, you could've killed me!" I barked at him in a playfully exasperated way.

"I can't even, man," he said in a low murmur, bowing and shaking his head like a child admitting a mistake. "I'm too old for this shit, I could hardly drag myself out of bed this morning." If green were a color attribute for a handsome face, then that was the color that washed over him. In a near reverent horror, he pointed his hand at the closed double doors behind me, "and if this wasn't enough."

Damn straight that was enough. Now, I'll fully admit, until then I'd coped by ignoring it. Not because I found the matter easy, but because the very idea of touching a deceased human body was tormenting. So much so I cited it to test out of the dissection lab in my college gross anatomy class by using fake models. To be fair, I tried. I tried for a month, believing facing my fear would diminish it, but each encounter only intensified it. Still, I couldn't quit. Chalking it up to pregnancy hormones, I made a case that was appealing, allowing me to pass a required class for dental school without really completing all the steps. The whole experience didn't sit well. In fact, I felt like a fraud forever after.

"Let me make it through Anatomy," I told any person who asked anything about my first year of dental school, "things will be fine once I'm done with Gross Anatomy. If I make it through that, I can do anything."

And I did. By going vegetarian and wearing a mask lined with Mentholatum over nostrils stuffed with cotton, fixing my eyes on the end. When I got there, a grand excitement washed over me, like I'd been filled by a spirit. I knew I'd conquered something life changing. That awareness buoyed my confidence and made me want to reach out for other achievements. The kind that, until then, felt impossibly out of reach. That's when I started to run.

"Earth to Ruby," Craig said, his voice drawing me back to reality.

"Oh, god. My mind's racing. Sorry, this whole 'decapitated head' business got my head spinning. Why did you have to remind me? This shit is the worst."

"Just tell yourself it's not real," he said, a graveness softening his angular features, "That's how I've always got along."

The garish color that had previously washed over his face was starting to turn more neutral. His eyes glanced toward the entrance doors with less trepidation than they had before. The statement he'd made was obviously as much a beacon of hope for him as it had been for me.

"Genius," I said, "thank you. We've got this!"

Right then, a voice rang out over a loudspeaker. "Five more minutes until we are ready to open the doors."

We both looked around, as though searching for the source of the voice. It was nowhere to be found. Next, both of us started looking around aimlessly.

"I gotta disappear for a sec," I said after a long pause, seeking an elegant point to excuse myself. I needed to disappear after dodging the head hussy, which to him might look unusual. "I'm evading the annoying sales people." I said in an explanatory way, "I'll be inside in a moment - save me a seat, will you? Yesterday he said we need groups of four, I think we've got a tidy four-some. It's dental school all over again, and that's something we know we can do."

"Yeah, sure. Thanks," he said, "See ya in a few," he added in conclusion, turning back toward the restroom.

When I returned to the lecture hall, after the double doors had been opened to let in the attendees then closed tight to keep out the smell, I realized I'd made a mistake. Ty, my chatty former classmate climbing the lecture circuit ladder was chatting up Craig, Nick, and Jack, his loupes and binders and jacket occupying the fourth spot definitively. Craig apparently wasn't up to the whole saving-of-the-space promise he'd made before. I locked eyes with Nick, whose somber expression reverberated my disappointment. Unwilling to let them think I cared, I strode up to their group with a smile.

"You four are all locked down, I see," I said, flashing my eyes across them, then around the room. The hotel conference room that was so orderly the day before had transformed into a scene from a horror film. Groups of three to four were standing around long tables with morose centerpieces—severed heads on a platter—with implant placement equipment scattered about like cutlery. Desperate for a welcoming face, I scanned each group while projecting the facade of a woman unfazed, despite the fact a mounting nausea threatened to consume me.

At last I made eye contact with Chad, who was among the scrub wearing doctors. He was set up nearly kiddy-corner to us, joined by an unfamiliar doctor, and Gregg. I mouthed the words, "can I join you," and he smiled back kindly, making a great sweeping motion with his arm to indicate I was welcomed over. I started to walk their way when I was stopped by Nick's voice.

"Hey Ruby, meet us upstairs at the restaurant afterwards."

"Sure thing, that sounds perfect," I said, fighting with my lips to stop at a nonchalant smile. I turned to walk away casually, but, as I did, I became aware of two hot spots burning through my back, as though penetrated by lasers. I couldn't shake the notion someone was staring. Assured I was making it up, I turned back with an innocent sweep of my eyes, only to lock Nick's firmly. They were squinted, and his stone hard jaw was set tight. His expression seemed of genuine intrigue, like he didn't know what the hell to make of me—a sentiment my whole body echoed. Judging by the rush of heat to my face, I was sure he saw me go crimson. I turned back again and strode away more briskly.

The remainder of the morning passed quickly. Once I started honing in on the minutiae of surgery, the greater picture became less overwhelming. Chad proved a great resource as well; his surgery foundation far surpassed mine, and he was unrestrained in offering an education tailored to my needs. I listened intently, grateful for the wealth of advice.

The sycophantic sales hussies and their male newcomer, Dr. Blankenshine, were wandering among the tables, pushing the Cuba trip. They ushered him around the room like royalty, as though we should be blessed when he paused to offer advice. His brown waves framed a round, youthful face. Too youthful, puerile even, such that he'd never have a hope for facial hair. He didn't possess a glimmer of potential for being classically good-looking and had zero legitimacy to the claim he was capable of supervising surgery. I found it all very bothersome, especially since such great lengths obviously went into ensuring his female personnel were over the top.

What was the intention behind this guy's lecture circus?

When they neared our table and engaged the group of doctors behind us, I eavesdropped. They were working over my contemporaries, enticing them on an experience centered on partying and getting laid.

Figures. I concluded obtusely.

When all our surgical tasks for the morning were complete, I packed up my stuff, rushed past the booths in haste to evade the conversational advances of every sales person, and locked my eyes on the glass elevators, looking only to meet up with the guys.

We shared a hurried lunch in the back wall restaurant before splitting ways. As I warily picked at a bowl of fruit, the realization that this was our last shared meal enhanced the sickness I was battling. I deeply regretted having changed my itinerary to D.C. These guys woke my restrained side, and I was not ready to let it go. As I detailed my revised itinerary, I added subtle hints to press them to make the same adjustment, finishing with an iron-clad selling feature: Cherry Blossom Season. "The single greatest event in our nation, nothing captures equivalent splendor," I said, mimicking the voice of a travel agent reading from a brochure enticingly.

"Not me," said Craig. "We booked a family vacation over that weekend ages ago; my wife would kill me if I changed it."

"Okay, you have a legitimate excuse. How 'bout you guys?" I said, motioning between Nick and Jack with my fork.

Nick paused from attacking his salad like it was his last meal and looked up at the air.

"Well, I'm doing the Cuba Trip next month–" he began.

"Wait, what?!?" I said, cutting him off mid-sentence. "You are actually buying into that?"

"Oh yeah," said Jack with a wink, "really though, he's just going to hang out with the 'head-head' guy."

"What? What am I missing?"

"Just a little nickname we gave Dr. Blanken-whatever, the guy who set up our whole area this morning. We're pretty sure he runs a side gig supplying this crew with severed heads," Jack explained.

"That is fucking genius."

"That guy," Nick said with a shake of his head.

I could feel Jack's eyes boring into me, so I was looking around everywhere to avoid eye contact. Nick was piling up his last forkful of salad with the fervor of one taking out aggression on a plate. Craig was sipping on a soda thoughtfully. Jack was still staring. Social norms dictate I occasionally glance his way, so I did. When we finally made eye contact, my insides boiled.

"Anyway, there's no way I can make D.C.," Jack added, regretfully. "I could barely afford these seminars, but Chicago was driving distance. It was the only thing that made it obtainable in the first place."

Relief rushed over me.

"Maybe you should change back," Jack said in a coaxing voice, "The seminar schedulers are very accommodating."

"Oh, I'm sure they are," I said with a laugh, jabbing at a strawberry, contemplating whether I could suppress my disgust and swallow it. "*Very* accommodating. I'm sure I could switch things back in a quick conversation with the 'head-head guy.'"

"Don't do that," said Nick, abruptly. His face seemed to harden at the very thought.

We shared a glance, and I sensed he was holding himself back. Seeking to douse any notion I had interest in things like that, I responded quickly.

"Oh, don't you worry," I said sternly, "I'd never."

Our lunch passed in relative silence after that. There was talk of surgery and travels and other cursory tidbits colleagues share, but it was clear everyone had mentally wandered. When lunch was over, I passed around a napkin and asked the guys to write down their numbers so we could stay in touch, then we bade each other goodbye in a basic, professional way.

My flight didn't leave until much later that night, so I gathered my things and transferred from the table to a solitary seat at the bar. Exhaustion overtook me the instant the need to uphold social interactions receded; it was all I could do to uphold my posture in a manner fit for functional life. I ordered a gin and tonic and hoped it would serve to both calm the nausea and calm my frazzled nerves.

As I waited for it, I turned the napkin over and over in my hands, studying the way each guy transcribed their information. I'd heard somewhere that handwriting could be used to decipher elements of personality, but I didn't remember in what way. A need to analyze handwriting had never presented itself, so I'd never expended mental resources retaining the science of it all. Right then, I wished I had. Craig's number was written with the blocky perfection you would expect from an architect, and Jack and Nick wrote in the stereotypical scrawling of guys. But whereas Jack's looked like there was nothing but lack of care behind his messy lines, Nick's had flair, like he intentionally wrote in an incomplete style to accompany his vibe.

I programmed each one into my phone and then sent out a group message to tender a proper farewell. It was simple; "Ruby," just to ensure they all had mine. A group text was essential, I didn't want to make it seem like I was playing favorites.

"Your gin and tonic ma'am," said the bartender, placing a fresh napkin down in front of me before setting my drink upon it. "Thanks," I said, looking up enough to have appeared to look up, then honing focus back down at my immediate space. I set my phone down and picked up the drink, starting in with a long, slow sip. The cold, crisp liquid had an initial bite, but as it washed down, a relaxed calm settled over me. I closed my eyes to savor the effect, exhaling slow and steady to embrace it. My eyes popped open at the sound of a ding; their focus drawn to the illuminated screen of my iPhone. A message from Nick came into the chain:

"Nick likes bowling."

I laughed out loud and shook my head at his absurdity. Another ding came after quickly. It was Jack, and he chose to message outside of the thread. I wished I could ignore his, but the brief message occupied the line adjacent to the icon labeled "J," there was no need to open it.

"We almost made it," it read, causing my stomach to twist and roll. I swiped it to the left and deleted it.

CHAPTER 14

As I sat catatonic in my spot at the bar, stunned and star-struck at what had unfolded, I took great pleasure in meticulously deleting Jack from my phone. Completion of the job, followed by a thorough inspection to ensure correct completion, provided healthy satisfaction.

"Hey! Lost you at lunch," Chad's voice called from somewhere off behind. I turned to greet him, stopping just shy of direct face to face contact.

"Yes, I had to dart out of there. Sorry."

"Not to worry," he said cheerily, "you're here now. Care if I join you?"

"Of course not. Pull up a seat," I said, motioning to the tall bar stool next to me with a half wave.

"Excuse me, sir," Chad called out to the bartender, who was polishing glasses with his back to us, "can I get a Bud Light?" The bartender turned to face us, setting his glass atop the lacquered wooden surface. "Sure thing," he replied, glancing from Chad's face to mine, to my near empty glass, then back to mine again. As if reading his thoughts, Chad winked at me and added, "Plus one more of whatever she's having."

Chad clasped the back of the adjacent chair and rotated it his way, placing his hand directly in my sightline. The visual was transfixing. A craftsman's finest tool is their hand, and when it comes to surgical technique, doctors are venerated by their lore. "Dr. So-and-so is the finest in town, everyone says he has the best hands." We all knew things to be this way. And, in comparison to the plethora I had seen, Chad's appeared iconic. It was a living reproduction of a masculine hand graphic artists use to depict manual labor.

Things like that struck an odd chord with me. I understand that, in many aspects of surgery, stronger, manly hands should prove superior. Yet, dentistry is the opposite. It demands mastery of restricted spaces made exponentially troublesome because they are animated and emotion driven. Here, the elegant, spindly fingers of a feminine hand fit perfectly. The idea he performed an array of complex surgeries with hands like his was awe inspiring. Purely from a job requirement fact, those hands were an obstacle he overcame daily. To add one more item to the minefield of intricacies we face was a thought trail I would never entertain.

"Would you like a glass?" the bartender asked, holding the bottle of bud like a trophy to his chest, waiting for Chads permission to release it.

"A glass would be much appreciated, thanks," Chad replied.

We both watched as the bartender produced a glass from beneath the counter, set it atop a white square napkin, and poured out the contents in one swift motion, such that the foam bubbled right up to the rim. Chad picked it up and raised it my way, "Cheers!" he said.

"Cheers," I replied, lifting mine and then polishing the rest off. I slid the empty tumbler to the edge of the bar, leaving an open napkin for the next.

"You flew right out of there today," Chad said, slapping

my shoulder and tossing his head back with laughter.

"So, you caught that, huh?" I said, shaking mine apologetically. "The whole cadaver business is something I've never been able to get over," I confessed, citing a viable cause for bad behavior unrelated to my departure, believable enough to animate my face with conviction. "I couldn't take it anymore, just had to escape. And I haven't been able to eat anything since." I added those last words because Chad invited me to lunch during lab. Instead of shooting him down, I'd answered indirectly and then shot out afterwards to avoid dealing with it. It was an awful thing to do, yet aware as I was, I watched myself execute it.

Right then and there, looking at his gigantic smile, his bright, laughing eyes, and hearing his crisp voice ringing with the clarity of one incapable of sexual impropriety, I felt like the world's biggest idiot. I boxed him in as a nerd and dismissed him in favor of guys I had no business fraternizing with. Guys that were all-American jock types whose doctor's mentality was superseded by "playboy first." I should have known better. Guys like that didn't go to conferences for education. For some reason, I was back in high school, labeling people as cool kids, nerds, and jocks, but that doesn't hold sway in a grown-up environment. Sure, I could share laughs and feel important because I had the attention of three hot guys at a lunch table, but what in the world was that doing for me? I needed to be spending time with guys like Chad, guys who would bring out the best doctor in me.

"Yeah, you look a little pale," Chad said in a reassuring fashion, nudging my body with his words. His voice carried over the air with a comfortable familiarity, as though declaring himself a safe space. The relief I felt inside of it was revitalizing.

"God, it's been two days of forever!" I said, massaging my temples and clenching shut my eyes, mentally playing it back over.

"I can't believe I didn't get in one single run; it's too freakin' cold here too. I'm supposed to be marathon training, but the weather won't let up and I can't get in the long runs," I blurted out in exasperation. "I was gonna go back and do the Phoenix marathon this month, but I have to let that idea go." The words were as much a confirmation for myself as they were a confession to him. He nodded back at this statement, frowning in a consolation.

I looked at his tender expression and sensed he wasn't going to offer advice on that matter, so I prattled on.

"Really, the race wasn't the big deal, it's just that running is my outlet and last week I lost my associate. In theory, I don't have the space for us both, but I'm moving to a gigantic clinic this summer and then I'm gonna need someone else producing in order to cover overhead."

Chad nodded at this bit of information.

"Sounds like you've got a lot of things bouncing around in that head," he said, and we both looked at each other and laughed.

"If you only knew the extent of it," I said, addressing my drink as I drew a line through the condensation with my fingertip. "And to make matters worse, he was perfect! I *liked* him."

"Believe me," Chad said, his eyes growing wider as we talked, "managing associates isn't easy. I've been through three, and I learned something new with each one.

Partnering up with another dentist is more delicate than a marriage."

"The very idea of going on the hunt again makes me want to quit. I have no clue what to do now," I said warily, folding my hands in my lap, surprised at how much I let spill out to a relative stranger.

"I've got an air-tight contract drafted and a very detailed job outline that gets reviewed extensively whenever I have a new associate start. Clear cut communication is essential," Chad said, picking up his glass and taking a big drink. When he set it down, the weighted glass contacting the wood made him blink. He blinked a couple more times and then turned to meet my gaze, "I can share it if you'd like. Having a framework—any place to start—would probably help."

My heart leapt at his generous offer. Lawyers make a killing off of drafting those documents, and a framework would certainly help. I hardly knew him, yet I'd learned enough to revere his business acumen. Whatever he was doing seemed like whatever I should do. I had no proper response to such a selfless offer, my face felt stuck in some type of expression that passes quickly before shock is exposed.

"Shoot me an email," Chad said, drawing a business card from his wallet and extending his hand.

"Thanks, I will definitely do that," I said, taking it from him, pausing to run my finger along the embossed lettering. "This is a great design," I said, flipping it over a couple times before tucking it into my iPhone jacket.

As our conversation unfolded, I allowed the complexity of my life to surface. Chad's expression remained impartial, and through our dialog, I was able to process and see alternate routes through the roadblocks piling up.

When we finished our drinks, we agreed to reconvene in an hour to split an airport shuttle and take advantage of the United Club. Once settled in there, we drifted comfortably to the topics of kids and family, and as we talked, I found that I couldn't stop my eyes from wandering. I was fascinated by the board listing all the United flights departing.

I thought of Nick. He was probably on a plane right now, headed to a home that was warm—a notion so fanciful to me I couldn't wrap my brain around it. How different would my life be if I had moved to California like I dreamed of when I was a girl?

There was a 7:30 flight departing for San Diego, the sight of which broke my soul. *That is not ever in the cards for you girl. You are going home.* I scanned back to the Fargo flight, departing at the same time, and realized the departure status had switched to "delayed."

That's odd. I thought, *usually they send out a text to let me know.*

"Looks like I might be here longer than expected," I said—motioning to the board flashing the real time flight details. I idled right up till 7:15pm, watching my phone and monitoring the board's activity closely. As fear started to surface that my return could be compromised, my mind flashed back to the tricky flight path I'd taken here. How that inconvenient layover in Minneapolis nearly ruined things . . . how silly and uncharacteristic it was I would do that . . . how in order to do that I had switched flight carriers to Delta, because United doesn't fly into Minneapolis . . .

"Shit!" I hollered out, jumping out of my seat like a

woman possessed. "I'm not flying out on United! My 7:30 flight is to Minneapolis not Fargo, and I am flying through Delta."

I waved my hands about in a frenzy and gave Chad an abrupt farewell before flying out of the lounge with my carryon. Busting out of the United Club like a runaway bandit, I hauled ass to the other side of the airport where the Delta flights were departing. As I breathlessly screeched into the gate area, the flight attendant paged my name over the intercom.

CHAPTER 15

Minneapolis–St. Paul International Airport is rarely a place to pursue an indolent layover, but on my convoluted flight path home, I was incapable of much else. Chicago derailed me; my coherent vision for life was suddenly jumbled and confused. I needed to reset because something in me morphed, the walking was helping me process. I was drifting in a surreal state, pace heightened by the moving walkway, surroundings passing in a nebulous haze. As if I was an inhabitant in an alternate universe, questing to reconnect with the version of me vanishing in its space.

In that frame of mind, I started to wish more than anything I could talk to my best friend Olivia. She was the one person I trusted would help me return to normal. Though we'd only been friends for one year, she knew my inner workings like a sister. As far as people go, befriending Olivia was akin to winning the best friend lottery. Never before had someone's mentality and pace of life aligned so seamlessly with mine. Of course, things hadn't always been that way.

She and I first met briefly at Logan's work Christmas party, an encounter I do not recount fondly.

"I'd like you to meet Olivia," Logan was saying, leading me to a table of girls dressed up in eccentric holiday gowns, "the one who shares office space with me."

He didn't actually need to throw in that last detail, I knew who Olivia was. Since they started sharing office space, I heard about her daily.

"Olivia's band is playing in the parade this weekend . . . Olivia and her friends made up their own version of 'True American' and from what I gather, it's amazing . . . Olivia is throwing a hipster themed party next month . . ." Oliva sounded like the coolest girl he'd ever met, and frankly, I was intimidated.

And then, he led me over to a table full of ladies and pointed out this impossibly skinny and perfectly tailored, dressed to the nines girl wearing Christmas tree baubles as earrings. Her hair was wildly styled and cut into an asymmetric bob. She had vibrant green anime eyes paired with a smile that lit up the whole of her face. She was the most adorable and enigmatic girl I had ever seen. One cannot *not* love her. Period. End of story. How could I not despise her?

"Logan!" Olivia called as soon as she saw him, scooting around the other ladies at the table to make her way towards us. "I'm so glad you're here," she said, embracing him in a manner I found too friendly.

He stepped away from her and pulled me from my post a few steps behind, wrapping his arm around my waist.

"Olivia, this is my wife, Ruby."

Olivia's youthful face beamed as she stepped up toward me. "I'm so excited to finally meet you!"

"Oh, me too. I've heard so much about you!" I replied, with such forced effort I instantly doubted she bought it.

My memory of the remainder of that evening plays like silhouettes dancing across a film reel stored in an attic too long. Being amongst his coworkers had me on edge, and the sinking fear he was more in love with her than me held my spirit down like a ten ton freight. Through it all, one feeling permeated the night, I was certain Olivia and I would never be friends.

Then, nine months later, Logan and I were dining at one of his company's hotspots and we had a chance meeting with some of his co-workers, Olivia among them. Everyone was chatting about work related things while I was scrolling through my phone, but then Logan tapped my shoulder and said, "Olivia is training for her first half marathon."

"That's amazing," I said, looking up to offer a dispassionate "atta-girl" smile before turning back to my phone.

"Ruby's running the Fargo women's half-marathon this weekend for her half ironman training," Logan said, tapping me again, looking back and forth between us, waiting for me to react. I wanted to kick him under the table.

"You should join me," I said, the words awkwardly tumbling from my mouth, words I instantly regretted.

"Oh totally, I would love to!" she said, with abandon and her winning smile.

There was no taking it back.

We shared information and race start times, then the morning of the race arrived. It was a "women's race," so naturally, people wore pink and matching gear, looking fashionably put together—as though it is expected women "get ready," even if it's to run. I wasn't on board. My idea of "getting ready to run" was putting on a black sports bra, race bib, and sunblock. I suspected Olivia would show up in something gloriously feminine and coordinated.

But then she shocked me. She showed up wearing the exact same shoes and her running attire was an inverted mirror of mine—dark grey sports bra and simple black shorts—as though we had ESP in planning. During the race she was on fire, abiding my cues for pacing and exhibiting indomitable spunk. She pushed me during the early miles by running faster than I'd typically pace, but not unrealistic either, certainly not so fast I'd succumb to the suffering. Then I pulled her through to the end after she hit the wall by crafting ridiculous scenarios about the fire-department personnel waiting at the finish line with our medals.

When the finishers' gate came into sight, we shared a glance and then burst down the shoot, all-out sprinting to egg each other on, crafting a legendary photo finish. Beyond the line, shirtless firefighters with glistening abs draped pink ribbon shaped medals around our necks.

"Congratulations, you girls did amazing!" the one who gave Olivia her medal said, his sandy blond locks falling into his eyes. It was all I could do to hold my tongue; I was dying to ask what sort of invite went out that ensured only men who looked like him arrived. Instead, Olivia and I exchanged a knowing glance, until she burst out laughing.

As we shuffled into the after-party zone/backdrop for a music video—complete with showers of mist raining down from a fire truck while *Don't You Worry Child* by Swedish House Mafia blasted over the speakers—I got an idea.

"Do you know what would make this moment even more cheesy?" I asked, gesturing around the space with a wave. "Running into those damn misters and actually dancing. Dancing like fly girls and owning it!"

A shimmer flashed across her eyes one second before she took off running, straight into the mist. I followed close behind and we arrived at the same time, just as the frenzied techno beat dropped. For thirty uninhibited seconds we 'werked' our asses and celebrated a momentous feat: instantaneous best friends.

From that day forward, we were twins conjoined at the hip. I created a workout regimen and she showed up faithfully. She took me shopping and inspired me to reconnect with the joy of dressing up like an elegant woman. We trained together, raced together, sang together, did fabulous evenings out and drank craft beer together—*together* we conquered everything.

Connecting with her infused my world with all the parts of me missing since my transition to parenthood. She made me realize how much I had checked out of the world at large. I had faded into the shadow of Logan and me vs. the world; I hadn't cultivated my solo identity since college, and Olivia's entry brought me back to life.

She and I were a force of nature; though ten years apart in age, we were every bit equals in life. We were often given crap for being such an inseparable couple, with Facebook comments on our shared posts of "I wish me and my fiancée shared the love you two do." Plus the low-ball punches of "What does Logan think of this union?"

He honestly never minded—he knew the version of me existing before her; I was a wilting flower when we met. She embedded vitality into my world—ergo ours—and gave us renewed purpose. Olivia fit with Logan and me perfectly. He loves to throw in the technicality that they were friends before she and I were, but the fact of the matter is, the three of us were nearly as tight a knit as she and I were alone.

She was well aware that there was no interest for me in anything physical with Logan. Olivia operated under the pretense that I was simply incapable of attraction to men; she had never seen that side of me.

Oliva was precisely the person I needed to divulge the crazy experience to and then be bitch slapped back into reality by. As a client relations manager, she was always traveling. If my mind served me right, she was heading home from a business trip herself. Since Fargo isn't a highly trafficked final destination, there are only a handful of major airports everyone funnels to before boarding a tiny craft bound for our final destination. Optimistically, I texted her.

"Where are you?" I typed into my phone.

The waving dots popped up on the screen instantly. Hope filled my body.

"I'm in Minneapolis—one last flight before I get home," she replied.

"Me too!"

"Which gate are you at?" She messaged.

"I'm heading right now to C4," I sent.

"Well, I guess I'll be seeing ya there."

Amazed at such serendipitous luck, I quickened my steps and did everything shy of breaking into a run. As soon as I came upon the gate, I was overwhelmed by a barrage of impatient, travel-weary passengers. I scanned them hurriedly but to no avail, so in desperation, I cried out, "Olivia!?!"

Among the sea of bodies emerged a tiny figure wearing a mod-inspired boutique dress, jean jacket, and an infinity scarf; she looked like a Hollywood actress emerging from a crowd of extras. Her beauty and confidence and charisma were now counted among the things I admired and loved her for. Her face was beaming as she raced toward me and we embraced like long-lost friends, enacting a big dramatic scene before bursting into giggles.

"Where's the nearest bar in this joint?" I asked, clasping her shoulders firmly.

"Right beside you," she laughed, motioning to a white counter lined by metal bar stools.

"Thank god. Come on," I said, pulling her behind.

"We need two Goose Island IPA's," I hollered to the bartender as we approached. His androgenous face was framed by a center parted pixie cut, squared up by two squinting eyes that took us in with scrutiny, as though measuring whether we'd had enough to drink. I gave him the most gracious of smiles and articulated clearly, "Please sir, this is an emergency."

His demeanor relaxed and he nodded back, "Two Goose Islands, coming your way."

I waited for him to be out of ear shot before initiating girltalk.

"Holy shit, I've had a crazy weekend," I said, plopping into the smooth metal stool nearest me. "I feel like I'm waking up from a dream."

"Sorry to interrupt," the bartender's voice cut in, "but the Goose kicked right as I started the second glass. I'll leave these here,' he said, placing pint glasses in the space between us, one full to the top with amber liquid, one mostly filled with frothy foam, the effervescence quieting while it settled. "This one's on me," he said, lifting the foamy glass and inspecting the liquid level as it formed. "If you want another, we just tapped Surly's Overrated, it's local. If IPA's are your thing, that's what I'd suggest."

Olivia and I exchanged glances.

"I love Surly," she said, flashing him a winning smile.

"Have you tried the Overrated?" he asked.

"No, I've only had the Furious—"

"Furious is their flagship, but Overrated's the shit. Apparently, they got in big trouble with their first label, and ended up with this," he said, pointing to the stars and stripes framed logo on our pint glasses. He pulled out his phone and typed something into it, all the while talking while he scrolled. I turned to catch Olivia's attention, but only caught her profile; she was staring straight ahead, fully enrapt in his presentation.

While I waited for him to finish, I racked my brain for the proper way to present my escapade. My morning had been spent practicing surgery on decapitated heads. I could spare that morose detail. What of the whole experience would she find worthwhile? What did I remember most? When I closed my eyes and focused, Nick's face was all I could find. The intent expression he held when we spoke, the somber way he stared at me during lab. Those were not things I was feeling liberated to share.

"You know those things where, unless you're experiencing it for yourself, you'll never fully relate?" I blurted out, cutting off their laughter.

They both turned and gaped at me. The bartender still had his arm extended, holding his phone where Olivia's gaze had been.

"Oh goodness, excuse me. The label, can I see?" I asked.

"Of course," he said, shifting his outstretched hand my

way. A pale pink unicorn with a hot pink mane was framed by a sprawling rainbow. Its anime face smiled contentedly at me, while a tiny fairy hovered above the rainbow to the left.

"What the hell?" I said, choking on my drink. "Were they trying to rip off *My Little Pony*?"

"Exactly! Apparently the powers that be thought no one of beer drinking age would be drawn to this. The Feds rejected the original artwork and made them do something less appealing to children," he said, motioning again to the label on the glass he was holding.

"Well, when it comes to IPA, I can't imagine any label you put on it will make it appeal to children. Pretty sure it takes an adult to appreciate this taste," I said, raising my glass to take a drink. "Cheers!"

"Cheers," he added, turning back to the kegs.

With his attention elsewhere, I turned back to Olivia, who was still gaping.

"Damn it, I wish you had been with me!" I said, setting my drink down forcefully. We watched the amber liquid slosh up the sides, crashing like waves on a wall.

"Classy," Olivia said, the frozen shock expression on her face melting.

"Yeah, I've got style," I said, winking. "Anyway, how was your weekend?" I asked, looking to shift the focus.

"Nothing out of the ordinary," she said. "I found an amazing place in Boston Harbor for oysters. Someday, I'm going to have to take you to experience them."

"Were you wandering around Boston by yourself?" I asked, slightly concerned because she really did have that kind of tenacity, yet a girl like her was not safe wandering alone in big cities.

"Of course, this time I wandered all around Little Italy. Boston is amazing. There are so many unique places to see."

"I love that you have no fear of big cities. Seriously. I do. But, dude. When you are out wandering alone, keep me in the loop, please. I just need to make sure you are safe. Promise??" I said, clasping her shoulder and turning her my way.

"Yes, mom," she said, tilting her head and looking up at me with raised brows. "But this isn't supposed to be about me, what's gotten into you this evening?"

"It's just, I ended up going out for dinner with these guys, and then drinks. And I probably stayed out too long. Some drunk playboy tried to make a move on me—"

"—What?" She asked, a concerned scowl washing over her face.

"It was nothing. I shut him down, but it was so strange—like something out of a movie. I'm sure this sounds ridiculous, but, I mean, I just never imagined people actually acted that way. It's ludicrous. Like, fucking cliché."

"Girl, you need to stay away. Why would you even go out with guys like that?" She said sternly.

Mentally, I screened potential reasons that didn't paint me horrendously, settling on the most innocuous one.

"I was bored," I said frankly. "Which is quite possibly the lamest thing I could say. But, ya know, we would never in a million years hang out with guys like that. I thought maybe it would be an entertaining shift of perspective."

"Seems to have worked out in your favor," she said in jesting tones.

"I know; it was stupid. Playing with fire or whatever,"

I said, lowering my head.

I felt so ashamed. How was it that she was ten years younger than me yet more capable of skillfully navigating these things? Olivia traveled the world, attended biotech seminars routinely, and never seemed to have any issues with men trying to seduce her. How was she totally safe, while I was entirely naive?

"Ya know what, for as strong as I believe myself to be, I don't think I'm equipped to handle myself in this scenario. Maybe the whole shenanigans of this seminar crew finally got to me. I don't know."

"Aaawwww girl, don't think that way," Olivia said, putting on her best reassuring voice and patting my back.

"How fucking ridiculous—"

"Guys like that are ridiculous!" she said emphatically. "Honestly, keep to yourself for the rest of these seminars, okay?"

"Ya know, not all the guys were horrible," I began, looking to reclaim some sense of decency. "Jack, the guy who hit on me, he was the douche bag. The other two, Nick and Craig, despite being insanely handsome, were also genuinely nice. Craig is a father of four and doesn't seem like he's ever thought of anything besides sports and family and dentistry. Nick, well, Nick's on another level, but he felt like the polar opposite of Jack."

"Ruby, do you need me to remind you? Guys are interested in one thing. Fuck them. I mean, don't *fuck* them. You get what I'm saying," she explained. "Trust me; if you're bored, call me. There are better ways to pass the time safely."

"Okay, okay. And, don't worry, I've changed my next two courses to D.C., so I won't have to face him again anyway. Thank god I've dodged that bullet."

"Cheers," Olivia said, raising her glass.

"Cheers indeed," I said, raising mine back in reply. "And ya know, I'm not kidding about wanting you with me. What are your travel plans like over the next couple months?"

CHAPTER 16

As fate would have it, Olivia was lined up to be working in D.C. the same week of my next seminar. It took little to no effort to align our itineraries, and we coordinated a girl's trip that buoyed my spirits for the whole month as I waited for it. The excitement was the kind that inspired me to prepare, so that morning, as I took to the skies, nothing frenzied occurred.

My Delta flight path started at my favorite new hotspot—the 5:10 a.m. Airbus A320 at my sleepy little airport. That jet carried me along the first leg of a most intelligent flight path. It was thirty-eight-minutes, then a layover in MSP, then a second flight duration of only two hours and twenty-two minutes, landing me in D.C. at 10:12 a.m. Olivia and I had an entire day before my seminars began to explore the capital city, and we were poised to seize it.

The mere act of stepping outside the Reagan National airport was exhilarating. A delicate rush of spring air carried the perfume of the budding trees, and it spun in eddies around my face. I closed my eyes and inhaled deeply, tracing its path as the rush entered my chest and then spread all throughout my body. Fresh eyes opened, ones keen to dive into novelty, and I used them to scan my surroundings.

The most remarkable observation was the ground, the

red hexagonal tiles laid down perfectly, their pattern shrinking into the distance as the platform converged at the vantage point. I couldn't bring my eyes to look away. They wanted to scrutinize everything. How the red tiles weren't all exactly red, but rather shades of brown with differing red saturations. My eyes traced the lines interconnecting them, following from the tips of my toes to the end of the platform and back. This very simple act swept me away. It wasn't the clay appearing reddish brown in some tiles and dusty rose in others that struck me though, nor the pristine structural beauty of the lines, rather, it was the lack of anything related to snow, and how clean and dry and neat that left things. The sheer absence of snow made me want to jump for joy.

When I turned to face the airport across the way, the structure of the airport roof caught my attention next. Two static layers of white wavy lines suggested the possibility of movement. Like, if giants stood on either end and pulled each layer back and forth, it would make the perfect waterscape for a children's production of *Moby Dick*. I imagined the roof to be floating independent of the building, though I knew this wasn't the case. What I saw was only one side.

Dentistry requires some grasp of spatial reasoning, in fact, the DAT, the dental school admissions test, has a section dedicated to assessing perceptual ability. I never really crushed that section, but I didn't perform so poorly it omitted me from candidacy. I showed a grasp of perceptual ability—enough to get allowed into dentistry—but architecture of this nature was another thing. How the intaglio of that design crafted a functional ceiling was beyond me.

As I stood on the second story Metro station platform, pondering the waving landscape of the airport across the way, I wondered if men's brains differed from women's in that regard. Maybe men in general had a knack for complex buildings? I couldn't bring myself to accept such a hard and fast rule. Everyone has a different skill set. To believe gender alone could separate these things was illogical. Then I wondered how the guys fared in Chicago. Instantly, I cursed my mind for drifting to them. For no logical reason at all, thinking of how I'd never see Nick again sent my stomach to my knees.

What foolishness! My D.C. trip was going to be amazing. Olivia and I had gone to great lengths to plan a weekend we would deem legendary. Our goal was to meet up, check into our hotel, and then take off running. Run until we could no longer hold ourselves upright, then return and celebrate with a decadent evening out. Anticipating that should be enough to make my heart pound.

The screeching of metal brakes gripping the rails was enough to turn my attention around. I looked up at the yellow line coming to a halt, and scanned the cars, wondering which one Olivia would appear from. Since she was here for a conference already, we had to find a place to meet up. The airport was as good as any, and since I'd never taken the Metro before, our first adventure was going to be her teaching me how. As I watched people flood out of the doors, I sent her a text to let her know where I was among them.

"Hey, I'm hanging out on the platform next to an antiquated phone booth, staring at the waving lines of the airport. Where u at?" I sent.

"I've made a mistake!" she texted right back.

"Something's messed up on the yellow line today, so I took the red. I just realized I missed my stop to change trains though, so I've got to circle back!"

Of course. I loved that girl for so many reasons, but her ability to conquer the world while simultaneously being swept away by it was by far her most endearing trait.

"Not to worry," I replied.

"It's gonna take at least 30 minutes for me to get there now. You want to try and meet me halfway?"

"Sure, why not!"

"Let me research what you need to do and get back to you. Give me a couple minutes."

"Sounds good, I'm comfortable."

Not that I didn't trust her to navigate, but now was as good a time as any for me to figure the mass transit system out. I wandered over to the map posted in the center of the platforms and studied it. It took a moment to get my bearings, but once I located the "you are here" bubble, comprehension began to take form. I saw that the blue and yellow lines both came to the airport, whereas the red traversed the opposite side of the city, with overlap in the heart of the metro. No doubt this was where Olivia missed her change over. We were going to be staying downtown, and I guessed that all those overlapping areas were close enough to where we needed to go. Just as I was mapping out the possibilities, the ding of a text caught my attention.

"Ok, I've got it. Take the next blue line and get off at Metro Center. Text me when you get there."

I checked her route against the map and saw both the red and blue lines converged at this point. Her mapping skills checked out.

"Sounds good. I'm on it! See ya soon. I'm so excited."

"Me too. Safe travels."

I stashed my phone back in my purse and checked the display sign for the next blue train's arrival. The blocky lettering informed me I had five minutes to kill. Accepting this, I looked around for a place to rest, but the metro rail platform must not have been designed for lounging, as the lack of benches became its next overwhelming detail. In defiance, I rolled my carry-on over to a nearby beam and propped it against it, using the canvas top as a makeshift seat and resting my back against the cement pole.

I pulled my phone out of my pocket and tried to start a game of candy crush to pass the time. The cement was cool against my spine, too cool; it set my leg off bouncing and the movement was too much for smooth control over the game. I closed the app and interlaced my arms, finding as much skin on skin contact to spread my warmth around. Despite these efforts, my leg continued to bounce. I thought again about the guys.

What harm is there in texting Nick? I thought. *The context is appropriate. It's okay to say hi.*

I pulled up his number and stared it down.

This is ludicrous; what could you possibly have to say of relevance?

What could I say? The third Chicago weekend had taken place a couple weeks back, a reasonable person might inquire about the content.

Sure, go with that.

I started to type:

"Hanging out in D.C. . . ." - delete

"How was Chicago? . . ." - delete

"Just arrived in D.C. and it's gorgeous. I'm already

wayyy more excited about being here than I could ever be about Chicago. I've even got a girlfriend joining, so we're planning to carpe the fuck out of the diem. Hope you guys didn't miss me too much in Chicago. If there's anything I should prepare for in advance - let me know. Happy Friday!"

It took three tries to compose the whole message. Nothing I could say honestly felt right, so I just had to accept it. I finished it off with a winking face emoticon, hoping to convey I knew my words were silly, and hurriedly pushed send. In the seconds that passed, my heart raced unconventionally.

The familiar screech of an approaching train kicked up the rhythm momentarily, and I rose from my seat and drew in a deep breath seeking to correct it. It was time to get going, and I needed to have my wits about me. Stashing my phone deep in the center pocket of my purse, I made my way to the train door. As I walked, I fumbled around the velveteen folds to ensure the phone nestled deeply inside them, outside of easy reach. There was no way I could repeat Olivia's mistake, and if I was going to arrive at Metro Center on time, I needed to be free from distractions.

* * *

"The first thing we need to do is get out of here," Olivia said the moment the heavy door to our twelfth story room banged shut.

"Agreed," I replied, walking past the foot of our plush king-sized bed to the paisley drapery covering the entire far wall. Its heavy folds were stiff with starch and felt as though they'd bend with pressure rather than slide aside. Great effort was required to push all the coverings to the corners of the wall, and when I did, my heart sunk at the dismal site.

"This place is a dump," I said apologetically. "Hard to believe they can still charge four-hundred and fifty dollars a night when the lobby is replaced with scaffolding and tarps and the construction noise drowns out all hope of enjoying the elevator music."

"All the more reason to keep ourselves outside. We wanted to go running; now we have no choice."

"Precisely. I'll set my stuff up over here," I said, motioning to a corner adjacent to the drapes. "I need ten minutes to unpack and change and then I'll be ready for anything."

"Sounds good," she said, walking toward the open corner along the other side. She laid her bright purple suitcase flat and unzipped the top, its contents nearly exploding out after being freed from their confines. I couldn't help but stand in my spot and observe.

"Don't judge this shit!" she said, tossing items into a pile on the side as she searched for pieces of running gear. "I had five minutes to pack everything up this morning so I could come down and meet your ass."

"Touché," I said, turning back toward my luggage.

After getting into running gear, Olivia and I sunblocked liberally in the bathroom and then captured a selfie in the gigantic vanity.

"This is us now," she said, holding her phone out for display. "I'm gonna create an album and send it to you," she explained, swiping and typing into her phone like she was playing some game. "Now we need to take a bunch more along the way and recreate this one once we're complete. It'll be a fun experiment, documenting the whole thing."

My phone dinged as she wrapped up her plan, so I pulled it out to accept her file before silencing it. As I did, I noticed my screen displayed two bubbles of content, one revealing her file, and the other a text message that obviously never carried over the construction din echoing through the hotel.

"Hey, I'm laid over in Salt Lake City. I won't be in D.C. for a few more hours. Enjoy the carpe diem-ing. If you guys want, I'm going out with a friend later tonight. Maybe we can all meet out?"

Wait, what?

"Olivia," I said, my voice hardly able to project above a whisper. "I think I kicked off something unintentional."

"Ruby, what are you talking about?" Olivia's eyes darted from me to my phone. I held up the screen so she could read for herself. As she did, I focused on calm breathing.

"Who's Nick?" she asked, her eyes fixed on my face.

"Perhaps this will all best be explained after we've done some running," I said, curling my lips into something I hoped resembled a smile before turning away from her gaze. I ducked out of the bathroom, hid in my corner, and shot off a quick response.

"That'd be awesome. Headed out running now. I'll message later."

My message was quite possibly the worst, but I didn't have energy to care. Olivia was waiting and the run was my priority. I hit send, ensured all alerts were silenced, and stowed the phone in my running pack.

"Let's get this party started!" I called out across the room.

Olivia and I ventured off unknowingly onto the crowded streets of downtown. Unknowingly because I wanted an uncharted adventure. I wanted to tackle a run and experience that city in a way most tourists couldn't dream about. I'd roughly plotted the outline in advance, but my overarching goal was that all turns were open for negotiation. When I explained this to Olivia the weekend before we left, she was eager to come along for the ride.

Just outside of downtown we found ourselves stopped at a trail traveling along the Potomac, stretching north and south. We opted to head north along the crowded path, delivering us to the Georgetown waterfront. When the sidewalk ended, we switch-backed up to a quaint canal path lined with historic boats and antiquated locks and dams that fed out to the major roadways. From there, we maneuvered a death-defying street crossing to the base of Key Bridge and used it to transport into Arlington, where we paused to marvel at the dilapidated "Welcome to Washington, D.C." sign, where we took our first photos for the album.

Next, it was a short jaunt along crowded footpaths that fed into an opening toward a small suspended bridge feeding onto Teddy Roosevelt Island. We ventured onto a dirt track, laden with twigs, and became unequivocally lost in the tidal marsh, such that the purported "one-mile circuit" took us more than two, before circling to the entrance, completely missing the vast clearing that housed the monument.

Deciding not to miss the main attraction, we took the extra time to seek out the physical space in which the seventeen-foot stone effigy of *The Man* resides. There, we contemplated the sentiment of the four engraved monoliths, and muffled our disappointment at the decidedly empty fountains, before capturing more photos and carrying ourselves off again.

We headed southbound on the Mount Vernon Trail until we approached the Arlington Memorial Bridge. Exiting there, we wound our way up and around and through Arlington Cemetery with sights set on the Tomb of the Unknown Soldier. We observed the changing of the guards and took more photos before heading back down toward the entrance. It was during our final quarter mile of running through that sacred space that we were approached by a security truck, the driver rolling down his window as he slowed to a halt. His sunglasses and hat shaded the top half of his face, presenting only a thick neck and jawline that melted into the shadow.

"There's no running in the cemetery," he called out to us from his window.

"We had no idea; I'm so sorry," I said, standing erect while wiping the sweat from my brow.

"We're kind of lost," Olivia added with a smile, "would you be able to point us to the nearest exit?"

"Keep following this road," he said, pointing in the direction we'd been going, "it's around that corner about another half mile."

"Got it, thank you!" she called back with a wave, grabbing my arm and rotating us in the direction he pointed, making a grand display of walking gracefully down the road.

Uncomfortably strolling and restraining itching legs, we found ourselves eventually at the entry. Once through the gate, we picked up the pace and crossed over the Arlington Memorial Bridge, delivering us back to D.C. between the gold statues of Sacrifice and Valor, ornate luminaries welcoming us back. Finally, we weaved in and out the monuments, in and out of crowds, and along the Potomac's turbid waters, landing us back at the T we first went north on, where we turned back into the city and finally back to our hotel.

Our run lasted nearly four hours, and it was both organic and amazing. We obtained the pinnacle of running perfection that afternoon. When we fell back to our room at last, we wandered into the bathroom and beheld our wayworn faces in the vanity.

"Good god I look horrible," I said, trying to smooth down the strands of wild hair framing my flushed face.

"A well-earned kind-of horrible," she said, nudging me into the spot we took our photo from earlier. "Now smile." Olivia draped her arm over my sweaty shoulders and made a serious face into the mirror while snapping a selfie of our reflection. "This one's for our eyes only."

We took turns rinsing off and then changed into comfies and crawled into bed for some well-deserved rest and relaxation. Once we'd both settled in, I decided it was time to start filling her in more realistically.

"So, apparently one of the other guys from my Chicago courses came to D.C. as well," I started, then paused, waiting to see how she'd absorb the news. No response came from her half of the bed, so I carried on. "His name is Nick, and he's NOT the creepy drunk player who hit on me. He's from San Diego—definitely has the SoCal bro vibe and there's a chance his hair cut was inspired by Macklemore—but also, he's one of the most hilarious people I've ever met."

"Mmmmm hmmmm," came a soft voice muffled slightly by a pillow.

"You saw the text; he invited us out tonight. I mean, I have no clue who the 'other guy' is, and I have no idea what things are like in their life, but it's an opportunity to go do something totally outside of our normal. I'm pretty sure if we go meet them out it'll be highly entertaining."

"I'm game for whatever you want to do babe," she mumbled sleepily.

I rolled onto my side and contemplated a girls-only evening out, but the very idea of doing so set fire to my skin. No was unfathomable.

"Okay, I'll text him and set up a place for tonight. Get some rest. I have a feeling we're gonna need it."

A decision had been made. I could hardly believe it, but Olivia said "whatever you want," and I wanted to obey my instincts. Once I had been given free reign though, it was hard to not lose control. I could tell by the deep, rhythmic breathing coming from the mound of duvet next to me Olivia had no trouble drifting off. I wished I could be so lucky. As much as I wanted to follow my own advice and get some much-needed rest, I had better hope of running another four hours.

CHAPTER 17

We stepped outside the revolving glass door and into the last hours of light. The cool spring breeze was suffused with the perfume of budding trees, weaving fresh hope through the weft of my world. Tall buildings obscured the sky, but not in the way skyscrapers eclipse the heart of every major cities' downtown. Their absence is likely D.C.'s singular most recognizable feature, due to the Height of Buildings Act, passed in 1899, amended in 1910, limiting buildings to one-hundred and ten feet, or twenty feet higher than the width of the adjacent street. Encyclopedia sources quote the desire to "maintain the city's European feel" as the impetus for this measure, but Logan always told me it was because no other building was allowed to be taller than the Washington Monument.

From where I stood, my eyes could not locate the obelisk. I circled once, with my eyes scanning up and down, looking high and low for a glimpse of it. But all I noted were chain hotels, familiar storefronts, and streets packed so tightly with cars even crossing at a crosswalk seemed unwise, but no monument. Also of note, nothing characteristically European. Perhaps I hadn't seen enough of Europe to give a worthy comparison? I couldn't say for sure, but what stood out most was that D.C. felt strangely like home. The mere act of beholding the cityscape calmed the storm inside me.

"Can you give me the name of Nick's hotel again?" Olivia asked, her sights set on the screen of her phone from her position beside me.

We had decided to spend the evening at Georgetown Waterfront because, as we ran by, it looked amazing, plus, given that it was within running distance, it should be within easy reach. I had offered this reason to Nick and he accepted without question but expressed a need for transportation. So, he and I devised a plan: Olivia and I would get a cab, pick him up, and then the three of us would head off together. His friend, Nick explained, lived just outside of Georgetown, so he was going to make his way there after the three of us arrived in one piece.

Olivia traveled so much she took the lead on transportation detail. Earlier that week, she'd learned of an app called Uber which, according to her, "was revolutionizing the cab world," but obviously required a little front-end work to get up and running. The act of setting up two stops in advance had absorbed all of her energy.

"He's staying at The Darcy," I said, pulling my phone out and calling up a map to see the distance between the two hotels. "I think it's only six blocks away, perhaps we walk there instead and then we just get this Uber thing from there."

"There is no way in hell I'm giving up now," Olivia said emphatically. "Worst case scenario, the driver has to change our final destination. This is all new, let them work the bugs out."

She hit a button on her phone and then looked up and around and then back again to her phone.

"Done!" she declared, "Now we wait . . . for a black

Honda Civic with the plates 194 918. Our driver is on his way." Olivia held her phone out for me to see, and we watched together as the little black car icon maneuvered through the streets. "ETA 3 minutes."

"Okay, Olivia for the win; your app seems super cool. But does it really work? That's my question."

"You'll see, you are gonna love this. Promise."

"Alright, promises promises! I'll let Nick know we're on our way."

Just as I finished shooting off an explanatory text, a black vehicle pulled up alongside us. He rolled the passenger window down and inquired, "Olivia?" to which she responded, "Sew-hi-all?"

"So-hell," the man replied, his thick brows bunching together as he spoke. "It's Persian," he explained, as if that piece of information would help us properly enunciate the vowels.

"Right, my bad," she said, dazzling him with a smile while flashing me a quick glance at her phone. The screen was prompting her to say her driver's name for safety; her driver, whose name was Soheyl. "I wouldn't dare pronounce that out loud," I whispered. Coming from a world where everyone was named Matt or Brian or Ryan or Gregg didn't equip me for that curveball.

The two of us climbed into the compact back seat. "Would you care for water or a mint?" our driver asked, handing back a basket lined with miniature bottles and individually wrapped peppermints.

I turned to Olivia with a puzzled face.

"Oh yes, thank you!" she said, reaching out and taking two of each.

"Drivers get rated by passengers. Having

accoutrements makes them more appealing," she explained again under her breath.

"You are headed to the Darcy Hotel?" Soheyl asked, keeping his eyes ahead.

"Yep," I replied. "We're picking up one more passenger there, and then we're all going to the waterfront in Georgetown."

"One thing at a time ma'am," he said, then he looked all around as though his head were on a swivel before pulling out into the traffic.

Soheyl navigated the puzzling roadway through bumper to bumper traffic the short six blocks to the Darcy Hotel. As he did, Olivia and I commemorated our first Uber ride by snapping silly portraits with our goods while taking turns donning YOLO sunglasses she'd nabbed from a conference booth.

"I hate to interrupt ladies, but we are almost to The Darcy. Do you know where your friend is waiting?"

"Let me check," I said, putting on the YOLO sunglasses and sitting up tall to get a better vantage. "There!" I tapped Soheyl's shoulder and then extended my arm to point. "See that tall guy looking at his phone near the road?" I passed the glasses off to Olivia, who put them on and sat up tall as well.

"Who, him?" She said, taking the glasses on and off, squinting and pointing his direction.

"Hold up, let me check." I took the glasses from her again and we busted out laughing.

"Ladies, is that your man?" Soheyl asked, forcing a calm over his voice.

"Yes," I said, choking on laughter. "Yes, I'm certain that's him."

Nick was standing on the sidewalk outside The Darcy, and his silhouette was instantly recognizable. He had the distinct swagger of a boxer, which, on a street packed with preps and politicians, caused him to stand apart. As we closed in, the shadow lifted on his face, exposing a stone-cold killer expression. The combination of his physique and face completed a look that was borderline offensive. He was certainly not someone I'd define as classically "handsome," yet he was deeply enigmatic on an existential sort of level. Seeing him rekindled the fire from the previous trip, and I was instantly thrilled.

"I see you," I texted Nick.

I watched as he reviewed the content and then looked up and laughed, scanning the scene to locate its origin. As soon as he spied the black Honda Civic with my arm flailing out the rear window, he wandered over and hastily hopped in front.

"Hello everyone," he said cheerily, "how are we all doing this evening?"

"Aah-mazing," I said, playing with emphasis as I tried to come across both excited to see him and nonchalant. "This is my girlfriend, Olivia." I said, placing my hand on her shoulder and presenting her like a contestant on a show. "Olivia, this is Nick, my fellow dental continuum attendee from San Diego."

"Hey," she said, "pleasure to meet you."

"Same," Nick replied.

"Ruby," Olivia said, turning toward me and making a stern face, "you didn't introduce Soheyl."

"Oh my god, forgive me," I laughed. "Nick, this is Soheyl." I took great care in articulating it properly.

"Hey man," Nick said, turning toward him as he

tendered his greeting.

"Nice to meet you," our driver replied. "Now, we are heading to Georgetown?"

"Yes!" Olivia and I replied in unison and then burst out into laughter.

"Wow, okay. Looks like I'm in for a fun night," Nick said, addressing Soheyl as he slipped back into the dense line of traffic.

"That you are my friend. We are about fifteen minutes away."

During the ride, Nick and I fell back into witty banter like no time had passed. Olivia joined in without missing a beat, exuding a confident manner of grace. She blended like she had been part of our crew the whole time. When we arrived at the Georgetown waterfront, the three of us piled out of the vehicle laughing like reunited best friends.

"Enjoy your night," Soheyl called after us as we left.

"Thank you," Olivia said with a wave, stashing her phone and walking away.

"See, wasn't that the best? And all the payment already took place. No more awkward pauses where the driver takes your card and asks for a tip."

"You have introduced me to something truly life changing," I said, wrapping my arm around her and snuggling my head into her neck. "Thank you darling."

"Would you two stop with the love for a second and tell me where I'm going?" Nick said, shaking his head at our display.

"Well, now we just want to find a great seat in any one of these bars," I said with a wave, directing his attention to the sprawling boardwalk ten steps away.

The Georgetown waterfront is, in essence, a strip-mall

of analogous bars, each with a quaint outdoor veranda on the inside slip of the boardwalk. They all offer views of the muddy Potomac River flanked by the Key Bridge and the Kennedy Center, which was particularly resplendent as the sun reflected off its mirrored paneling that night. Simple cabin cruisers, ornate yachts, pontoons, and touring boats were mingling along the water's edge, completing a picturesque backdrop.

Looking at the crowds of unfamiliar people inside bars where professionally dressed hosts tended their podiums like club bouncers kick-started my anxiety. I wasn't sure we'd be allowed inside what appeared now to be an exclusive hotspot. But Olivia was confident. She walked up to one host in the center of the boardwalk and sweet-talked him into admittance—basically, a despondent sounding invitation to "search"—and like a flash, she snatched a coveted location before anyone had a chance to tell us it wasn't available.

The three of us took residence in the two deep crimson couches on opposite sides of the fire table. The delicate flames danced in the center trough ethereally, seeming to originate from a pile of rounded gemstones, not fully expressing their color with twilight still illuminating the sky.

"I'll let Mike know where we're at," Nick said, settling into his spot on the couch facing ours and pulling out his phone.

"Okay," I said, shifting weight as I tried to get comfortable in my spot. I watched the flames waving in and out, fazed by the reality that we were now seated at the perfect spot with a perfect stranger, and I had no clue how we were supposed to go about having this evening when we had no true common ground to banter about. And a fourth person was still yet to come. The dissonant hum of unfilled airspace felt so loud in my ears I could scream. I needed to calm down.

I looked up and around. Patrons both lounging and standing filled the space, with no obvious servers weaving amongst the throngs. A bar was set up backing the boardwalk, which appeared to be the epicenter of the hub.

"Do you think people serve us here, or should we just go to the bar?" I asked Olivia to break the silence, pointing toward the boardwalk.

"I think we should take our chances at the bar," she replied.

I looked at Nick who was zeroed in on his phone and decided this was a ladies only assignment.

"Hey Nick," I said loudly, "you hold down the fort. Olivia and I will be right back with drinks. Don't let anyone near our coach." I ran my hand along the length of the crimson back proprietarily then pointed at him and scowled. "Guard this with your life." Sarcasm and humor were the weapons I trusted myself wielding in our world.

"Okay boss," he laughed. "Can I have a drink in return?"

"Sure thing, Sir; first one's on me."

With his order secure, Olivia and I made our way toward the bar. As we stood waiting, the Key Bridge was in direct line of sight, and beyond it, the horizon was streaked with pink and orange as the sun melted into the Potomac. The view was resplendent, and I lifted my phone to capture a photo.

"This place is stunning. We crushed the setting this evening!" I said.

"That we did," she replied, rotating in place to take it all in.

Even with the two of us assured we'd crafted our perfect evening, I was terrified about how the guys would perceive our idea of an idyllic night. What if they thought it was stupid? What if someone got bored? I felt like I needed to apologize in advance, fearing the fanciful backdrop we were wandering in would be stripped away any second.

"This is gonna be a strange evening," I said, grabbing hold of her arm and halting her pirouetting. "I don't know these guys from Adam; I have no idea what we're in for. We just need to get a drink and make the most of a strange evening. Okay?" I rambled emphatically.

"Ruby," she said, placing both her hands on the sides of my head. "Everything is going to be fine. Nick seems hilarious. Relax and enjoy the night." The green in her eyes conveyed an assuring warmth.

"Okay, I've got this. Let's do this thing!"

The crowd proved denser than previously noted, and it took quite a long time to get to the bar. So much so we decided it was best to double up on drinks, saving on future wait time. By the time we returned, fire and twinkle lights were the only source of illumination, and Nick's boy Mike had joined him on the couch. As I walked up carrying two tall cans of beer and a tall glass filled to the rim with an orange mixer, I had to restrain my jaw from dropping open.

"Ladies, this is Mike," Nick said, completing the introduction as we dispensed the drinks.

"He and I met last month on the Cuba trip," Nick explained.

"Yeah," Mike added. "It was such a good time he had to come here instead of Chicago. After spending three days in surgery, any more time in lecture seems like a waste. But at least we all get to hang out," he said, laughing and tossing his sandy blond curls.

"You haven't mentioned anything yet about how things went in Cuba—" I said.

"You didn't ask," Nick replied.

"Well, do tell. Please, I'm dying to know. What was it like studying beneath the head-head guy?"

"—The head-head guy?" Mike cut in, his perplexed expression carving thin lines above his brow.

"She means Dr. Blankenshine," Nick explained. "A story for another time. Since Olivia has no ties to the dental community, what other things are going on?"

"I really just want to go dancing . . ." Mike said, leaning forward and winking.

After that, all my worries about the four of us having nothing to talk about dissipated into the black sky.

Mike evened out our crew effortlessly. After breaking the ice and settling in, he and Nick proved a hilariously lethal duo—they played off each other with deadpan comedic timing yet were the perfect yin and yang. Nick was the personification of crazy, pointed and edgy with obvious issues. He was either owning the moment or looking entirely out of place, and he couldn't sit still for longer than five minutes, attending to his phone or occasionally wandering off.

What would be construed as off-color mannerisms to ninety-five percent of the world were eccentric coping strategies with which I identified. Simmering beneath his integument of humor and confidence was a dark and brooding soul that was hauntingly attractive to me. He was all of the things—the big personality, confident, fit, bat-shit crazy, but somehow pulling it off in life—a virtuoso. I was hypnotized.

Mike was his polar opposite. Where Nick was a labyrinth of convoluted crazy and screamed bad boy from all his angles, Mike was a straightforward line of obvious. He was heavily flirtatious, wildly inappropriate, cavalier about sex, and attractive as hell. His sandy brown hair was just long enough to have perfect waves, and his wide-set jaw softened by deep dimples. His face was nearly always sporting a charming smile that flashed in concert with his electric brown eyes. Nothing about him was sharp or edgy; he was solidly round and inviting. The epitome of a guy who was easy.

Olivia created a dance move we all emulated, and hours slipped past with conversation centered around Pitbull and dance music, general science nerdery, and something about yelling on planes. We drank . . . a lot. We laughed so hard my whole body hurt.

When my eyes started staying closed longer and longer with each blink, Olivia and I opted to abandon the boys and make our way back to the hotel. We weren't done yet, though; we needed one more drink and serious girl time to reflect on the night.

Nursing our final IPAs, we took up spots in cozy loveseats near the front window of the bar of our hotel, reveling in the modern ambiance of it all. Half slumped over with exhaustion, but persisting for the sake of sisterhood, we carried into a discussion of the night.

"Those guys were a blast," she said, stating the obvious, "but if you had to involve them in your daily life, they would be more work than they are worth."

"Absolutely," I agreed. "Those two guys are not real. Not like you and I know real. They live a fairytale existence. They are guys who will charm you for a fleeting instant, but as soon as they knew they could, they would turn around and leave you for dead," I said, to agree with her, and support my lifelong held belief about *those guys*. But I found myself desperately wishing it weren't really so.

Overall, we determined that our night was insanely fun, but in the same breath, it was an illusion. Nick and Mike were the prototypical enigmas of men you could never be with in reality. Girls like us usually avoid *those guys* on principle. They can, and only ever will, break your heart. Avoidance is essential because we are smart enough to know that the temptation can be overpoweringly ruinous. But we were making an exception for them since they were my new friends, recognizing that it was all transitory.

We rested our conversation sensibly there and declared ourselves content with our safe and supportive men back home. We took tipsy selfies and sent them off with words of love, and then officially called it a night.

CHAPTER 18

The next day at the conference I met up with Nick, and we got seats for him, Mike, and me, at a long rectangular table near the middle of the sparsely filled room. Nick seemed both genuinely concerned for my wellbeing and shocked that I was in class and functional, cluing me in to how much I must have drunk the evening prior. He passed me over a couple of acetaminophen tablets from his briefcase and said, "I think you probably should take these just in case."

"Is it safe for me to be accepting unmarked pills from a strange man?" I asked, looking at him quizzically to convey his concern was entirely out of place.

"Sure," he replied without skipping a beat. "As long as you're cool with waking up in California tomorrow," he said in soft tones, ending with a light chuckle.

My stomach flipped inside out as the last tones of his laughter dispersed.

"You promise?" I asked, holding the firm gaze of his reckless brown eyes until I blushed crimson and unlocked them.

As I threw back the pills with one deep drink of water, I closed my eyes and desperately willed them to possess such magnificent power.

Conference attendance and long spans of attention have never tallied in my "strengths" category. To top it all off, my cellular signal was dead thanks to class being held in a concrete locker of a conference room tucked in the bowels of a downtown sky rise. Not having a connection to the outside world kicked up my anxiety, and I found myself checking and rechecking my phone, desperate for a momentary signal to ignite so I could ensure messages were coming through.

Nick was dialed into my struggle; he laughed at my vibrating legs and stir-crazy antics and calmly encouraged me to leave when it became obvious I couldn't hold calm another second. So, I took breaks. I'd get up and leave until I felt relief, then return able to hold focus. I tolerated class way better than usual. I drew pictures, like always, and though it was a very long day, having him beside me made it okay.

Nick and I passed our phones back and forth, flaunting photos of ourselves that snapshotted our lives into perspective. Each pass of the phone allowed for a deliberate brush of hands, and I felt my skin come alive in each spot that we touched. I felt euphoric around Nick. I was so attracted to him that his presence had a physical component to it, a force field that scrambled my moral senses.

Mike did his best to compete, and he really had a special space, just that it was limited to physical attraction. Mike was a puppy dog, it was impossible not to adore him because he was so damn cute, but he seemed also naive about it all and my primary emotion toward him was protective.

During our first break that morning, Mike dove straight into sex topics by opening the door of porn.

"I mean, it's just a part of everyday life," he said,

leaning around Nick to catch my eye.

Not looking to further the discussion, I deflected with something I assumed sarcastically grotesque enough to force him to change themes.

"Oh yes, but what about gay porn? I mean, you two are both attractive guys. Do you like to only look at the women, or are you okay with guy on guy?"

"Oh, come on," Nick said, "what do you take us for?"

"Guys have no shame. Whatever gets you going, I'm not judging."

In the middle of our ridiculous discussion, the head hussy strode over and broke up our banter.

"In case any of you are curious," she said in a sultry voice, "I wandered over to the seminar next door and it appears to be some type of sex conference. There's booths offering lube samples and discounted toys, and some sexy outfits I may have to return for."

There was no holding up my jaw as she spoke.

"Wow. Sounds pretty desperate," I said under my voice, flashing her my coldest stare.

"Well, if you're over there again, be sure to nab us some samples," Mike said.

"Hilarious," Nick chimed in, in a disenchanted type of dismissal tone I'd never heard from him before.

"Will do," she said in a sing song voice, flipping her glossy hair as she turned to waddle away.

Nick and I exchanged glances. It seemed like we were united on the matter that she was not welcome with us. Mike, on the other hand, looked like he needed a napkin for the corners of his mouth as he gawked at her rear end. When he finally came to, he kicked back up the conversation like no disruption occurred, leaning in toward me and sporting a smoldering stare.

"Well, of course, *I* like it, but really it's not about what I like, it's *you* that matters. What makes you happy? What do you like?" he asked.

I gaped at him and busted out laughing. "Are we still talking about gay porn?"

The day passed with the two of them viciously flirting. When class wrapped up, my entire body was sore from laughter, tense from desire, and my mind was liquefied. Two very engaging men were pressuring me hard from both sides, which sent me into an invidious state. All good judgement condensed outside my body and evaporated into the open, rendering me incompetent in a peculiar situation.

* * *

I returned to Olivia as fast as I could, and she and I took to the trails for more running. Cleansing air and exhilaration from the run settled the storm raging in my brain. Finally, outside of their bubble, I was able to take relaxed breaths.

"Those two are exhausting," I complained. "I needed a moment away to recoup. I don't know how much longer I could have survived them. They are relentless! I don't know what they are playing at, but the two of them wouldn't leave me alone today. It was starting to get awkward."

As we ran, I grew silent and started thinking over the plans for the night. After class, Nick, Mike, and I decided to all meet out again, this time at a place of Mike's choice because D.C was his stomping grounds. Nothing more was decided, but it sounded like we'd be hitting up a bar or a club in some type of environment primed for shit to go down.

Since the "Night of Crazy Flirtation from Hell," credited to Jack, I realized I was treading precarious ground. It seemed as though I was open to being with someone else, which was something I'd never allowed myself to consider before.

Mike was plausibly on board; he was so blatant with his sexuality it floored me. He was certainly capable of a no-strings-attached one-night stand with a married woman on hiatus, but was that capability extended to me?

I was sure it was. My read on him after today was that he was moving in for the kill. It was entertaining for sure, but as I had felt with Jack the weekend prior—no spark or desire beyond curiosity prevailed.

Nick was on a whole other level. My attraction to him bordered on dangerous levels. His appeal was way beyond physical. I knew him—he *got* me. I yearned so intensely to be a part of his world I could scream, but the very fact that I felt so deep a connection with him made it a potentiality I had to shut down. He was a reminder of everything I missed out on, as such, I didn't see my soul stopping there.

Not that I had one iota of experience when it came to such matters, but my understanding of the intellectual rationale was that affairs be cut and dry. Emotion free. Some means of release or expending of energy resulting in instant catharsis without risk of lingering attachment. I needed to set my mind to the task of shutting things with Nick down.

As a means to an end for both dilemmas, I decided it best to throw myself at Mike, both to invite the experience and divert the Nick pandemonium.

* * *

We met up with the guys later that night at a trendy bar nestled on H Street. A large contingent of Mike's friends from the area joined us out, and we found ourselves huddled with a ragtag bunch of doctors and scientists on the outskirts of an unquestionably random mix of patrons: flamboyantly attired middle-aged men rubbing up against authentic hipsters, East Coast-styled college kids, riot girls and boys, and two random girls flanking Mike that wrecked my well-laid plan.

With Olivia occupied by two sciencey-guys intrigued by her bio-tech credentials, Nick and I spilled out of the commotion and took up a post near an ornate outdoor heater with one stream of vibrant flame dancing inside. I was internally downcast that my plot had been ruined, but I resolved it wasn't smart anyway. Mike was a playboy and entitled to his fun; who was I to interfere? Instead, I carried on an innocent flirtation with Nick.

I kicked it off by comically detailing massages I get from a beefy man who has an affinity for my ass.

"The first time I went to this guy, I didn't wear underwear," I explained, "and apparently, that's code for 'handle the ass.' Sometimes I request a focused area, just to see how he reacts. He'll halfheartedly attend to it, but it doesn't take long for him to resume his usual routine. Shoulders . . . back . . . ass ass ass . . . ass . . . ass. I mean, dude, I'm an athlete!!!"

I started out with a comical detailing to make Nick laugh, but it actually bothered me that my massage therapist didn't listen. I was annoyed that, despite the fact I explained in detail to him areas in need of massage, that got overlooked just so he could handle my ass.

Nick just stared at me with a blank expression, the root of which I couldn't guess. So, I concluded my story.

"I find it confusing, but strangely arousing, and so I return, time and again, waiting for the shock factor to wear off."

"AAANNNNDDD. . ." Nick asked.

"It doesn't."

Olivia burst out just as I finished this story and informed us that she and her guys happened upon an open table inside the adjoining restaurant. There was just enough room for Nick and I to join, and she wanted us to come quickly.

Before leaving, I snuck back to where Mike was hanging out and grabbed him firmly. I leaned in close to his ear and whispered, "You fucking ruined my night." Then I embraced him seductively and grabbed his curly hair, tugging hard and pulling his head back before turning on my heels to leave. I'm not even sure what possessed me to do that, but I distinctly recall wanting him aware that he was missing out on his chance with me. I think I made my point clear.

Near the end of the night, Mike and the other remnants of his crew joined our table. By that time, I was relaxed and happy, confident and secure, in the zone and owning my night. Mike had one frisky girl remaining at his side, so I shoved in his face that I could be that too and acted out my own display with Nick. We took playful selfies and texted them back and forth and cuddled up together on the couch. I freely enjoyed playing out my attraction to him, like it was the obvious thing I would do in those situations.

But as the night grew long, Olivia snuggled up into my side and passed out. Early on she hit a wall, but persevered, drowsily keeping up, allowing me to continue my shenanigans. She had put up a valiant fight, but this final act was my wake-up call that it was time to go. It was late, and I recognized I should end things before I carried out my display too far. I hailed an Uber back to our hotel.

Shortly after leaving, the ding of a text message caught my attention. I pulled out my iPhone and gawked at Nick's words, scandalously inhabiting my screen.

"You looked hot tonight. I don't sleep much either. You should text me after Olivia passes out."

A yell escaped my mouth—this was not supposed to happen! Olivia was startled awake by my response, and so I passed her my iPhone to get her take on the matter.

"I don't approve!" she yelled, half dazed but crystal clear on this detail. So, I texted him back.

"Olivia does not approve."

"You showed Olivia?" he messaged back. If an incredulous emoticon face existed, I guess that too would have been included.

How could I not show her? She's my girl. We shared everything, and I needed her to know. It kept me honest. Secretly, I was dying to know what would happen if I did message him, but Olivia was not only my best friend; she was my husband's friend. She knew my other world inside and out, and my read from the previous evening's summary was that she did not believe they can co-exist. She was the angel on my shoulder convincing me that staying away was the correct decision. I was determined to make the responsible choice.

CHAPTER 19

Back on the twelfth floor and back in our room, where the veil of night put the construction crews on intermission, Olivia flopped onto the bed and fell asleep in an instant. Her deep breathing was amplified in the absence of banging and screaming drill bits, and I decided to try and wield that to my advantage. When my boys were too wired for sleep, I would hold them tightly and breathe deep breaths until their little bodies went in sync with mine. Nine times out of ten it did the trick, but the flipside was that I always wound up out for the night alongside them.

Applying some modified version of that tactic ought to be a good starting point for putting myself to sleep, I surmised. So, with one large pillow resting atop me, I laid flat on my back and matched Olivia breath for breath, counting one sheep each time. It was soothing my body for sure, yet it quickly became apparent that no matter how deep my breathing, my brain wasn't giving into the allure.

While I lay wide awake with sheep piled in the two-hundreds, my count finally scrambled. The hitch allowed my thoughts to swim off course and wade in the acute awareness of Nick's absence. All I wanted to do was reach out. Trying to deflect again, I started back at one and went five sheep more before all together abandoning my experiment.

I grabbed my phone from off the side table and Google-searched Nick's full name. The search didn't produce any images of him, but it did offer a photo of a hairy old man that I took a screen-shot of and sent him in a text with the caption, "Apparently the internet thinks this is you."

Dots started waving beneath my words immediately.

"That is me. How did you not know?"

"Good lord. I must be tired. Forgive me."

"No problem. That photo was taken ages ago."

"I see. Well, I got momentarily concerned and couldn't sleep without letting you know. I'm glad we got that resolved. Probably should go back to sleep."

"Yeah, that sounds better than what I'm doing," Nick said, then texted the same photo of our lecturer that smeared our world so pervasively one would assume the guy was running for president. "Just spending quality time with this guy."

"Oh gawd. Oh gawd. WHY?"

"Lol. That bad?"

"Just message me and stop with that shit for the rest of the night. K?"

"Deal."

Nick and I maintained an innocent text flirtation for the next hour. Messages of funny pictures, stupid nothings, and jokes, anything to make each other laugh. He didn't invite me over or press me to join him the way Jack had. It was easy and fun and comforting enough; I was warmed to know he was simply there. Eventually, our conversation died, and I fell into a deep sleep.

I woke up feeling refreshed around 5:00 am, which was 7:00 am in my world, given the time change. Olivia had not moved all night, and judging from the rhythm of her breath, she was still fast asleep. I thought maybe she'd rouse shortly and we could head off for a run together, so I laid still waiting, but after a seemingly endless span of time—trying to stay rigid so as not to disturb Olivia's slumbering form—I reached a point where I could no longer wait.

I felt a magnetic pull toward Nick. He was the demon on my other shoulder, willing me along to improper action. Akin to his kindly nudges to get out of class when I became painfully restless, tossing in bed thinking of him, I knew I could no longer hold still. I needed to move. I needed to act. I needed to feel like I was progressing toward *something*.

I checked the weather and mapped out the sunrise, and then waited for the bewitching hours of D.C. twilight, when it would be safe enough to head out alone for a walk. When the time drew near, I crept out of bed and quietly composed myself in gear fit for either casual walking or running. Then, I gathered my phone and my ear buds and snuck toward the door, trying to slip away stealthily. Unfortunately, my skills were not up to par, and Olivia woke and peeked her head up at me as I was passing through the door, a disbelieving expression on her face.

"I'm just going out for a run," I whispered in a pacifying tone. She accepted this reality and calmly rested her head back down. Then I slipped out into the hall and messaged Nick, inviting him to join for a walk or coffee if he was up.

I passed through the large glass revolving door and ventured off in the direction of his hotel. I ambled, indistinctly stricken, along the liberating streets of downtown D.C., anxious for him to respond before I got there. The ground felt cold beneath my feet, and my eyes were still adjusting to the dim of twilight, as the first rays of dawn crept into the sky. When I was one block from his hotel, and he had not yet responded, I called up The National playlist on my iPhone. "Terrible Love" was always how I started, and that morning was no different.

The National is my drug of choice, and "Terrible Love" is their silver bullet, always fixed to deliver. That song has a sound capable of simultaneously eviscerating and completing me. It builds and ends on such a thrilling, complex layering echo that I feel I could lose my soul in the reverberations. They travel through me like adenosine, stopping and then resetting my heart. That morning, as the song climaxed, I closed my eyes to truly experience the effects. I let the melodrama wash over me like a soothing wave, and then, out of no intention at all, I started to run.

I ran past his hotel and headed toward the entry to the National Mall. The Cherry Blossom ten miler was getting set up to run, but for the first time in forever, I was completely uninterested in a race. I was running for different reasons. The race start forced a pause directly in front of the Washington Monument, so I used that time to gaze upon it and wonder.

Its immense structure is transfixing, but what my eyes always get caught up on is the color change almost a third of the way up from the bottom. This is another D.C. fun fact Logan loves to elaborate upon. He told me it was because construction stopped during the Civil War due to financial constraints, and that the bottom part sat unfinished for twenty-five years before enough money was garnered for construction to resume. When it did, the bricks were thought to match seamlessly, though they came from a different quarry. With the passing of time, however, weather erosion revealed the seam, and now the color change is woven into the monument's lore.

I snapped a photo of the monument eclipsing a resplendent sunrise and sent it off to Nick with the caption, "Hope your morning is going this good."

I continued on my run. I ran over to the Tidal Basin and traversed its inner track. Multitudes of photographers lined the pond, all setting up to capture the transcendent beauty of the cherry blossoms at sunrise. While they set out to freeze one pristine snapshot, I set out to absorb it all, to be transformed by its rejuvenating power.

I wanted to impress that moment with the cherry blossoms into my very core. I took it all in. I inhaled the intoxicating fumes and envisioned myself ascending among the trees. *I am not amid the throngs of spectators here. I am but a ghost, navigating silently above them.* I felt everything, and I let that powerful emotion flow through me. I was at one with my world and myself, and I was truly at peace.

That was my provenance of therapeutic running. I ran to celebrate being alive. I ran to overcome disappointment and loss, to be centered in a space where I was wrapped up in only one moment. I found absolute peace that morning.

Occasionally, I stopped to take pictures of the monuments silhouetted in the sunrise. Then I stopped to do yoga on the lawn at the base of the Washington Monument. And I waited for a response from Nick. I yearned for him to awaken and discover my texts. But my little green message box remained disappointingly empty that morning.

I finished up my run and stopped by Starbucks to grab coffee for Olivia and me. If there is one constant in my world, it's the ability to always make her smile with coffee. I returned to our hotel room with two Venti flat whites, and proceeded to get ready for the day, rejuvenated from my run, but dejected by my lost opportunity.

Class was much like the day before, Nick and I flaunting photos, him laughing at me for squirming like a child, and sexual tension clouding us in a thick fog.

"Are you going to be in Chicago next weekend for our final seminar?" Nick asked during the morning break.

"Wow, next weekend already!"

"Yep, another reason why I made this switch, two weekends back to back and then it's a wrap on this shit."

"Wow, I wish I would have thought of that."

"It's not too late, maybe you can still change," Nick said, his expression inviting and soft, conveying the unspoken—that he'd very much like for me to change it.

"I've already made my travel arrangements for the final weekend," I said, exhaling and turning away to avoid exposing my despondent expression.

When class ended, we only had a short time before all three of us needed to get to the airport. Mike insisted we have one last drink at Old Ebbitt Grill, Washington's oldest saloon, in homage to the city's grand history, before we had to leave.

"We have to get to a bar," he insisted, "because we are great at bars."

The ornately decorated Victorian interior, with its priceless collection of art livening up the walls, was packed floor to ceiling with patrons. We wound our way through the main area and set up in a secluded tavern hidden off to the side. Nick had gotten frantic by the end of class and insisted on finding a TV to watch golf. Our group parked in the far back room and set up along the center, bordering a standing height bar. Nick rested against the wall behind me, his hand holding tight to the brass beam running along its length, his gaze fixed on the TV screen mounted above the bar.

When our drinks were gone, we parted ways with Mike, and I grabbed him once more, hugging him provocatively and tugging on his hair. I leaned in and whispered that even his voice was sexy, and I was sorry I had to say goodbye. With a wink and hair toss, I turned away, and looked at Nick and Olivia, who were staring at me.

"What?" I asked, jokingly. "I'm not actually taking myself seriously."

Our foursome became three, and we returned to the hotel to collect our bags and catch the Metro. The Metro, which drove Nick to new heights of crazy. He was visibly on edge, be it from the crowd or the unclean surfaces or the inability to be exercising control—one couldn't know for certain—but I knew he was off. His deep brown eyes darkened to near black as they darted around, analyzing all the fine details.

In an honest effort to soothe, I offered to hold him using humorous tones, hoping to pull him out of his funk, but I realized too late it was the wrong move. Nick glared at me like I was dead to him and I shut right up, staying silent for the remainder of our ride.

Once we arrived and exited the train, warmth flowed back into his eyes. Olivia and I accompanied him to the check-in kiosk for his flight. We were on different airlines, which were out of two separate terminals, so it was there we had to split off completely, ending our obscure adventure. When we parted, he embraced us both and planted gentle kisses on our heads before turning and sauntering away.

My eyes fixed on him as he receded into the expanse, longer than anyone should observe a departure.

CHAPTER 20

It was highly illogical, but the simple act of separating from Nick felt like someone cut off my air. I felt naked and lost and anxious as soon as his absence sunk in. I had texted him a selfie of Olivia and I at the airport bar before our flight home, really just trying to give him one last photo for posterity, and he texted back that he was hanging out with our lecturer and his staff at the other end of the airport. That was that. I assumed it had to be.

But on Monday, I woke suffocated and flattened and knew I needed to find a way to re-establish my Chicago itinerary.

To be fair, it all made sense. The final D.C. weekend fell over our anniversary, so Logan and I had thrown around the idea of him attending with me already. If I went to Chicago this weekend instead, we could still head there as planned, but I'd have no conference obligations. It was a genius plan in reality.

"I don't want to be obligated to anything," I explained to Logan first thing that morning. "If I go to Chicago this coming weekend and finish the course, then we can go to D.C. together next month and utilize the entire time for ourselves."

There was a sinking sick feeling about it all, but I also didn't truly believe myself capable of anything. I wasn't that girl. Nick was a friend. He and I were invested in these lectures together now, I wanted us to finish out as such. Us being in class together made me more attentive. Plus, I wanted to see the other guys once more, especially Chad. I had several reasons to make the change, several grounded and logical reasons which made the one giant awful reason as fickle as dust in the wind.

"That's a great idea," Logan agreed, and he helped me set it all up.

With the change in itinerary, the final Chicago seminar was only three days away. I sent a text to Nick before I went to bed that night.

"Hey - fyi, I'll be seeing you Thursday. I couldn't resist, I mean, it's Chicago. I hear that place is amazing."

On Tuesday morning, I woke to a text:

"Good morning sunshine, you just made my day."

My heart skipped from his cavalier usage of a term of endearment.

When I got to my office, we picked off where we left off in D.C. via text, messaging pictures, jokes, and work-related topics back and forth, only our communications were limited to the short down time between patients.

He mentioned that he had waited to book his Chicago hotel and was having trouble securing a room at the conference center. Like an idiot, I said he could share mine, since I always got one with two double beds anyway. I didn't think much of this. I never thought he'd take me seriously.

Nick fixed his flights to depart the same time as mine Saturday morning and made a whole host of plans for us in the city, including dinner at a restaurant where I needed to "dress up," and tickets to see his friend in a play.

The ardor he put forth in executing these

arrangements and our unremitting text match made my head spin. I was fraught with confusion, and the dial on my anxieties was cranked to *extreme*. I was deleting his texts as fast as he would send them, trying to ensure Logan never saw.

On Wednesday, Nick kicked off our morning chat by asking if the hotel offer still stood. There was no way I was going to say no. Just as my morning was wrapping up, I walked in on Logan hunched over my desk, hard at work doing something on my computer. My computer, which my phone was plugged into and set up against. It was displayed front and center, a billboard with a scandalously wide screen, flashing with unread messages I knew were from Nick. Most likely in regards to sharing a hotel room that weekend.

My anxiety ratcheted up to its maximum range, from *extreme* to *about to explode*.

Looking to diffuse the situation, I formulated an on-the-fly plan.

"Let's go to Moe's!" I yelled, because anyone who's been to a Moe's knows that's how their employees greet you.

"Goodness sakes Ruby, patients can hear you!" Logan said, looking at me standing in the doorway like a scolded child.

"Nope, everyone's done for the morning. I'm just waiting on you," I said, making my way around his back and slipping my phone from the desk.

"I'm installing the drivers for your CT. I just need a couple more minutes," he said, turning his attention back to my computer.

Judging by his body language and tone, he appeared

unaffected. That was a good start, but one can never be sure.

"No worries, I can wait. I have a couple things to tackle in the lab."

I wandered back into that space, reveling in inhaling the mix of plaster and stone, a welcoming scent similar to that of tilled earth absorbing fresh rain, and opened the messages on my phone. With meticulous industry, I deleted everything Nick had sent, and then deleted his name from my contacts. I hoped my actions would alleviate my distress.

"All done," Logan called out from inside the office.

"Perfect, I'm starving," I said, even though my insides were churning.

During lunch, I ignored my phone, working hard to stay present. We shared our typical order and splurged on an extra queso. I kept the topic centered on exciting things we could do for our anniversary trip.

"Olivia and I have that city locked down," I said. "I've got amazing running routes, and now I've been to some local restaurants that you'll love."

"That all sounds great, anything you are this excited about is good by me."

"I wonder what Olivia is doing that weekend? Maybe she'll be there again and can spend a day or two with us as well." I said this and then second guessed it.

"That's not weird, is it?"

"With Olivia and you? No. You two come as a pair; I don't think anyone would be shocked," he said with a little shake of his head. "All I ask is for one day alone. The rest of them are up for grabs. You know me, I'm highly entertained by the Ruby and Olivia show."

"I love us!" I said, elated that he was willing to consider this plan. "I'll check with her later today. I bet anything we can work out something."

All in all, lunch was invigorating. The idea that our D.C. trip could be legendary too enlivened me. But then, when we got back to the office, I made the mistake of attending to my phone. There was one text from an unfamiliar number occupying the screen.

"If you say okay, then I'll hold off on my reservation. Chi-town here we come!"

I hit the end of my fuse and detonated. When I went to do anesthetic on my next patient, I started to shake. I backed away and regained my composure, then prepared to try again. Only, I shook worse. I was losing my grip.

On my drive home, I called Olivia to help me gain perspective "Where are you?" I asked when she answered.

"I'm just heading out of the office. What's up?"

"I need you!" I nearly shouted into the line. "Can you meet me for pedicures?"

"Absolutely. I can head straight over if you're ready," she said.

"We need drinks as well—how about you hit the liquor store, I hit the gas station, and we convene in the parking lot first?" I proposed, hopeful my juvenile plan didn't sound too trashy for her.

"Love it! It's on. I'll catch you up in a minute," she said, laughing into the line.

"I love you!!" I said, half choked up with emotion and half dying from laughter at the ridiculous escapade we schemed.

After meeting up and mixing Malibu into our 32-ounce Big Gulps, we entered into a nondescript nail salon that typified the genre. While lounging in large black leather massage chairs, with our feet resting in hot tubs of sudsy water, I disclosed to her my dilemma.

"I don't like this at all," she said, raising her eyebrows and lowering her gaze sternly. "There is no way this is going to end well."

"I know," I said, holding my remote and fumbling with the settings. "But I don't think he's really 'that guy.' I sense that there is something more here. And I trust him; I'm sure I sound corny, but to me, he's genuine," I said, resting my remote on the arm console before turning to face her squarely. "Actually Olivia, I *really* like him. There is this intense thing between us. It doesn't make sense, but I feel like he's something *missing* from my life. I might have to figure this one out."

Exhaling slowly and fixedly holding her gaze, I watched as the concern in her features softened to cautious assent. It was obvious she was still guarded, but I also recognized a need to acquiesce. She was onboard in knowing it satisfied my conflicted soul.

"If you do this, you do this for *you*. Logan can never know. This is not something that you share with him. I will always be here for you, no matter what happens, but you have to protect him from this," she said.

"I personally think you should tell him, be upfront and say you are sharing your room with a guy who had trouble booking the right place. Maybe if you are open from the start it will keep you honest, and you can avert any crisis from happening," she said.

I didn't.

It was a great ladies' night, and a valiant effort to try to deter a train wreck, but honestly, at some point or another, I was going to run off course.

Crawling into my bed merely hours before I was set to arrive for my flight, I checked the contents of my message box and discovered a long, frenzied text from my mother. Tom had been to the eye doctor and his retina was detached, again. Emergency surgery was impending, but they needed to formulate an aftercare plan. I was tempered with the hard truth that it was my burden to intervene.

I should have canceled the trip. I knew I needed to stay and coordinate their admittance into a nursing care facility. It was the right thing to do, but nothing in me would do it. I was desperate to experience the upcoming weekend. Nick elicited emotions that, to me, were entirely foreign. Emotions I felt my life was lacking. If I let this pass, I feared the unknowing would be more tortuous than the aftermath. One of those hauntings that, later in life, would give credence to the mind's propensity to forget.

For the first time in as long as I could remember, when facing the need to sacrifice myself for others, I could not find the strength to do it.

The NASA astrophysicists recently released a video of a computer simulation visualizing the collision of two neutron stars. This event is violent and spectacular, surmised to be one of the most ferocious to occur in our universe. When these two stars occupy overlapping space, they begin swirling toward each other, appearing first to be initiating some delicate dance. Their rotational velocity increases rapidly until their outer layers begin to intertwine.

They warp, mutate, and then forcefully unite and simultaneously disperse. The end product of this union is the absolute destruction of both stars; they are incapable of coexistence; instead, they violently rip each other apart.

As the stars collapse in on themselves, they emanate a tidal wave of intense energy and transform into one tiny point of inescapable singularity, capable of bending the very fabric of the universe.

It is fascinatingly divine and exceedingly rare, speculated to occur only once every 10,000 years. Two immensely powerful objects combine, destruct, and leave in their wake a black hole—a singular point that obliterates everything within its reach, a pull so strong not even light can escape.

A point which is notable only by its absolute blackness.

This cataclysmic maelstrom is evidenced by one visible radiant ring, and a wave of powerful energy it concentrically radiates

The afterglow.

CHAPTER 21

I awoke giddy Thursday morning and readied myself in the now usual pre-flight ritual of showering and dressing in my most hipster-esque, conference-appropriate yet air travel-friendly, attire. On that chilly April morning, I selected a thick black dress with an ornate brown cross-hatch, accenting all the right places. The dress had a short A-line skirt flaring sharply from my waist and ending not too much further beyond. It was delightful—check, heavyweight and weather appropriate—check, chic—check, but conference appropriate? Questionable.

I allowed my hands to sit idle at my waist, extending my fingertips their full length while observing the figure in the mirror mimicking my actions. The skirt's hem extended barely beyond those fingertips, by half an inch at most, but beyond them nonetheless. Conference appropriate—check. The dress crafted a classic look that emulated Audrey Hepburn's style. I was feeling quite confident that I would be perceived as artistically charming.

That particular morning, I drove myself to the airport, keeping a better pace than my previous trips, yet still nowhere near the recommended travel pre-arrival window. I found myself entering the front doors to our cozy little airport thirty minutes before my flight departure. I was jittery and anxious, eager to get this final conference over, and eager to see what would transpire with Nick.

I didn't know what to expect. His bombardment of texts leading up to my departure left me in a state of consternation. I had kept it going all week and then shut it down hard on Wednesday. His last message to me was about sharing a room. I didn't know if he still intended to stay with me, and if he did, and I had no idea how I would respond once I faced the real situation of being alone with him. I centered my thoughts to focus on a singular purpose—*keep it together*.

My plane descended through the familiar dense pack of fog and mystically contacted the tarmac with impressive skill, delivering me with ample time to spare. Passing through the jet bridge, I was hit with the same rush of cold that greeted me four months prior, even though it was a dreary April morning. As soon as I entered the expanse of the airport, I ended my silence by shooting off a text to Nick.

"Just arrived—it's freezing here. I totally did not dress appropriately."

“Ha ha! I'm picturing you in a naughty nurse's outfit standing outside right now.”

“Nice. Any epic debauchery last night?"

"If you count eating pizza alone in my room, then, yes."

He sent another text in rapid succession. "Also, I got my own hotel for the night."

My heart sank with anguish and sighed with relief at the same time. My head was infused with vaporous fog, mirroring the sediment idle in the sky.

"Thanks," I replied.

I stashed my phone and headed off in my usual routine of wandering aimlessly around the exterior of the airport baggage claim, seeking the elusive shuttle pickup spot for the hotel. I was quite familiar with the routine of getting lost to wind up found, and it was something I did with a profound level of efficiency. At shuttle gate one, I breezed onto the bus that I had taken previously to and from the airport. I knew the bus well, and I greeted it as an old friend.

I was welcomed by the driver with the familiar perfunctory question, “Which hotel are you going to ma’am?”

I confidently replied “The Hilton Garden Inn,” because that was the hotel I had booked for the weekend. Logan and I had booked the trip in somewhat of a frenzy, and initially we encountered trouble getting the conference hotel, but after changing the dates to stay over Friday night, everything lined up. I had checked and double-checked myself—so I thought.

“There are two Hiltons in this area,” he explained monotonously, and then motioned to a large photo of the conference center plastered to the wall behind the driver’s seat, “This shuttle is for the Hilton O’Hare; is this the hotel you are going to?”

I inspected the photo with careful consideration and confirmed assuredly, “Yep, that is my conference center. That is where I am going.”

I must be confused. I booked the right hotel.

Accepting this to be true, I positioned myself on the large bench covered in worn gray leather, absorbing its cold into my bare legs. I was situated directly behind the driver, in plain view of the photo of the large conference hotel with the two round side towers, connected by a large atrium. I sat calmly scanning the photo in a meticulous fashion, considering each detail and confirming my position, assured that I was on the right bus.

I closed my eyes and focused on my purpose, shivering with cold and fidgeting with anticipation, forcing calm over the flurry of excitement clogging my muddled head. I would be seeing him shortly and then everything would feel okay.

This is real, I am real, everything will be fine, I promised the April air.

Once at the hotel, I headed straight down to the conference level and over to the check-in table attended by the fabulous ladies that weren't. The head hussy, who had been an impartial observer of the previous weekend's schemes, didn't take stock in me at all, but instead, looked obtusely at me and asked, "Where's Nick?"

My face couldn't contain the shock at that moment, so I stared blankly and said, "I don't know," before turning to walk away. I pulled out my phone to text him again, "How did I beat you here," I began to type, but before I could send it off, I was pulled to the moment.

"There she is," I heard Nick say, his voice floating across the air.

I lowered my phone and exhaled.

My whole body contracted in alternating flurries, driven by electrical currents proliferating in his presence. I calmed my nerves and turned up my gaze, meeting his welcoming grin with a nervous smile that quickly transformed to a fazed glare. He wasn't walking toward me alone. Jack accompanied him, and his knowing expression took me in with equal avarice and my stomach lurched at the memory. "Ugh, I can't win!" I groaned under my breath.

We all three exchanged greetings and then proceeded inside, parting ways to set up accordingly for the conference. Nick liked to sit up near the front to get pictures of slides and take decent notes. I liked to sit in the back, so I could leave often and be my naturally ADD fidgety self, out of the lecturer's watchful eye. We compromised and sat nearly at the front, completely off to the side.

Jack and Craig were set up in the back. Chad and Gregg were one row behind. Ty was front and center. I chatted everyone up giddily during breaks and found it ironic that, four months prior, this room of strangers felt so off-putting. I was a reticent girl in an adorable sweater dress, putting off my best RBF, and rebuffing anyone who dared to approach my invincible wall.

Chad was the first to vanquish on that fateful January weekend, Jack number two one month later. After that, a veritable onslaught ensued. More people achieved occupation in my closed-off world than I had ever allowed. Suddenly, I was the fucking homecoming queen—smiling brilliantly and owning it—everyone was my friend, and I was as happy as a skylark. What a difference four months and the anticipation of a love affair makes! I exuded an air of confidence that was a complete 180 for my character. It felt natural and easy—comfortable even.

The lecturer took his podium and resumed speaking without grace, while Nick and I picked up right where we left off, passing notes back and forth, cracking asinine jokes, and me sneaking out randomly so I could calm down. We were again reveling in an energy field surrounding only us, playing at some fantasy that was too good to be true.

During the first break, I went to check into the hotel while Nick headed off to his room. There was a lengthy queue for the check-in podiums, so I impatiently waited my turn and frantically fumbled with my phone. I was reviewing the morning's texts and searching for hidden meanings, trying to make sense of my situation. The line moved quickly in that fashion, and in no time at all I found myself face to face with a composed check-in agent with a pristine glossy bun and no-nonsense makeup to match.

I smiled with confidence and gave her my name while passing over my ID, awaiting a reciprocal gesture with the key to my room. Only, that wasn't what transpired. "You don't have a reservation here," she said, her face pallid with indifference.

"What do you mean I don't have a reservation?" I asked. "I know I have one. I booked the Hilton. It's on my Priceline reservation."

With a heartless delivery, she rattled off a familiar story. "Well, there are two Hiltons in this area, and this is the Hilton O'Hare. You probably have a reservation at the Hilton Garden Inn up the street." Apparently, this mantra is rehearsed as part of the Hilton new hire initiation, and they say it so often its delivery became mechanical and virulent.

Internally, I began freaking out. "No," I insisted while pulling out my iPhone. I called up the itinerary screen and shoved it across the counter to display my reservation.

She took one look at my evidence and confidently verified that I managed to screw things up royally. "It says so right here," she said, motioning to the screen. "Your reserved hotel is the Hilton Garden Inn, which is only a short cab ride away." With a delicate fanfare, she dismissed me, indicating the direction I should go.

I moved away from her podium with dejected footfalls and stopped a few feet shy of being in the way. "Idiot!" I cursed under my breath. Then I pulled up the message screen and alerted Nick.

"I don't have a room here. I booked the wrong Hilton."

He messaged me back instantly.

"Come to my room, 121. I can keep your bag here for now."

He let me in, and we sized each other up, encased in air weighted with misty swirls of trepidation. I was exhausted from the previous night's stress and the morning of hectic traveling, so I asked if I could relax for a bit in his bed. He glared at me through chaotic eyes and said: "Sure, you do what you need."

I lay down in his bed flat on my back and closed my eyes. I slowed my pulse and regulated my breathing and tried to embrace the surreal events of the morning.

During this time, Nick sat at the desk, then stood, then paced around in agitation. I caught a glimpse of his expression, which was overwrought with distress, and I knew it was high time to start making our way back to class.

An hour before lunch, he looked at me and asked bluntly, "Should I get rid of my room here tonight?"

I mulled over his words, unable to envision a scenario where I would separate from him willingly. There were forces at work entirely outside my control. A fire indeed was kindling. No part of me felt capable of holding my demons behind closeted doors. It was as though my alter-ego forced one foot outside the door, caught sight of freedom, and became wild with excitement and possibility. All I could do was watch her go.

"It seems likely that we will end up in one room together," I answered, purely from the gut, keeping my eyes trained ahead. I could not bear to meet his gaze as I made my wonton confession. But I was speaking my truth. I only knew what I felt, which was that I was incapable of leaving his presence for as long as it was available. Nick took away the confirmation he needed and immediately bolted to get out of his reservation.

He never returned to class before lunch, but my attention was trained to the ding of a text, "My reservation here is undone. I will meet you out front by the cabs with our bags. Come outside when class breaks for lunch so no one can see us leaving together."

My stomach ached at his words. Knots were forming that burned and twisted my insides. I felt something like the thrill of auspicious excitement bordering something like the beginnings of impending death bursting outward from one focus of pain in the center of my body.

As I was walking away from class, headed toward our rendezvous, Jack appeared at my side and casually draped his arm around me.

"You came back," he whispered, "what made you do that?" His delivery was cool and confident, assuming I'd respond in a manner fit to continue our charade. I shirked away from his touch and slid out from beneath his arm.

"I wanted the camaraderie," I replied coolly, maintaining a steady distance as we ascended on the escalator toward the restaurant along the back wall. Once at the top, he carried forward, and I turned the other way, heading the opposite direction of the crowd.

"Aren't you coming to lunch?" Jack called after me.

I relayed the story of the screwed-up hotel reservation and excused myself to solve the problem. “Likely I won't make lunch,” I confessed, silently wondering how odd he’ll find it that Nick doesn't make lunch either.

CHAPTER 22

Nick and I hailed a taxi over to my hotel, which was a short three-minute ride away. The place was a tacky business class hole in the wall, situated in a rundown neighborhood of suburban Chicago. Immediately I hated it. I refused to cancel it, though, fearing that to do so would arouse suspicion with Logan. In hindsight, I should have walked away and let it go. We should have stayed somewhere, anywhere, else. It set the stage for failure on ambiance alone.

At the front desk, the hospitality agent asked if I wanted one king bed or two doubles, right at the time where Nick sauntered over from the modest convenience store set up around the corner and announced loudly, "We need to find a new hotel. This one does not have extra-large condoms."

I cringed at his haughty arrogance. I gave the lady an exasperated look and replied firmly, "Two doubles please." *Seriously, the nerve of this guy!*

Focus. *Breathe.* Singular purpose.

We walked the short distance from the desk to the elevator, making small talk as we covered the floor.

"I don't do this kind of thing. So that you know, this isn't me. I've never been unfaithful," I said, all matter-of-fact like, as though perhaps I could put him off by expressing this sentiment now.

"I'm not expecting anything," he said earnestly. "I'm here to keep you company, that is all."

"I trust you," I told him, because I honestly did. "I don't know why, but I trust that you will do the right thing."

I wanted him to know I was vulnerable. I wanted him to know that if anything did happen, it was not because he was just another guy at the end of a long line of guys—he was *the* guy—and he was special to me.

We dropped off our bags and snagged a quick bite at the hotel restaurant for ease. Lunch was awkward, and I couldn't eat. My stomach was writhing in searing knots, and the center of pain was pulsating fiercely. We both ordered salads, and he devoured his while I lacked the capacity to even pick at my own.

We returned to our conference, resumed distracted attention, and survived to see the end of another day, securing plans for an evening of drinks and dining with our fellow colleagues. Then we dodged conversational advances from anyone around us and bailed entirely on the fancy soiree to commemorate the final class. Even without him I would have never considered going—but with him, I didn't have to worry—we were on the same wavelength.

We ventured back to the little dive hotel and readied ourselves for an evening out. Jack messaged Nick shortly before we left, "Can you let Ruby know when and where we are going to meet up?" As though he couldn't have done that himself? But he knew. Nick had become my connection to the group. We had spent the day together, disappeared at lunch together, existed in our little space during lecture, and bailed when it was over—*together*. We were so visibly together only a blind man would miss it.

We were out with the now familiar cast of friends I'd acquired through the experience, all except Chad. I could not bring myself to clue him into my scheme. The night was spent in a restaurant billed as an "Irish pub" but felt more like a TGI Fridays. We were sampling craft beers and dining on crab cakes, joking and carrying on with the same black humor—only suddenly, my self-confidence deteriorated.

A sinking paranoia was overwhelming me, and I started to fear that it was only a matter of time before Nick would turn against me. Suddenly, I was back in my formative years, a defenseless, shy, timid girl. A girl who was tormented, bullied, and spit on by guys; a girl who was called a hooker and a whore. I was so sure Nick would discover I was flawed and then turn around and spit on me too. Fear paralyzed me. I stopped acting like the nonsensically confident "zero fucks what you think of me" woman I grew up to become and sought escape from everyone's eyes.

Before the night had a chance to draw long, I called it. I apologized profusely, declaring myself exhausted and wishing everyone goodnight while Nick hailed us a cab to return to our arcane world. We fell into the derelict gloom of our business class suite and prepared to crawl into our respective quarters. I knew if I remained awake and alert, eventually one thing would lead to another, so as a last-ditch precautionary measure, I took a hefty combination of sleeping pills in an already drunken state.

Nothing can go too far if I pass out, I convinced myself.

When I walked out the bathroom door, I heard Nick's voice coming from the back side of the bed where his luggage was set up.

"Time to take these jeans off and put on my Lululemon pants!" he announced cheerily.

I laughed back at him. "Clothes really are the worst. We tried to get my oldest son to wear skinny jeans, and as soon as they were buttoned up, he fell to the floor, writhing like they were filled with ants. I couldn't stop laughing, but I identified with his pain. He was the outward expression of what wearing jeans feels like to me; I just suck it up for as long as necessary. Also, why I prefer dresses–" I could feel my face getting hot as I rambled nonsensically about things he obviously wouldn't care about. And why did I just mention my son? Unable to let my aimless thought train linger unfinished, I carried on.

"That was a long story with no great punchline to explain that I don't sleep wearing pants," I said, holding up my hands and offering an apologetic face. "Anything touching my skin will keep me tossing and turning all night. It's a tank top and panties over here." If I could have whacked an off button to my mouth I would have done so, but the damage had already been done. I felt compelled to clarify my neurosis; however, I was sure all Nick heard was a lugubrious monologue ending in "I'm stripping down to panties."

"I like panties," Nick said, a boyish smile taking shape on his lips.

"Behave," I said in a soft, jesting tone while I crawled beneath the covers of my bed.

"I am. See." Nick made a big production of crawling into the double bed next to mine and reached over for the TV remote. "Let's see what we have on TV."

He flipped through all the channels twice, but nothing held appeal.

"I have Netflix on my iPad; we could project a movie to the TV from that."

"Yeah, let's do that," Nick said.

I got out from beneath the heavy coverings and wandered over to my gargantuan purse to get the iPad and cord. Deciding it more feminine to carry a purse than I computer bag, I had rigged the thing to double as both; however, it wasn't properly designed. The contents started out highly organized that morning, but then, as the day went on, my bag packing got sloppy. Though the iPad was easy to locate, my cords weren't in their right places. I was pulling out fliers from salespeople and chargers and my loupes case, all the while keenly aware of Nick's eyes soaking up my bare legs. I rifled through the contents until I could no longer stand it.

"Maybe just set the iPad between us and watch it that way?" I said in defeat, turning back from my purse to meet his eyes. The lust filled expression on his face melted the reserve of my defenses.

"In that case, I'm coming over there," Nick said, throwing back his coverings and rising up out of his bed. "And if you aren't wearing pants, I'm not either." In a flash, he stripped down to his damn sexy briefs, uncovering a tattooed body so chiseled in perfection my vision blurred from observing it.

He playfully leaped into the bed I'd just vacated while I stood holding the iPad in one hand, trying to wipe the shock off my face with the other. He sat propped against the pillows, looking at me expectantly.

"Okay then," I said, crawling back onto the other side. I set up the device between our bodies, and together we scrolled through the movies.

"What are you feeling, comedy, action, girl movie?" Nick asked. I had zero interest in content; whatever occupied the screen and gave us purpose to lay together fit the bill nicely.

"Just go with the first one you'd like," I said, sinking into my warm impression forming on the mattress.

"Have you seen this one?" he asked, pointing to an unrecognizable movie jacket.

"Nope, there are gaping holes in my pop culture experience. If you recommend it, I'm on board."

"Done deal."

The movie selection got under way. After adjusting the volume to an acceptable level and trying a few ways to prop the thing up such that we could see it, we opted to rest it on the nightstand between the beds, using the lamp as a prop. In that set up, we both had to be turned to the side, which opened the gates for the flood.

Nick crept up on me from behind and swallowed me whole with his enormous arms. Inside his warmth, I allowed myself to unravel completely. The greater world could have been in rapturous chaos, and I wouldn't have batted an eye. In his arms was the safest place I knew. In his arms, I felt at home. I closed my eyes and soaked up that moment where everything was perfect, everything was euphoric, everything transcended everything, and a new me reigned.

After laying in blissful silence for the blink of one eternity, he stepped things up by gently kissing my back. Each place his lips brushed burned slowly, then flickered, then fizzled, eventually dissipating, unable to sustain life with each new location that lit up. I allowed myself to drift into a wondrous place contemplating how this act wielded transformative power, how his lips could awaken my skin—skin so usually lifeless and dull—compelling it alive with renewed significance. At that moment, its purpose was to relay ecstasy from a slight brush of contact, a covert functionality it had been hiding from me all these years.

Things heated up quickly from there. I could feel his erection pushing hard against my back, and he was unyielding in his tight hold against me. He flipped me over and kissed me passionately and, soon, I was on top, writhing against him, still protected by one thin layer below.

It was getting intense, and eventually, he suggested that we get ourselves off individually. Jumping into parallel masturbation with a stranger was a place I couldn't free myself to go, so instead, I suggested we move in another direction, one in which I was better versed.

In the span of an instant, we shed the last layers and he swiftly entered me with no talk of condoms, no thought of safety, and no consideration for my entire life. I lost sight of every single care in the world; my overriding and singular purpose at that moment was the need to experience him absolutely. A pull so strong that to deny it might result in a fate worse than action; I needed him inside me like I needed air.

He lifted my knee and thrust himself in so deep I felt ecstasy mingled with pain. He was so aggressive that I found myself actively focusing on separating the two so my body could hone in on my one. It was no easy task. He flipped me around skillfully, and in each new position, I was blown away by how darkly euphoric it felt. It shred every inch of my soul.

He wrapped the length of my braid tight in his fist and

pulled while I clung to his back. The moment before he came his hand caressed my neck—the span of it capable of cutting off my air in one firm grasp—but the gentle act of not, of simply resting there, set my whole body on fire. He asked if he should pull out and I assured him he was fine; I was so out of control with him. When he did it was the most thrilling part of the experience. I could feel the undulating current as he came inside of me and the stiffness in his arms as his whole body went rigid with pleasure. The intensity of the thing skyrocketed me. Nick fell into the mattress and I laid out across his warmth. There, our overlapping torsos rose and fell in unison, my consciousness obliterated.

It was like birth. It was like death. It was the most spectacular thing I had experienced in my life. I was a goner.

He was ready to go again in minutes, and the second time was much like the first, ending again in his classic climax. We collapsed into each other, and he started talking animatedly in his impossibly sexy voice. "That was hot. I felt like we really connected—like we weren't just fucking, but we were something more. I think we both honestly needed that."

He was so sincere and genuine; I actually *believed* him.

But I was satiated. I was wasted. My mind was opaque from the combination of sleeping pills and alcohol. In my head, at that moment, I was resolved to knowing that he had complete power over me. If he asked, I would have walked away from my life. I would have given it all up and followed him anywhere, and I had no idea *why*. My intense response to being intimate with him terrified me. I wasn't thinking clearly, but one string of words scrolled through my mind in neon block letters that commanded my conscious attention—END THIS NOW.

I knew there was no universe in which I could be a functional person when someone possessed that kind of control over me. He made me feel neurotic. He woke up something I had put to sleep ages ago, something I was no longer able to identify. All I knew was it wasn't right. I convinced myself that we had a fun experience, but this was fantasy, not reality. I had a safe, respectable, honorable husband, and Nick would ever only ruin my life.

I looked into his eyes one last time, fighting back the tears that would expose my frailty.

"Being with you is like breathing," I whispered.

Then I flipped on my side away from him and inhaled one large breath, let it all out, inhaled once more, and proceeded to lay into him hard.

"You are the life I was supposed to live—the life I set out to have but never got to experience because I am a girl interrupted. My family is falling apart, and I am terrified that I'll go through this all and wind up at the end of my life having never felt passion. I don't enjoy anything I do. I don't feel pleasure. I don't feel love. I don't feel excited about anything. I so desperately want to *feel* something."

I dumped this all out on him in one quivering breath, then inhaled deeply to refresh before carrying on.

"I need you to promise me one thing."

"Sure," he conceded softly, "what is it?"

"After this weekend, I need you to never contact me again. I'm going to delete you from my world, and you need to disappear." I said this, and he stayed silent, so groggily, I carried on.

"This is too much of a distraction. I can't focus on my

work with you texting me all day. I need to be tuned in at home right now—my family is falling apart and I'm trying to hold everyone together but I'm not even holding together myself.

"I have a contract in place to move my clinic in two months, and I've got to be preparing for that. I have to hire another associate, and until I have one, I'm going to have to work overtime.

"I couldn't deliver anesthetic yesterday morning because I got a hand tremor. I've never had that happen before. And I think my husband saw your text messages . . . I just . . . I can't handle this—" I carried on rambling.

And then, with the flipping off of some physiologic switch, everything was cloaked in soundless black. My toxic concoction crafting a merciful end.

I am an epic dick.

CHAPTER 23

That night I woke up alone and naked, freezing on a little strip on the outside of a lonesome double bed, huddled beneath a threadbare sheet. Nick had moved completely across to the other side and was peacefully slumbering with the majority of our coverings. I crept alongside him and snuggled into his back, attempting to return to a more palatable body temperature. At the moment of contact, he thrashed and angrily yelled out, "What are you doing?" Then, he forcefully snatched up a pillow and wedged it between our bodies.

"One pillow of separation," he asserted firmly, before collecting himself and lying back down, drifting instantly back to sleep. I tried to find a comforting way to do this. I held the pillow in the vicinity of his space. I maintained a position near but distant. Rather than feel comforted, I felt alarmed. I lay trembling in my out-of-his-way spot, startled and empty and alone.

I tossed and turned until I was seasick from the torrent of confusion and drained from chasing the elusive construct of sleep. I snuck off to the bathroom and drew myself a hot bath. As I lay half submerged in solitary waters, trying to wash away the pain, I launched into an inventory of my emotions. *What am I feeling right now?* Pain, regret, loss, betrayal?

Nick seemed to be satisfied; he was blissfully

slumbering away. Nothing in his life was going to change.

I, on the other hand, would likely never know peace again. The rest of my life would never be the same, and it was a consequence I would bear in his absence—he would never see the heartrending wake of destruction in our afterglow. And I was floating in a bath alone at 2:00 a.m., contemplating the status of my emotional state, which made one appalling measure of success.

I had to concede that I felt fucked.

I felt utterly alone. I felt abandoned and isolated. I felt hurt, used—*worthless*. I was circling true rock bottom blackness. As I let out the waters, I imagined myself swirling in the eddy, circling the drain and heading toward the void.

Class the next day was shrouded in gloom, overshadowed by a descent of discomfiture. Instead of the confident and happy prom queen of the previous day, I was the cheap whore who was duped by the king. I could sense that everyone around us knew. And he wasn't at all shy about it. During class, he had the audacity to say, "last night was hot" in earshot of our new group of friends.

His comment hit like a blast of ice, and I let him know with a frozen glare. He continued, more quietly this time, "I don't care what these guys think; we're never going to see them again, and they aren't your close friends." Which might have been true, but they were now my professional colleagues, and what they thought of me did matter. I was disappointed.

He left class often that morning, making arrangements for his practice. He was wheeling with a guy to sign up for SEO at $3500 per month, and he recommended I do this too. I expressly detailed how much I felt that was unnecessary. My practice had me running on roller skates as it was, and I didn't even market. My philosophy was grounded in being *genuine,* and I couldn't see how promoting it that aggressively aligned.

I had hoped he was more authentic.

When the class break for lunch came upon us, we decided that one million "but-um's" was officially the breaking point, and we walked out of that lecture hall on a mission. If a mic had been nearby, I'm sure one of us would have dropped it, just to emphasize our point. And it's not that I felt the true need to be so exacting, but the combination of my now very public affair and the exhaustion of an educational experience that wasn't, left me feeling imperative that this dissolve cleanly. We cut out and excised our ties, and my general feeling was *ugh, I totally failed that interaction.*

I casually chatted with Craig and Jack while I waited for Nick to wrap up his business calls. We all had a reserved curiosity for the Cuba trip, but no one individually was serious enough to commit. I threw out a challenge to get us there together should anyone else declare chicken. Then we swore to keep in touch, and I embraced them both deeply, saying my final goodbyes. In the span of four short months, we had grown together; they are tied to a version of me that exists only on these pages, and in their minds.

Neither of them passed judgment, though their expressions were knowing. And I wondered how their conversation would go as soon as I turned my back. I feared I had lost my credibility with them; though, paradoxically, I'm sure they thought Nick was a god.

Lunch was at a little bar and grill near our dive hotel,

aptly named "Bang." Immediately, I ordered up one gin and tonic, downed it, and in no time, was onto another. I barely picked at a salad for lunch, again, overwhelmed by the writhing in my stomach, rendering me unable to chew and swallow without pain. I could not eat in his presence, but apparently, I was unimpeded in the consumption of alcohol.

That day, instead of the light-hearted banter we maintained in the presence of peers, we ventured into depressing new territory. We started out by discussing my racing, but then I confessed that my friend died tragically in a bike accident, and I hadn't felt comfortable racing since. He told me a heartbreaking account of a friend who recently got engaged only to have his fiancée die a couple months later. I detailed my disjointed stay at a California treatment facility, my failed attempt at adoption, and how the inability to part with my child resulted in me becoming the mother and wife that I had never intended to be. He told me about his previous arrests and battles with alcohol in his youth and confided that he had been married briefly to a woman who used to beat him.

Everything lost its luster. We were no longer laughing or bragging to capture the other's attention. Now we were competing over tragedy after tragedy, two wounded soldiers comparing battle scars, story-topping each other's ugly to see who would be scared off first. We matched heartbreaks blow for blow and had to call a draw because it was obvious we were both as twisted and jaded and dark as we were outgoing and fun.

Back in the seclusion of our dive hotel, we gave up the fight to maintain segregated spaces and united passionately as soon as the door clicked in place. It was the same dizzying ecstasy as the previous night, sending me to heaven for one fleeting moment of time. He came quickly, and while I lay in his arms, he expressed frustration that I hadn't.

Softly, I explained to him that it wasn't easy for me. I needed to use a vibrator to enjoy anything with my husband, and with years of passionless sex, I would need to figure it out. So, we tried again. I didn't climax, but to be honest, I didn't care. The way I felt when he took me was enough; the simple act of being there for him made me feel fulfilled. I lay dizzy in his arms and then mystically fell asleep. Being wrapped in his embrace put my mind to rest, and that elusive construct I chased more often than caught, finally was there in his arms.

That evening, we ventured into downtown Chicago to see his friend who was starring in a play. The venue was a theater in the round and was fronted by a kitschy coffee shop & bar reminiscent of my favorite one from college, freeing me to morph into the quixotic spirit who so desperately sought to connect with the arts.

The indie rock staples of my youth provided the haunting background music, and each new song was evocative of a significant time or place or event. Within the first few measures I relayed the corresponding backstory and ardently expressed my love of music—carrying on about how music shaped my life and how I define eras by the songs and artists that supported it.

Trying to project my creativity, I confessed that I used to do the singer/songwriter thing but threw in the towel when I became frustrated at my ineptitude and loneliness. Having no one else to collaborate with left me uninspired, and I opted to abandon my craft.

"I deleted all my recordings and hung up my guitar almost ten years ago," I confided to him. "I desperately miss it. I would give anything to have someone to play with me."

"I love to play guitar and write music," he said thoughtfully.

"Of course you do!" I cursed at him, "You do all the things I wanted to do. You live the life I wanted to live. You are all of the things I wished for in a partner," I cried out in exasperation, and then watched as confusion washed over his face, realizing too late that my outburst was crass.

But I was struggling to contain my feelings; I recognized I was projecting onto him something he knew nothing of, but for me, he was a beacon of hope. A sign that someone out there fit my salient mode, and that someone actually may have wanted me back. He was the type of person I would have desperately sought had I not bowed out on passion, choosing motherhood and stability instead. He embodied the life I dreamed I would live.

And there we sat, me and the man of my dreams, in a backdrop I recognized as home, only that dream could never transform into reality. The impossibility of it all arrested my fluttering heart.

His friend's play was *The Three Sisters*, a work by the Russian author and playwright Anton Chekhov. It was written in 1900 and first performed in 1901 at the Moscow Art Theatre. The piece revolves around the pathos of three sisters, Irina, Masha, and Olga, and in four acts dissects the disturbing shortcomings and complexities that ensue when life serves up offerings you didn't expect and withholds the longings for which your heart truly desires. From the antiquated follies of arranged marriages, the timeless heartbreak of unrequited love, and the too close for comfort "secret affairs of the heart," nothing for them resulted in fulfillment.

He held my hand endearingly through 90 percent of the play, like we were a real couple out for a date. That simple point of contact lit up my body and sharpened all of my senses. Near the end of the third act, Irina cried a dreadful monolog expressing the disquiet in her soul:

"*Nothing I do, nothing at all gives me any joy, and time goes flying by and all the time it seems as if you are abandoning real life, life that is beautiful, you are going farther and farther away from it, over some sort of precipice. I am in total despair, and how I am alive, why I have not killed myself before now I do not understand.*"

Her dialogue reverberated my previous night's unveiling and jarred my brain from the poignancy. Nick, too, recognized the parallels, and turned to me, whispering, "That is exactly what you said last night."

The fourth act was a blinding grand finale of histrionics which took the experience from relaxed beholding of heartbreaking beauty to a sucker punch hard in the gut. The Lieutenant-Colonel with whom Masha maintained a private love affair arrived and reported he was scheduled to relocate immediately. He outlined his transfer informally and then moved to leave, apathetic and composed. As he rounded on them after his declaration, Masha flipped her shit.

She clung to him, panic-stricken, then she fell to the floor, overwhelmed with grief, refusing to let go of his leg. He looked to her sisters and pleaded for their help. Jumping to action, they willingly obliged. They disentangled him from her embrace and restrained her in that state, freeing him to leave. For an uncomfortable lifetime of tragedy, she howled in unchecked anguish, trembling in a heap on the ground. It was disturbing to witness and resonated so deeply the bittersweet irony was like sugar-laced aspirin, burning the inside of my mouth.

And he was clued in, I think, to the inevitable horror of my demise. Even though we were witnessing the reproduction of a 1900s Russian play, those girls were me, and I shared their fate.

Disparate passion and life dissatisfaction are not a disease of a culture or era; rather, they run universally rampant—persisting across all of time—from beginning to middle to end.

From there on I lost him completely; he let go of my hand and petrified. The play ended. We stood. We exited. At the door we met his friend briefly, but he hurried through the introductions and excused us seconds after she came out. He called an Uber, and we climbed in the back—sequestered in separate corners—with a bottomless chasm between us.

CHAPTER 24

Our forty-five-minute ride back to the suburbs passed uncomfortably; dense air intermittently cut through by my desperate attempts to breathe life into our asphyxiating world. I talked about dentistry because I knew it was common ground, but he responded with aggression to my attempts. I pressed on. I expressed how passionate I get about mimicking natural beauty—how much joy it brings me to match existing imperfections. I confessed that those challenging cases inspired me the most, but he just scoffed under his breath in response.

He thinks I'm an idiot! I assumed in a panic. *Here I am, making senseless confessions to a guy who spent the morning setting up SEO to sell artificial beauty to affluent women in California. Why would he even care about natural beauty?*

I had failed. He constructed an impenetrable wall and was done with me. Accepting his disenchantment, I fell silent.

While he engrossed himself in the world of his phone, I huddled in my backseat corner, surreptitiously analyzing his features. He won me over with his personality, not his stunning good looks, so now that he transformed into a closed-off jerk, I had to wonder, what was it about him that was drawing me in so intensely?

He was constantly distracted by his iPhone. At present,

he was ensuring he did his part as an important guild member because there was a war going on in the village game that he played. He'd been getting momentarily lost in it all day. And in truth, when he first explained it, I found it lovable and slightly sardonic because I used to do the exact same thing to the exact same degree. Observing him was like looking in a mirror.

"You are me," I said aloud.

"What?" Nick asked, his delivery short while his eyes stayed locked on his phone.

"You are me," I said again, this time more clearly.

Nick looked up and sneered, as I'm sure, to him, my declaration was nonsense. But it wasn't nonsense to me. For two years, I had entrenched myself in the same type of activity, but one day I forced myself to stop. I realized that playing a virtual game was interfering with my presence in real life. I didn't want to need a fantasy game and a guild of strangers to feel complete, I wanted that completion to come from the physical people who needed me more. I let the game lapse, and when I did, my whole world slackened. My body was freed from unseen restraints, and I could finally stretch out neglected limbs.

I didn't speak those thoughts aloud to him though; his snide response implied he thought little of the matter, so I casually made my observation and carried on studying his profile.

The deeply trained creases that formed near his eyes were suggestive of a lifetime of humor. They were not flattering, but they endeared him to me because they signified his character. The patches of gray highlighting his temples were most assuredly out of place; they suggested a physical age and maturity he simply did not own. There was such an air of petulance to this man that those patches were a complete invasion of his otherwise low-profile demeanor. His body was massive, so unlike anyone I had ever been with before. He was a perfect physical specimen but chose gym T-shirts, hoodies, and jeans as both his conference and going out attire; casual, borderline sloppy. So typical "guy who gives zero fucks."

He was my designer drug. I wanted him so desperately I couldn't see straight.

He looked at me and asked curtly, "Are you staring at me?" The delivery a kick in the chest. As I caught a glimpse of his black expression, I was acutely aware of a void within him that was an expanse I could never bridge.

Fuck me; I am such an idiot!

I think I stammered words fit to respond—honestly, I cannot remember. Even though I was hemorrhaging, I sought to exude an air of control. Internally, my mind was clouded. I felt like, somehow, I messed up. I had failed at something, and he was done with me. I wanted his attention, but he was in a realm entirely his own; my nose was pressed firmly against the glass. My efforts to draw him out only resulted in him retreating further inward, a feat I never dreamed possible.

The death of us was as impending as night.

We got back to the hotel and he insisted he was tired, lying down hurriedly to go to sleep. I crept alongside him and lightly complained that I was still unsatisfied. He turned toward me and jumped at the chance, but his exertions were half-hearted at best. He went down on me briefly but didn't work hard at making me cum. While fucking, I tried to direct him into a position in which I could climax, but again, he wasn't willing to stay there. He flipped me over onto my back and fucked me so hard and so deep I felt him for a week.

When he came, he apologized; apparently taken off guard by how quickly it was all over, then he rolled away, back toward me, and closed himself entirely off. I tried to snuggle up with him, but I couldn't find a way to do so without breathing awkwardly on his back. He was instantly annoyed and got up to put on a shirt to protect his skin from my breath. I took the hint and moved into the other bed.

When sleep did not come, I accepted defeat and retreated into the shower. In the comfort of the cleansing waters, I fell into complete despair. I cried—loudly. I gasped, panicked, and lost all control of my senses. I pounded my head and fists against the cold, smooth wall, letting the water run and the tears flow for a seemingly endless period. I was a disaster, a failure of a person, a tiny point of inescapable singularity—the moment of connection was over. What had I done? Who had I become?

When I emerged from the refuge of the shower, I resolved to flee. I needed to end the pain. What value was there in continuing this charade? We were a disaster of a pair, the air between us was noxious and toxic, still teeming with the massive energy of an afterglow. I needed to escape it, or at least, I needed to act like I had the possibility of escaping it. I got dressed, packed my bags, and readied myself to sneak off to the airport. I was to leave him there—alone—and perfectly happy. Without me.

But as I made my way out the door, knowing this act would be the ultimate catastrophic act of finality, I hesitated. I didn't want us to end on a note that resonated so painfully sharp. What if he really was tired? What if I had been reading the situation all wrong? Maybe if I stayed, I could fix things with him? Maybe tomorrow would be a new day?

Ultimately, I couldn't go through with it. I stepped back into our hole of a room, unpacked, undressed, and tried again. I took a pillow and lay next to him, this time keeping my separation. He didn't even respond to my presence. I moved back into my bed and lay on my back, meditating on sleep and working every mantra I knew. I eventually dozed off, but the sleep I achieved was fitful and unnatural at best.

My alarm never got the pleasure of fulfilling its purpose that morning, as I beat it at its own game. I got up and readied once more. I was nearly done by the time he roused, and I kept silent and closed off, maintaining my own secluded world. His cold-hearted expression while packing seemed to convey disgust at my presence. *He hates me. Why the hell did I stay?* I realized in a panic. I wanted it done, so without consulting him, I ordered an Uber.

By the time we arrived at the airport, the awkward air surrounding us was unbearable. I sought to escape him at the first opportunity, so while he proceeded to the front to check in, I fled to the furthest security checkpoint line, assuming he would lose sight of me by the time he turned around. My solitary respite lasted only a few minutes, though, as he somehow ended up right behind me.

While waiting in the line, he tried to make nice, kicking up small talk while we waited.

"Maybe we should be CE buddies," he said. "You said you're going to the digital dentistry symposium next month in Phoenix, maybe I should check it out"

I had already booked it as a mother-son trip, and the very idea of overlapping those two worlds shook me like an earthquake.

"Oh, no. No, no, no. Not that one. When I go to Phoenix I stay with my sister, and I've already booked my youngest son to join me. That would not play out nicely," I said, shaking my head and trying unsuccessfully to mask the hysteria from my voice.

I didn't know it then, but his absence from my life would prove ever more devastating, and I should have just graciously agreed. But everything's lucid in hindsight.

"I hear Frank Spear's Occlusion seminar is legendary. I've never taken anything on that topic before."

"That guy?" Nick replied with a cough. I decided not to press the topic further.

"So, when you get home, you'll have the whole weekend ahead. What are you going to do with yourself?" he asked.

A whole weekend ahead? The prospect of facing that flooded me with a whole host of new emotions. What had felt like a lifetime's worth of a twisted love affair unfolded temporally over two natural weekdays. I had two full weekend days at home before I could throw myself back into work, my mental reprieve from the *proper Midwestern wife's* starring role that was slowly dismantling my essence.

Internally, I was rattling off the truth.

I'll be processing the destructive events of this weekend in my real world surroundings, putting on a happy face and pretending this never happened, staging an intervention to get my parents moved into a nursing home facility, and generally returning to a world that I've catapulted into tumultuous ruin, attempting to navigate that space without completely cracking.

Outwardly, I said, "I think I'll head to the lake and run thirteen miles."

"Why the fuck would anyone want to do that?" he said, laughing at me.

"Because I love it," I replied solidly. "What are you going to do?"

He looked off in the distance. "I think I'll go surfing," he replied, his face so casual it appeared he didn't have a care in the world.

I fucking hated him.

After we had been through security, he embraced me hard and kissed me, catching me off guard. Even after all the mercurial shifts I'd suffered over the last twelve hours, his embrace completely disarmed me. He whispered in my ear in his deeply sexy voice, "Can I still text you?" which annihilated my newly built wall.

"Of course," I responded impulsively, "and I promise I won't delete you from my world."

It was forced. It was unnatural. And most pointedly, it wasn't true. We said those things because it's unorthodox to part and say words that are harsh. Instead of being transparent and admitting—"We failed, this ends here and now—" effectively slamming the door and eliminating any loose ends, we lied to ourselves and each other. We left our relationship open-ended and implanted an ingot of hope deep in my chest, then dispersed hurriedly to our respective terminals.

Only, this time, no more text messages were shared, no flirtatious selfies were fired off, and no feverish excitement lingered in my veins. I found the nearest Starbucks and fell deeply into remorse.

In the end, I only wish we had allowed ourselves to speak truly.

"I don't think we will ever make it; we were two neutron stars overlapping in space. We had our one glorious moment in time, but we destroyed each other in the process. All we have left is the afterglow."

But those are the words that never get said.

CHAPTER 25

As soon as the wheels of my Canada Air Regional Jet 200 touched down on the runway, I flipped off airplane mode and shot off a text to Logan. I was determined to return to Ruby: the wife, mother, best friend, and doctor. I was determined to return to *me*. The proper Midwestern woman. Getting in touch with him instantly was what a good wife would do, so I started there.

"Just landed. Where are you?" I knew he was somewhere among the soccer fields adjacent to the airport. We had planned earlier for me to head straight there upon arrival. It was only 9:30 a.m. I had a full day ahead in which I needed to project sufferance.

"We are at field 3A. Cade's game just got underway. You should make it here to see him in plenty of time."

"Excellent, see you soon!" I shot off, grateful to have purpose and intention coursing the synapses of my mind.

Waiting anxiously for my gate-checked luggage in the compact jet bridge, I texted Olivia. "Just landed. I need to go for a run, are you up for it?"

She answered right back, "Sure thing—what are your thoughts?"

"Meet me at my place in an hour. We can run from there to meet Logan at the soccer fields and then do brunch if you're free." Then I messaged Logan again to keep him abreast of my activity. He's used to this kind of spontaneous action, so the additional plans hit him as no surprise.

I desperately needed to clear my head. The events of the last two days had shifted the axis of my world; I sensed an urgency to realign. The longer I strayed from my fixed trajectory, the harder it would be to bring myself back into orbit.

I used the pleasure of mapping a route in my mind to quiet the distress in my soul. Privately, the motivation behind this run was monumental. I was going to go home, unpack my luggage, put everything in the wash, and run away from it all. I needed to purge myself of this taint. I was hoping to physically and metaphorically run myself clear.

Olivia was unaware that anything transpired with Nick. He was so concerned I would tell her that he begged me to send her a lie: "He's a perfect gentleman," I professed the morning after we slept together.

She messaged me back plainly: "I'm glad."

Lies

I was a liar and an adulteress. I was no longer Ruby, the decent human being, who sat so uncomfortably in her pseudo-suburban professional, wife, mother, and athlete reality. I was mentally a full-scale outcast, resolved to endure a clandestine existence.

The night before I left for Chicago, Olivia advised me that if I slept with Nick, that reality was only for me. Logan could never know, and I had agreed. To tell him was to destroy him, which was a sentence I refused to issue.

Olivia met me at my house and in true ESP best friend fashion, we were both sporting new running shoes and excited to break them in. She loved her Nike Pegasus and was predictably donning a new pair in pink. I had been pleasantly surprised with my last pair of Mizuno Wave Sayonara, which were worn precariously thin from marathon training and awaited retirement. The night before I left for Chicago, I bought a new pair in Green Flash/Electric from Amazon. When I arrived at my house that morning, I entered the kitchen and found them, pristine in the box, unwrapped and on display for my discovery. I gingerly removed them and inspected the seams, overcome with a thrill of excitement too grand for the prize. But heck, I'm a girl who happens to love shoes; it's not like I'm breaking any social convention.

Running shoes are an extension of me, a gentle cushion protecting me, covering me, voyaging with and completing me, a constant companion while pounding the pavement. This pair was glorious. The green was impossibly fluorescent, like the color of watermelon gum. The pink was the ideal accent, contrasting the green in all the right places, and truly living up to the broadcast hype of "Electric." They were vibrant as hell, bordering on offensive, and adorably up to the task. These new shoes were to be my faithful companion for the next six months, the usual life span for a solid pair of kicks.

We started our run from the familiar concrete slab of my driveway. The route had us interweaving the college campuses and then shifting one block up, off Main Avenue, until we fed into the entry of Broadway. From there, we headed north, traversing through downtown and passing through the neighborhoods and college housing beyond, finally landing us on a seemingly endless stretch of highway that picks up near the outskirts of town. We stayed along this road the remainder of the way, ending us neatly at the soccer fields, adjacent to the airport, in just enough time to catch my youngest son's game.

It was a luscious April morning, and the route had us enjoying the greatest scenery our city has to offer. Even the final stretch was lined on one side by train tracks and prairie grass and offered a tranquil fixation capable of numbing the mind, a never-changing landscape dotted with railcars shifting from rusty reds to dusty blues and pale greens, establishing a progression across the vacant valley.

The run passed us by in near silence. Having not eaten or slept for two days straight on a diet of alcohol, I was starting to feel the ill effects of my choices. Nausea settled in and disquiet rattled the base of my brain. Olivia did most of the talking. I breathed not a word about my infidelity.

We arrived at the soccer fields just in time to take in the last game, and I was immediately clued into the presence of my ugliest nightmare—my high-school ex-boyfriend. Though we reside in the same town, we had not overlapped spaces for fifteen years. It behooves me to call out that this encounter was freakishly timed. He was the embodiment of the most disgusting thing I could fathom; my visceral reaction to seeing him was so severe I couldn't rightfully explain it.

I pulled up my hood and hid beneath my running jacket to make sure I stayed covered while simultaneously exercising restraint. I forced myself to stand in one spot, repressing the urge to walk over and punch him in the face; inciting-event unrequired. Pent-up rage and him being in the wrong place at the wrong time was all the motivation I needed. Seeing him heightened the brewing nausea and disquiet in my body to a place far beyond imagining.

I vehemently hated that guy, as strongly as I had passionately loved him, the way only a sixteen-year-old girl could when presented with the promise of an older man who fronts a rock band and does his own tattoos and graffiti art.

But then I grew up and tried to move on, and he clung to me for dear life, forcing my hand to decisive action. Our break-up was a tumultuous war, and at the end of it all, I cut ties with my friends, my hobbies, and everything related to who I was. I deconstructed and disappeared and hunkered down, reconstructing a new me. When I finally emerged and opened fresh eyes, I had shut down all romantic and passionate emotions. If I did not open myself to love, I could not open myself to loss. In securing that tenant, I ensured I would never experience agony in that way again. I hadn't been intimately involved with anyone capable of triggering such a roller coaster since.

Until Nick.

I went home and tried my best to sleep it off. The next day was going to prove even uglier, and I still needed to get my axis realigned. The run, invigorating though it was, had not proven fully restorative.

The following day was the one I had decided on to confront my parents and insist they transition into some form of care facility. I was certain that it was the only viable means of procuring them a healthy future; they were on a collision course with destruction and required intervention. The need was so blatant it was as though jet streams scrawled it across the blue sky, but the action, until then, felt impossible.

It's strange how people continue to dance, even when the music has stopped. We all knew this was improper, but to remove them from the situation and force a life-sweeping change seemed more overwhelming than watching them die. No one wanted to accept the end of the song.

But Tom's most recent crisis shocked me back to reality. I had been dancing as though they were fine for far too long. They were not fine. They were in crisis. All other means of care for them had failed, and they were hovering on the brink of destruction. It was time to take decisive action, and this one was on me. The next morning I drove down there, and I messaged Nick before heading off, "I have a long drive and a hard afternoon ahead of me; I could use a laugh if you have a chance to call."

Only, he never responded.

When I arrived, I talked with my parents and laid down the hard facts, then waited for my stepsister to arrive. When she finally arrived, I reiterated the plan to her; however, she had been envisioning things differently. She wanted my mom to go into transitional care while she took her dad home to live with her. My mother was terrified to separate from him and begged me to ensure they didn't part.

We gave each side serious consideration and allowed everyone to speak their mind. I tried keeping present and meditating as best I could, but it wasn't very good considering my head was on sideways and my mind was numb. But, in the end, this assembly resulted in them getting checked into a care facility by the end of the week, so overall, I qualified my venture a success.

But I didn't feel like I'd succeeded in anything at all.

Placing your parents in a nursing home at the ages of fifty-five and sixty-three isn't exactly what you envision for your life at thirty-four. I hated it . . . every last bit of it. I wanted so badly to abandon ship and move on. I was so unhappy tossing about in my chaotic world that each crashing wave dissolved bits of me like salt water corrosion.

But, for the time, I conceded that I was moored, and my only option was to endure. I promised myself someday I would be free, allowed to heed my unrelenting allure and seek happiness in uncharted waters abroad.

When I arrived home, I had reached a state of depression beyond consolation, from both the exhaustion of the mission I had accomplished and the rejection from Nick, who didn't even acknowledge my text. I walked through the front door, locked eyes with the caring and understanding gaze of my husband, and lost my will to remain passive. I needed to break down in front of someone, but that someone could not be him.

"I need to talk to Olivia," I said softly. "Are you okay if I meet up with her for a while?" I had been home merely seconds, but he sensed my urgency.

"Of course, sweetie," he consented. "Take all the time that you need." Secured with his permission, I turned right back around and reentered my car.

Sitting in my garage, I texted her. "Can I come over?"

She messaged right back, "Of course. I'm finishing up dinner right now." I backed out of the garage and raced over to her house, dying to get to her as fast as I could.

She was waiting for me outside the elevator on her floor, and as soon as the doors slid apart, I looked at her through tear-streaked vision and murmured, "I've done something horrible."

She took me in her arms and assisted me onto the soft brown couch centered in the picturesque living room of her neoteric downtown apartment. She brought me a plate of food and forced me to eat. Between bites of sesame chicken, I relayed the details of the past two days.

"It was horrible," I cried to her. "He told me he was on a reality dating show called *XXX Wife-swap of LA County*, and he was an abysmal asshole the following day," I said, detailing how distant he became. "He shut me out completely. He totally retreated inward. I was an idiot. You were right. He is just a selfish asshole, and I got played."

This admission to her was like a first-time confessional, my gross misread of him tore out my heart. I had entered into things with him sincerely believing that he possessed something more. I'd never been so fooled in my life! I couldn't imagine what I had been thinking.

"I tried to message him today, and he didn't even respond," I murmured softly to her, dropping tears on my face with each passing blink. I was broken, dejected, and despondent—a smoking hot mess kindling her couch.

She embraced me and reassured me and talked me off the ledge. Then we took a montage of silly selfies, sending them off in a blitz to Logan, reassuring him things were fine. Once I was composed enough, we YouTubed episodes of *XXX Wife-swap* and hated on him until I threw my phone at her TV. She took it away from me and deleted every picture of him and unfriended him on Facebook.

"This feels like death," she told me sternly, tentatively returning my phone. "You have to treat it as such." She was wise beyond her years. "You are never going to contact him again, okay?" I matched her impossibly green eyes and assented silently. “You had your fun; now you need to go back to your normal life.”

“I can do this,” I assured her. “It is over with Nick; he is dead to me.” The sentiment aptly fit, as the impact of his loss hit me the same.

CHAPTER 26

The first week after Chicago I was a busted-up shell of myself. There was no sound reason for it, but the absence of Nick was a black hole so powerful I couldn't function. Each moment without him sucked me in more deeply, pulling the last vestiges of light. Time was a relative term; sometimes the blink of an eye felt like it spanned an eternity. But I was determined to wait it out.

The Monday of my return to work, Logan and I had lunch at our favorite Chinese restaurant. Sometimes things like sesame chicken and pork fried rice have transformative powers. But it wasn't just the consumption of comfort food via wooden chopsticks that enlivened my spirit that day. For the second time in my memory, a parable written on a little piece of paper altered my perception of the world.

"You've got to read your fortune out loud, and don't forget to add 'in bed,' " I said to Logan, passing him one of the cookies from the tray and reserving the other for myself.

"Honestly? Aren't we a little old for that?"

"Not today! Give me today. Please. Humor me. I need to laugh," I said, unwrapping the cookie in front of me and holding it up by both ends, pausing there and signaling with my eyes for him to do the same.

The snap of the crisp cookie was oddly satisfying, and

I was pleased to see a perfect center break into two equal parts. There were rules surrounding fortune cookies, rules that were actually superstitions my friends and family held, but rules nonetheless used to entertain when nothing more could be said at the end of a meal. Things like you have to eat half the cookie and read the fortune first or it will never come true, or if the cookie crumbles in the breaking the fortune passes on to someone else. If a fortune is blank, it means you're going to die within the week. If you burn the fortune, it has to come true.

I turned the little white paper around in my hands and was relieved to discover there were words. *At least I won't be dying this week.* Before I had a chance to review them, Logan started reading out loud.

"Inch by inch, life's a cinch. Yard by yard, it becomes hard . . . In bed."

"Good lord. For real?"

Logan nodded slyly.

"Well didn't you just win?" I laughed. "I don't think they come any better."

"I might have made it up; you'll never know," he said, crumpling his fortune and stashing it away before I had a chance to snatch it.

"Dang it all. Whatever. That's fine. Today, I'm accepting. Thank you," I said, smiling up at him.

"Well, let's hear yours," he said encouragingly.

I looked down at the red lettering and read the fortune out loud without a silent pre-screen.

"Time will heal all things, just give it time . . . in bed."

I set the paper down and looked up at Logan. Neither of us were laughing. The flood of emotions that came after the reading threatened to drown me, but I contained it by cranking up the sarcasm.

"Well, that was utter shit. Why couldn't I have gotten something ridiculous like yours?"

"Here, take it," Logan said, producing the crumpled paper and tossing it at me.

"Sweet. This little bad boy is all mine," I said, flattening it out and re-reading it.

"Inch by inch life's a cinch . . . oh my gawd who writes these things? It's like they knew we were adding in bed."

"Yes. They are hoping for everyone to be easily entertained and immature," he said, shaking his head.

"Hey, don't judge. I have a case of the Mondays."

"Well, we need to get back. I have some TPS reports I need to get on top of," he said.

"Yeeeaaahhh. If you could have them on my desk by the end of the day that'd be grrrreat," I replied, doing a Lumbergh impression that was nowhere near on point.

As we joked, I furtively pocketed both fortunes. After lunch and back in my office, I pulled them both out and studied them again. Logan's was certainly just for laughing. But the reference to the healing power of time? How often do people need healing? Not that I was a great believer in things, but I trusted that that red lettering on the white strip of paper held my saving grace. Whoever governed the laws of the universe packaged that cookie for me.

Time. Time would heal all things. It made perfect sense. Life was never easy. Bad things happened every single day. And how did they cope? They survived. Survived by hanging on, until the storm blew away. This idea that I could wait it out, that soon my infidelity would be a distant memory, became a beacon of hope.

For ease, I tried forcing myself to believe Nick's vested interest was getting an easy fuck. It stung, but for sanity's sake, it needed to be an unconditional truth. His lack of response to my messages after our weekend corroborated the belief. But there lingered one small matter. I begged him and made him promise to do that.

Maybe, just maybe, he was *that good* of a guy. In the innermost spaces of my faulted heart, I refused to abandon that hope.

* * *

By the second week, dentistry-centric problem-solving was satiating my mind. I had ventured into these seminars with the intention of advancing professionally. Now, if I wanted to validate what I'd been through, it was time to focus my energies back where they belonged.

My new goal for week two was to formulate an iron clad treatment plan for my first implant patient. I had taken a cone beam image to know all the precise anatomical details and I had mounted study models to evaluate the bite and the size of the edentulous space. I had done the preliminary leg work, but I wanted to run the whole case past another set of eyes, just to ensure I didn't miss anything.

I needed an outside source, preferably someone with expertise. My biggest problem: I didn't know who I could trust anymore. I had promised Olivia I would treat Nick like he was dead to me, and I was embarrassed and feared I'd lost credibility with all my other new colleagues. One of the major reasons I cited for re-booking Chicago was camaraderie. To create an alliance of doctors who would challenge and push me forward—people who could be sounding boards for case discussions, to fill the void left by the departure of my associate.

After that first January weekend, Chad became my go-to guy. We messaged about cases, operations, and general day-to-day life. He had become a legit friend and selfless resource, but now, I was too humiliated to message him. I was sure he had seen the way I acted around Nick, and with him being such an upstanding guy, there was no way he would still consider me professional.

Disregarding Olivia's counsel, I decided to try again with Nick, rationalizing it was treatment-related and trumped personal agendas. And of course, I wanted to hear from him.

While manipulating images of a 3-D image superimposed on my CT-scan, I formulated an approach I deemed worthy of presenting.

"Hey, would you be willing to entertain some treatment questions for me?" I messaged, anxious to see if he would even respond.

"Sure," he replied instantly.

Relieved he acknowledged me and eager to acquire feedback, I sent him photos of the site along with a detailed explanation, highlighting my concerns.

Patient X: Congenitally missing tooth #29. Primary tooth T was in place until last year, so the space has been preserved, sort of. Potential complications:

1) Mental foramen is close - as circled on the screenshot enclosed. Given the anatomical constraints, I would need to use a 3.7 x 8 mm fixture. This is a bit smaller than ideal.

2) Patient has a history of clenching/grinding, as

evidenced by the flattened cusps. The mesial-distal width of the space was preserved, (hell - let's just say exaggerated seeing as it was previously a primary molar) however, from an interocclusal standpoint, the height is restricted (the opposing tooth had dipped some into the space, as T was below the plane of occlusion.) I can remedy this by using a screw retained fixture, but chances are I'll need a lab fabricated, titanium-based restoration with porcelain facing.

3) I have all the data to make a surgical guide, but I don't have a surgical guided kit. I'd like to at least fabricate something that will suffice as a placement reference, without having to invest in a complete surgical guide set up. How the hell do I do this economically?

After sending all of my material, he replied within the minute.

"Looks good. Go get 'em tiger!"

I gaped at his message insulting my screen. It was weak. Void entirely of substance. Either he was intentionally acting like a dick, or he was incompetent clinically. Regardless, it was not what I was looking for.

The patient genuinely wasn't a "slam dunk," which we had been instructed to start off with to ensure success. But, in reality, cases never are. Once you look at any problem long enough, hinders to success rear their ugly heads. Most people just aren't looking hard enough. So much else about the patient was perfect, and I knew it was doable. But hindsight is always 20/20, and for this case, I wanted a crystal ball. I wanted dialogue. I wanted to review the potential shortfalls and relieve doubts while broadening my scope of understanding because that was how I was going to get better.

"Thanks," I replied simply, not pressing him further for comment.

I was gravely disappointed. All my questions remained unfulfilled, and I refused to proceed with surgery without having one other person look over the case with me. With one door closed and no progress toward my goal, I opted to explore another.

The community of doctors in which I participate has an online forum where people post cases: successes and failures, treatment plans, and general dialog among cohorts. It's a decent forum, but all in all, it's a boy's game. They love to tear each other down and rip apart treatment like its fresh meat out for the picking. I don't appreciate it. Instead, I approach my posts from a different angle, ensuring they know I am not playing the same game.

I present as completely transparent. I presume this feature enhances what I offer the people I interact with. However, I am not reciprocated with equal fidelity ninety-nine percent of the time. I have tried in the past to shelter my true intentions to match wits in this male-centric world, but it's not a game in which I am holding all the cards.

If I am to succeed in this industry, I need to change the rules. I need to break down the walls that are constructed to hold me out, or redefine my role within this paradigm—craft a niche allowing me to play to my strengths. With that intention, I posted the same screen shots and content I sent to Nick, laced with my air of ingenuous inquiry, and awaited the flurry of responses.

It didn't take more than an hour for my post to be flooded with replies, and as expected, my case was gutted by vultures. Not that all the posts were bad, but to glean bits of useful data, I had to sift through piles of horse manure and ensure my big girl panties were snugly in place. I read over the entire thread and paused when I hit a response that was thoroughly reasoned and extraordinarily helpful.

The response came from a faculty doctor whom I had seen lecture before. Of all the guys who lead this group, he is one of two who has caught my eye before. He's witty and intelligent, and I can listen to him without straining. He delivered lectures conversationally. I was honored he even commented. Plus, his advice was given perfectly. He made my day with his kind words.

And then the strangest thing happened; right before I headed for home, I got a personal message from him.

"Ruby,

Your case would be good to use for the seminar next month if you don't mind. If so, let me know, and I can walk you through how to send me the files. Also, if you need any more help with the case, please contact me and we can discuss it more. Otherwise, if you want to wait, we can talk more at the seminar.

Regards,

Steve"

Holy Shit! I stared at the blocky words occupying my screen, incredulous that this occurred. I had been seeking validation and dialogue with someone experienced, and here it was! Instantly, I messaged him back.

"I would love that–please do so. You have already given me a great educational experience today. I would like to talk more and learn how to plan this the right way . . ." It was a long-winded message addressing the concerns he had originally posted in the thread about my plan and asking for details on how to share my files with him.

Ultimately, my post kicked off a texting, Dropboxing, and emailing flurry. Over the next week, we worked together, and he catapulted me into a treatment planning world that felt light years ahead of where I began.

He was an amazing teacher. He offered only the essential components of treatment that needed attention and did not belittle or offend. He genuinely displayed compassion to catch me up to speed, though he had no skin in the game.

He entertained other questions on which I had been stymied as well, like what surgical software to choose and what type of guide I should be looking to utilize. He took his time and explained everything at my level. He was candid, he was genuine, and he was kind.

Steve distracted me and showed me that the compassion of a stranger could alter the trajectory of your world too. For the remainder of that week, I was able to suppress my itching finger to message Nick.

And the cherry on the top? Chad saw my post and reached out to me personally. We resumed sharing cases and life stories via text and email, as though nothing in our world had changed.

A little corner of sunshine broke through my clouded mind, and I took one miniature step forward.

CHAPTER 27

Early on a Thursday morning, two weeks after the Chicago Affair, I traveled the same *#bestflightpathever* to D.C. with Logan to celebrate our eleven-year wedding anniversary. We had gifted ourselves four obligation-free days to spend in the Capital City, as it had been nearly a decade since we'd had more than two days of uninterrupted solitude. Frankly, the idea terrified me.

My saving grace on this trip was Olivia. I couldn't picture myself in D.C. without her, so gingerly, I asked if she could join. Having your best girlfriend on an anniversary trip seems a bit odd to most, but Logan had diplomatically agreed, requesting at least one day to ourselves. She booked a later flight and would be arriving the eve of day two. The three of us would then finish out the weekend in style.

Our itinerary was action-packed, which, given the current state of my mind, was truly requisite. Any momentary lapse of activity and I lurched into a domain veiled in blackness. Constant vigilance was key.

We slated an arduous long run on Thursday, as far as our legs would tolerate, followed up with relaxation and indulgence of equal magnitude—the proper way to recover from exercise. Friday marked the actual anniversary and was to be commemorated romantically at the Georgetown waterfront. Saturday night we had plans with our neighbors, who happened to be attending a wedding there and sat in front of us during the flight. They had an in at some fancy nightclub, so the challenge was thrown out to go big or go home. We were prepping for the former.

To the old version of me, this trip would have held legendary excitement potential. The premise had been so sincere: anniversary + husband + best friend, taking on a city that Olivia and I have come to love and recognize as our second home. The world was ours to own that weekend. Proper Ruby would have been ecstatic. Instead, I harbored only panic and dread.

I was tainted. I was back in a city where, three weeks earlier, I traipsed with Nick, leaving disruptions in the patterns of the universe, traces of our sick afterglow. It was a ghost town, and I was haunted by him the second I got off the plane.

The Reagan National Airport underwent significant remodeling in 1997 to become the streamlined, aesthetic beauty it is today. There are two separate concourse terminals feeding into the Metrorail system on an elevated platform, where one can catch the blue or yellow line. The station is positioned directly across from the airport entrance and is an excellent vantage point to behold the architectural beauty of the fifty-four Jeffersonian domes conceptualized by the architect, César Pelli, the man charged with creating an airport design befitting a national landmark.

The domes scallop the landscape and rising above their canopies is the air traffic control tower, a proud beacon of the Capitol City. On that morning, while contemplating the wonder of the undulating domes and omnipotent watchtower, my wits were provoked to unease.

Everything was too fresh; *he* lingered in the air. I sensed the watchtower plotting my demise, scrutinizing my every move; I needed more time before facing this. It was unclear if I would survive the weekend.

When I arrived three weeks ago and stood in that spot, beholding that landscape and awaiting the blue line, I kept occupied by texting Nick. Three weeks prior, I was flying on wings granted by the promise of cherry blossoms in spring. I felt excitement; I felt possibility. I felt everything around me collectively respire, clear and sturdy, with purpose.

Standing there then, I felt empty. Spring had evolved into summer, and the delicate flowers blanketed the ground. My heart wilted like their slight petals, and I was reft from the world by their death. Dense humid air clouded my throat, and with each breath, I encountered a hitch that thudded hard against a wall in my chest. I was suffocating.

Desperate to occupy fidgety hands, I grasped my iPhone and opened the little green message box. My fingers itched to create a dialog that could carry the potential for unanticipated excitement. I wanted to carry through the motions of shooting off a text, to reconnect with past sentiment. But I couldn't message Nick, so instead, I messaged Mike. It was also the final weekend of the seminars there, so he was likely in class.

"Hey, I'm in D.C. to live it up this weekend. I finished the classes in Chicago instead, so no more seminar attendance for this girl. Say hi to everyone for me. And please, try pay attention."

The blue line came, Logan and I jumped aboard and

traveled upon it toward Foggy Bottom Metro. From there, we navigated ourselves on foot to the Georgetown Melrose, a picture-perfect boutique hotel situated on the border of that neighborhood. The décor was luxurious and modern, so-right-now trendy. I adored it. We headed to our room, changed into exercise clothes, and took off into the humid mid-afternoon heat for my favorite D.C. activity: running.

From our quaint hotel, we ventured toward Key Bridge. Looking to avoid the Georgetown waterfront crowds, we opted for the trail alongside the canal, a hidden path, rock-packed and antiquated, forming an oasis lined with picturesque condominiums so flawlessly staged that the entire scene seemed surreal, as though nobody indulged in these retreats for fear of disrupting the purity. The whole of Georgetown is like this: gorgeous, fragile—quintessential east coast—but illusory, like I am observing a play.

The first mile of the run was the hardest I've ever endured. Panic instantly overwhelmed me, but I pushed on. Thick summer air hit my lungs like gasps of water, adding a visceral component to the metaphysical state. My vision narrowed and my thought swirled; time lost its referencing ability. Hours or seconds could have passed by; pounding the pavement was my centering metronome, constantly coupling me to the ground. I held silent focus and counted my steps, forcing myself to stay present.

Dark clouds churned overhead, and as we entered the wood plank boardwalk traversing through the marsh of Teddy Roosevelt Island, heavy drops of rain emptied onto us, a celestial offering in that sanctified space—waters that were cleansing and healing. My suffocated journey, with stygian thoughts and stifling air rallying to take me down, was emancipated by this shower and the refreshed air that followed.

I'd committed an act that had tarnished my soul. I had perjured myself and ruined eleven years of marriage. I was haunted by those crimes. They had shaken my core. But right there, in that rain, I could finally breathe. I resisted the urge to halt and stretch out my arms, train my gaze skyward, and soak it all in. Instead, I pounded on, and the scatter of the raindrops was enough.

The remainder of our run felt effortless, hints of my former self shimmered beneath my projected surface, gifting me the strength to persevere. I felt twinges of restoration, a glimpse of how it would feel to be whole. For a time, I remembered who I was.

That night, before heading out, I proposed we walk to our destination serenaded by music that had defined our past eleven years via headphone splitter. It was a fanciful concept, whereby two people drown out every other sound to enhance the experience of the scenery. Two souls, separated together, sharing a sacred space. He received this suggestion as completely romantic, and I was internally ecstatic. I had wanted to try it out ever since seeing Keira Knightley and Mark Ruffalo pull it off artfully in *Begin Again*. I was hoping to do the same.

I readied a playlist, and we drifted out of the baroque façade of the Georgetown Melrose, into the pretentious air of Pennsylvania Avenue. We breezed through the mile-and-a-half trek to downtown, serenaded by Radiohead, Blur, Rufus Wainwright, Bon Iver, and various other staples from our past. We passed by the White House, the Eisenhower Executive Office Building, and the U.S.

Department of the Treasury, occasionally pausing to capture selfies and observe the significant buildings of our history. We weaved in and out of throngs of tourists, civil servants, and traffic. We didn't even notice anyone else was there. It was us. And we were. And life seemed okay.

We settled into a high-top table at Shelly's Back Room Bar, overlooking plaid couches set up like a lodge, and I forced myself to find peace. We sent messages to Olivia and professed our undying love to the audience that is on Facebook. Then we reminisced our past eleven years.

Brandishing cigars and sipping burnt mixed drinks transported us back in time: before children, before dentistry, before Nick. We were the dirty scenesters that drank all night, smoked like chimneys, and philosophized the meaning of life over pretentious indie music.

Buoyed by the perception that this could mend—like I wasn't completely broken after all—we finished contentedly and took our leave. I was pleasantly surprised with the flow. Not only had I survived day one, I felt like we managed to kill it.

The next morning was our anniversary proper. We slept in, savoring time in a warm bed with a warm body, minus the added pressures of life—a lusciously lazy start. Around 8:30 a.m. we took to the trails, following the Potomac path toward the National Mall. Lincoln Memorial was our first stop, and there we paused to take in the site. Together we climbed the steps and pondered the presence of Lincoln in his dome before Logan guided me around to the back.

The early morning rays played in the flowing waters and magnificent beams arched across space, illuminating the Arlington Memorial Bridge and crafting a breathtaking scene overlooking the Potomac.

I was distractedly taking photos when he tugged gently on my arm to turn my attention his way. On the third tier of the marble striations, tucked amid two ornate pillars, rested my husband on bended knee. His face was lit up by the dancing beams, and his crystal blue eyes were as vast as the unfaltering sea. In an outstretched hand, he extended a delicate pavé diamond ring and, in an unfaltering voice, he delivered an emotional proposal.

"These eleven years have been the best years of my life. I love you with everything I am. You are my partner, my best friend, my lover, and my wife. I am so blessed to have had this time with you. I am so excited for the next eleven years, and the other ones after that. We have built a brilliant life together, and I cannot wait to see what the future holds. So Ruby, will you promise to stay married to me for the next eleven years? And all of the years that follow after that?"

"Will you please continue to be my wife?" he asked, in a voice so overwhelmed with the sentiment it split my soul in two. The significance of his words conspired against me, and I nearly slumped to my knees alongside him.

A million thoughts streamed through my head, begging mercilessly to be freed. My doubts, my fears and regret, my infidelity—rallied and wrecked me—crushing the tender hope of reclaiming my former self. And like the dense humid air, remorse encapsulated me.

Twelve years ago, on an unseasonably warm December evening, Logan and I mirrored this scene like two statues of a couple in love. Beneath the warm glow of a street lamp, outside our favorite bar, he closed out a drunken night of reckless idealism by proposing we get married.

Earlier that night, our conversational topic was "struggling to find a creative workaround to obtain health insurance heading into dental school." After countless drinks and envisioned scenarios, we concluded that the only practical solution was to be united on paper in the eyes of the law.

A lifetime of unfaltering commitment based on the need for health insurance coverage, another excellent example of my sound decision-making analytics.

But back then, I honestly believed our personality differences were surmountable. Together, we formed a nuclear unit capable of ensuring a *stable* childhood for my son, a primitive instinct so powerful I would have done anything to secure it.

I was a supreme realist shunning everything related to the idea of romanticism. A cold hard wall was constructed around my heart and Logan was content to set up outside. It worked.

So, on that night, as the dim of the light danced in shadows across his face, Logan asked if I would marry him, and I answered with a confident "yes." My soul never even paused to think.

Saying yes to his proposal twelve years prior felt effortless—the word was freely given from my tongue. But now, to speak it felt deceitful.

I wanted to say, "I don't know," or "let me think about it." I wanted to unleash all my horrible secrets, scream them at the top of my lungs from that third tier, proclaiming to the world everything that I was locking up. Logan should be the one to decide whether *he* wanted to remain married to *me*, no longer the woman he referenced.

His infallible love belonged in a world where I was absolved of my crimes. In my heart, I knew I was a desecrated woman and his confessed adoration for a wholesome figment of unreality only widened the gap in our disparity.

But it was hardly the time or the place to unveil my duplicity.

My mouth formed the word “yes.” I whispered it out loud while guilty tears traced down my cheeks.

But my heart did not agree.

CHAPTER 28

Olivia joined us late into the evening of our anniversary, and we met for beers at a studious pub near our hotel. On solid wood benches, drinking from robust glass steins, we recounted our travels and celebrated the final hour of the day. I found myself overenthusiastically gushing about the romantic events that had unfolded thus far, working hard to reinforce my lie.

But I recognized that this weekend could not suffer from the fault in my soul. I made a pact with my rational self to sustain my projection, my blissful masquerade. Don my best contented face and silence the screams desperate for release. For the sake of Logan, Olivia, and the plans we made, I would persevere, focusing all my energy on the enjoyment of living in the moment. The sad thing for me was that it shouldn't have had to be that hard.

We passed the next morning adventurously, recreating my zen running route from three weeks prior and wrapping it up with Starbucks and napping. For the afternoon, we elected to try out something decidedly novel and perfectly pedestrian—renting the clunky rideshare bikes and embarking on a zoo adventure. We had seen all the monuments, and the National Mall is best avoided during the broad daylight hours unless your thing is being in crowds of upwards of a million people organized into neat groupings of boldly colored T-shirts, bandanas, or other hideously emblazoned items symbolic of a group.

Plus, the major bonuses—the zoo was free, and for some reason, at the zoo, you could drink beer and walk around in public. It was like Vegas, only it was the National Zoo. Drinking beer and drifting around in public in the daylight—that was the dream, and we were chasing it.

We hopped aboard our cruisers and picked up the Rock Creek Park Trail off the M Street Bridge. The trail led us to a narrow, winding network of paths overshadowed by giant trees, sketching out the tranquil waters of Rock Creek stream like pencil strokes jumping off a page. The stream flows gently inside its bed and welcomes travelers and exercise enthusiasts with equal vivacity, injecting the energy of its current into those traveling alongside its bank.

The trail is heavily trafficked, for good reason, but unfortunately poorly marked. It took a little back and forth to locate the zoo entrance and then get our bikes parked in a drop-off terminal, but we eventually arrived unscathed. I now include a trek along this trail among my top recommendations for things one must do when visiting Washington, D.C. It is a rare beauty and certainly one of the nation's great treasures. Enjoying that afternoon didn't seem so forced.

Having drunk all the beer and seen all of the zoo, we decided that three tipsy adults were quickly becoming as exhilarating an attraction as any other of the exotic animals on display. Next, we headed out of the park, and while Logan and Olivia worked reconnaissance for a Starbucks, I scouted out a grimy little liquor store and purchased a medium-sized bottle of Baileys; a perfect item for safekeeping in my purse.

Sensing that any person overseeing our jovial little threesome must feel irksomely jealous as not to have such a tightly knit group, I recognized how fortunate I was.

The third outing of the day found us finally meeting up with friends at the Gryphon Club near DuPont Circle. What we had failed to take into account was that was the night of the heavily touted "Fight of the Century," Mayweather vs. Pacquiao, and this club was set up as a huge hub for the event, complete with hefty cover charge, velvet roped-off entrance, and muscle-headed behemoths of bouncers equipped with tiny headsets, stone cold in their mission for order.

The club was densely packed with sweaty bodies and locating a place to setup was an impossible fairytale of a task. Fortunately for us, just as we were about to give up, we were brought a table of our own, thanks to the good fortune granted those in attendance with the best friend of a bottle service girl. The table was complete with a black satin table cloth and allowed our small party to park front and center of this establishment: make-shift, first-rate seats to the entertaining crowd of gatherers, and the "Fight of the Century," which ended unpoetically when Mayweather unanimously destroyed his opponent.

This eponym has now been changed to things more befitting the event, like "The fight that wasn't" and "A complete waste of time and money."

The night ended with our party on the dance floor, but I was not feeling the mood. Olivia most certainly was, so I pushed her out with Logan, whom she happily pressed against while he appeared more than fine to allow that to unfold.

I firmly planted myself against an elaborate fainting

couch set in the middle of the floor to rest my aching heels and observe the insanity of my surroundings. *This is some people's way of life* I thought. *The bottle service girl has to navigate these out-of-control spaces, but her job is to serve shots and dance provocatively on tables. People love her, and she gets paid willingly.*

I also give shots. Except I inject people's mouths with needles and then wield tiny instruments in out-of-control spaces until I complete a task that I wonder if, on hard days, is even worth doing. I get paid begrudgingly. People expressly hate me.

Some days I wonder why I keep entering the fight.

Mike called early the next morning, and we talked for a while about life. He broke down the specifics of his practice, and I offered advice on ways to build it up to start honing his career path. He told me I had a fine ass and inquired as to when I would next be in D.C. I confessed that I needed a break—D.C. had evolved into my home away from home. On a Facebook photo post of Olivia, Logan, and I, a friend commented: "Do you guys live in D.C. and vacation here, or is it the other way around?" My traveling was getting out of hand.

I told him I'd likely be back in the fall. We ended our call, and I rejoined my friends for one last outing before the flight carrying us home. Before hitting the Metro, we made a ceremonial stop at Old Ebbitt Grill, a legendary brunch location whose fare and ambiance bills as D.C.'s finest.

Three weeks prior, Mike had taken us there as the final stop before heading home, but it was too packed, and we were too rushed to indulge. Instead, we only had one quick round and one hasty close to our riotous weekend.

I was forcing us there that day to erase those memories and rebuild: Logan, Olivia, and I, three best friends, at the most iconic restaurant in downtown D.C., enjoying a decadent brunch of crab cakes and eggs. And I was glad that I felt comfortable enough to eat around them, a luxury I wasn't previously aware of.

But I was also losing it again—like the entire restaurant was not right. The place had been possessed and reset, and I was occupying a space that didn't exist. Like, I was the only one who was real, and everyone else was just an illusion. The lifelike oil paintings on the walls were TV screens because the imagery turned dynamic. Like, the world didn't make sense, and I couldn't seem to find any grounding. Panic-stricken, I forced my gaze toward Olivia, and she locked me in with her anime eyes.

Focusing on the veil of calm on her face, I stabilized my breathing and reimagined the greater world around me—*this is real. I am here. Everything is okay.* Everything was going to be okay. I brought myself back into the moment. One more panic attack survived, but I didn't know how much more of it I could take.

As hard as I tried, I could never return to the old me—she wasn't willing to be found. I wasn't okay. I was broken. I'd fractured myself, and I didn't know if I would ever recover. I was still Ruby, but not the same one; the old Ruby was gone forever.

Our small party took to the Metro and poured out onto the platform, rushing past the domes and bee-lining for the security checkpoint at Terminal B. Two last things transpired that I found to be of significance.

One, The TSA agent in charge of the line verbally accosted Logan for not acting gentlemanly toward me—he cut ahead of me in line when she called "next," after which she reflexively put him in his place. But that was our way; he never doted on me—acting the chivalrous gentleman to my delicate lady—nor would I ever have wanted him to. But being around Nick awakened that side of me, and suddenly, I found myself desperate for that kind of attention. That even a TSA agent felt I deserved better was abruptly, and harshly, eye-opening.

Two, the highlight of the weekend—another more fortunate TSA agent recovered a medium-sized bottle of Baileys from my purse and proceeded to inquire after what I was thinking. One would assume it obvious that I wasn't, but he pigeonholed my egregious oversight as obvious intent, and looked highly unimpressed by my tactics.

We all laughed hysterically, and I told him to toss it, apologizing profusely for my mistake. It was classic. We thrived. Our anniversary trip was epic—definitely one for the record books.

CHAPTER 29

Olivia has found a boyfriend.

When she first started dating him, I was hesitant. She was my best friend and my paragon of solidarity. That girl embodied unbridled awesomeness, and I loved to watch her run. The idea that she could be saddled by a man terrified me. But then Dalton came along and wooed her away, and the two of them were pulling it off ever since. They found each other at a time in their lives where they were individually whole and free, neither in need of the other, but both sensing the universal pull to thicken the layers of the complexity in their lives.

They both possessed the requisite skill set allowing for a person to analyze a relationship from a healthy perspective, truly ascertaining their level of interest and commitment. Neither would be there if they didn't want to be, and they did. They *worked.* And Dalton evened out our old party of three.

What always used to be Logan, Olivia, and me, was now Logan and me, and Olivia and Dalton. The flip side, what used to be Olivia and me, was also now Olivia and Dalton—and me. I had lost my best friend at the same time that I had lost my foundation. I wanted more than anything to convey my absolute support for her, and them, so I plastered on my happy face; likely it came across as just sort of "meh."

On that particularly frigid Saturday morning in May, Logan, Olivia, her new boyfriend Dalton, and I, were running a half marathon as part of a huge citywide event. Logan, Olivia, and I ran the race annually, but it was to be Dalton's initiation. It was exactly the activity I should be doing, swallowing time in vast quantities, waiting to come alive while acting like my old self.

To celebrate post-race, we all convened downtown at a favorite local hotspot with a group of friends for a night of drinking and dining. We started at a classic, upscale restaurant with appetizers and drinks, and then moved on to the most "dive" of dive bars. While washing down a Kool-Aid flavored shot mixture with swallows of domestic beer, I found myself pleasantly falling into that place where I can relax, be free, and embrace the night with whomever is around me.

Dalton, Olivia, and Logan faded and wanted to call it a night; however, I was on a roll and ready for more. Although our threesome crew was tight knit, one of the women in our entourage that evening was what one might call a second-tier best friend. As a stay-at home wife, mother, runner, Leah was all around bad-ass. She and I had spent a fair share of time together, and most people who saw us out assumed we were sisters. But also, because she was as all of those things, we rarely got dedicated girl time. So, when Logan announced they were ready to go home, I grabbed Leah's arm.

"Look here," I said, pointing my finger at him and waving it back and worth. "I want to spend time with Leah tonight. They're all staying; if I stay, one of them can take me home. Can I, can I, can I?"

At hearing this, Leah wrapped her arms around me

and turned to face them.

"I never get this girl to myself! Let me have her for one night. I'll take good care of her. Scout's honor," she said, stomping down one foot and saluting, causing us both to break into laughter.

"You ladies are on another level right now," Logan said, patting our heads lovingly. "I trust you'll make it home. Be safe and have fun."

"Thank you!" we said, and then watched as Logan, Olivia, and Dalton made their way out the door.

"So, what should we do now?" Leah asked, her face lighting up with possibility. The guys were busy bouncing back and forth between Golden Tee, Buck Hunter, the bar, and the table of ladies, but she and I needed something more.

"Where can we go dancing?" I asked.

"I've got the perfect place!"

At the club, I befriended the DJ, requested all my favorites, and we took over the floor, dancing and partying and having the most amazing of times—right up until the moment when I *wasn't*.

One minute I was busy getting low and the next minute I was inundated by a deluge of inescapable blackness that threatened to knock my ass to the dance floor. In the span of an instant, I lost my grounding with the world, and I had no Olivia to help bring me back. In a panicked flurry, I removed myself from the situation, retreating to the ladies' room and locking myself in the stall. Once I was situated securely inside, I allowed the blackness to devour me.

I cried in breathless gasps with streaming tears, physically manifesting the emotional overload that was so vastly consuming and chaotic that the walls of the stall were the only thing capable of holding me together. I stood pressed against them with my forehead connecting in one cold spot, chest rising and falling in frenzied clusters of action. In the zenith of my dissociative meltdown, Leah burst in.

"Ruby! Ruby . . . Ruby," she called out time after time.

I tried to quiet myself and wait out her search, but she was clued into my game.

"Ruby, I know you are in here," Leah said, pressing herself against the cold outer wall and coaxing me to come out to her.

It took a few breaths before I could unlock the stall. When I did, I walked straight out with my eyes down, focusing on the tracing the tile patterns.

"Ruby. Look at me," Leah insisted. So, I turned her way and tentatively raised my chin.

She took one look at my tear-streaked face and her passionate and gentle gaze freed my tongue to let it all go. In one weakened moment, my concealed world died, and my proverbial cat was loosed from the bag.

Her husband drove us home and Leah came inside, sitting me down on my overstuffed couch then kneeling down in a ball at my feet, in a stance akin to an auspicious yogi. Taking my face in her hands and locking my gaze firmly, she spoke words of reassurance.

"You are going to make it through this. You are a fighter. Everyone you see is battling something; trust me love, you are not alone."

We cried, and we shared, and when words had no more places to go, she helped me upstairs, tucked me in bed, and snuck out through the garage.

I wandered into a fitful night's sleep while she wandered back to her home, a new allied soul in possession of my dark secret.

* * *

The next morning, I awoke groggy, confused, and determined that I was going to start making a difference. Lying on my back in my well-worn mattress rut—Logan fully settled into his—I decided I needed to begin figuring things out with him. I wanted to comprehend how we worked; I needed to start by figuring out what he *really* felt for me.

Logan has always been my best friend. My champion. And I love him deeply and emphatically and *platonically*. He was aware of that fact and accepted its reality, as he had been assured by me repeatedly since our inception that I was incapable of passionate emotion.

"I am asexual," I repeated to him often the first year we knew each other. "I am just not interested in that. I don't really think I'm attracted to guys," I would always say. Which wasn't a complete truth. It was more so that guys who were attractive to me also hurt me, so instead of taking both the good and the bad, I opted to stay entirely neutral.

I convinced him I would never feel attracted to anyone. I told him it just didn't exist for me.

But as I tossed and turned, fighting for sleep, I got the sick feeling that maybe he felt the same way for me as I had felt about Nick. I had always assumed him a stoic, impartial man—as emotionally unavailable as me—but maybe things I did cut him as deeply as Nick had cut me.

With this disheartening realization sinking in, I decided to start our morning conversation by asking, "Can I hurt you?"

He was rightfully a little confused by the question, so I elaborated further. "Does the way that I act or the way that I treat you cause you to feel pain? Like, if something I do makes you upset, do you feel deeply saddened? If I am gone, do you ache in my absence?"

"Yes, of course, I miss you when you are gone. And if you are short with me or you ignore, me it hurts a lot," he admitted.

"And can I make you feel passionate? Like, do you get excited by being around me, euphoric by my touch, miss me when I am not around?" I continued, exploring both sides of the thing.

"Of course," he said "You are amazing to me. I am very attracted to you. When you say you are attracted to me or compliment me, it excites me. I feel compelled to make you happy, and I revel in it." His admission was heartfelt and genuine and detailed precisely what I had been so terribly reminded being in love *could* feel like.

I had spent all our years feeling stable. I had conceded this aspect of our relationship as a consequence of my honest reality. I never wanted to be seen as an attractive girl, nor did I ascribe to any *conventional* beauty regimen. I was an oddball, an intellectual. I belonged to the geeks. As such, I had accepted a sex life hallmarked by a necessity to be wasted and I considered it a success when I didn't cry in the bathroom afterward from not wanting it *that much*.

But I had learned that explicitly was not true. Nick blew the cap off my bottled-up desires, and after catching a glimpse of how it invigorated me, I was catapulted into territory that felt entirely foreign. Having spent the previous twelve years in a dearth of passion, I felt instinctually driven to seek it unremittingly to compensate.

But how do you confess that to someone with grace?

"You are lucky," I said flatly. "With you, I feel *safe*." I said this to imply nurturing. He tended me like a garden. He watered me and fed me and sheltered me with love. But in the same vein, I felt like he overshadowed and enclosed me, and confining myself to his little garden plot was stunting my growth.

I am an ardent personality who always needs to be seeking the novel, and he is my polar opposite.

"You have never hurt me this much," I said with a grand gesture, holding my hands as wide as they go, "and I love that about you. I am safe with you.

"But you also could never make me excited or happy or impassioned this much," I gestured again grandly and then crumpled my hands down into the covers, training my eyes to that spot. "I have no highs and no lows with you. No mad love, and no epic sadness. I am, and I have always been, only safe in between." I did not say this to be adversarial. I said it to be frank. I wanted him to understand where my deep sadness was rooted. "I am envious of you. I do not think it is fair. You get to be with someone who makes you feel all of those things. I never will."

"Do you know why I have been so depressed lately?" I implored him further. I wanted so badly for him to figure it out on his own. I didn't want to have to tell him expressly about Nick; I wanted to simply confirm an already brewing suspicion. "Do you have any inkling, or thought, as to *why*

I am so tortured right now?"

"I have been assuming it is because of that night in D.C. where Olivia and I were dancing, and you were sitting quietly off to the side. I didn't mean anything by it; it was a drunken night of dancing, but you haven't been yourself ever since, and I guess I assumed you were upset with me about flirting with her. I haven't said anything because I thought it would pass."

My heart sank at his admission.

His dancing with Olivia made me feel nothing. He could have dirty danced with any girl at that club and I would have felt equally disimpassioned. That he thought I was feeling jealous over something he did only heightened my awareness of our disparity.

Until the Chicago Affair, Logan and I had been a couple defined by our unconventional ability to be candid with each other. Not being open with him about this matter was slowly consuming my essence. I desperately wanted to be honest with him, but I did not know *how*. I only knew that I was nowhere near confirming a suspicion, and I was not yet ready to point-blank confess.

So, I resolved to resume my clandestine charade. But internally, I committed to begin planting seeds. I couldn't hold out hope my secret would remain closeted indefinitely. Either he would find out from the two people in possession of my secret, or he would find out from me somehow. I recognized that there existed only a small window before all hell broke loose.

CHAPTER 30

May is a loaded word. In the calendar proper, May falls one month before the middle of the year and is considered by the majority (in the Northern hemisphere) as the end of spring. End, as in, the months preceding it are the ones during which spring began to unfold. Being not part of this majority, Fargo's preceding months were undeniably winter, but the adage "April showers bring May flowers," was something I did buy-in to.

As a child, handcrafted felt tapestries decorated with ladybugs and chrysanthemums and raindrops and rainbows transformed my school into a perfect spring picture on May Day. Each school day began with the pledge of allegiance, but during May, our youthful voices would also unite for "April showers bring May flowers," prior to the commencement of the morning's activities. My eyes zoned in on each iconic beacon in reverie, assured that, like the immovable and concrete stars and stripes, these things too were given.

The vivid felt picture must come to fruition, I believed, so as a child, each morning I'd burst through my front door awaiting it to appear upon the earth's frozen floor. Only, every year on the mornings of early May, I'd discover April's blizzards and ice storms and sparse smattering of showers brought dirt colored snow piles, the ones my mom referred to as snirt. A promise of flowers fulfilled by a reality of more winter crushed my hopes annually. Not that May couldn't conclude with flowers, it's just, by the time they finally pushed out from the soil, my disappointment was irrecoverable.

It had been a little over a month since the affair, and the promise of May flowers and seasonal transformation wasn't delivering. I was gritting my teeth with faith grounded in the healing powers of *time*, carrying on in a manner consistent with something like surviving, though I spent most of my days disconsolate. Running outside was feasible, but the canopy of branches overarching my street were bare and crooked and notched, the trees themselves writhing in disbelief at the indomitable winter.

If that wasn't enough, during my runs, the reprieve I sought was starting to falter, and more often than not, the ponderings flopping around in my persistently lapsing mind centered on whether or not anything in the world was real. I didn't know where my place in the whole of this expansive and obliterating universe was anymore.

Each new dawn, I would turn on for everyone and push through the mire, but the persistent projection of a persona was growing weightier instead of lighter. To shed some of the load, I gave myself permission to break down and cry when I knew no one was watching. Suffering took place in cosseted spaces, where I spent time opening a connection to the person I dreamed I was. In those hidden moments I flooded, and I desired nothing more than to reconnect with Nick.

But even if I did, what would I say? I didn't live in a world that could function in his presence. That was where I was, the life I had to be living, going through the motions in the life of Ruby; the good wife, the friend, the doctor, the mother. I was walking the walk and carrying out the actions of being all of the things. There were no other viable alternatives for me.

When the overwhelming urge to reach out to Nick hit, I'd turned to texting Leah. Since our night, we'd been exchanging texts daily; check-ins to say hi, links to motivational quotes, photos we'd taken during our times together—little gorgeous things that lifted the veil of darkness for a while. That particular May morning, I woke with my mind shrouded in darkness, so I stopped by a bakery to buy a dozen donuts for my team. There was one thing I knew for certain, and that was donuts were always uplifting.

When I arrived at the office, I propped it front and center in the reception area and took a photo of the assorted iced goodies to show off for Leah.

"#thisishappening"

"Atta girl," she messaged right back.

Chocolate frosted cake donuts with rainbow sprinkles must be laced with Prozac. Four of those lovely things were stacked near the front of the box, so I selected one and wandered around the corner into my office. It would be another hour before anyone else arrived. Opting to take advantage of some solitary time, I sat down, booted up my computer, and started in on savoring my treat while waiting for the login screen to pop up.

The screen of my phone illuminated in concert with the ding of a message. Gooey chocolate had coated the fingertips on my right hand, so I reached across with my left and fumbled through the prompts for the content. It took three attempts. Three annoying attempts, during which my useless block of a left forefinger missed simple targets repeatedly. By the time I correctly input the passcode to bring up the message screen, I was irked beyond reason by my ineptitude.

In college, I had taken to note writing with my left hand because I liked the extra challenge it presented. After a semester of this activity, left-handed manipulation was something I could do with ease, and I believed I had mastered a skill that would stick. I had hoped things of this nature would be like riding a bike, that my muscle memory would uphold and even though I hadn't used my left hand for some time, basic maneuvering through prompts on an iPhone screen would come readily. But I had held onto a fanciful notion.

Moved by the sudden wave of college memories, I became overwhelmed by a desire to examine those notes, to transport and submerge into the past for a spell. Fortunately, the tattered purple three ring binder storing them was tucked away with my dental school binders, all on the shelf behind me.

That binder saw me through four years of college, and I was committed to keeping it for eternity. When I first saw it in a bookstore, I was impressed by its sturdy backing and broad functionality: it was capable of organizing my entire syllabus each semester, a feat worth the ten dollars it set me back. I used it semester after semester, adding layers to a labyrinth of doodles I drew upon its cover. Upon graduation, I transferred all the notes I deemed worthy of storing for posterity into its three rings. They had moved to Minneapolis and back, but I hadn't done more than brush the outside of the covering to shift it from cardboard to shelf in years.

I reached up and freed it from its nesting place,

between a similar binder labeled Gross Anat/Et. Al. and a hefty textbook labeled Oral Pathology. As soon as my fingers clasped the smooth plastic shell, smells of the dank chemistry building came to life, proliferating at the very idea of sifting through its pages. Gingerly, I flipped the graffitied front open, taking great care not to separate the cover that was clinging by a thread to the spine.

I was pleased to find the section labeled "organic chemistry" came first, past Ruby must have instinctually known those were the notes I would be most nostalgic for. Eager to dive in, I flipped to the first page of lecture notes. Each day started with a date and title written in a meticulous script, except no dotted i's or j's. I'd long given up that excessive activity, as I had deemed dotting a waste of energy. By the third page of each day, an abrupt shift would occur to scrawling reminiscent of the ones before, only more like a child trying to reproduce an adult's writing. That was my left hand. It wasn't illegible, but it wasn't pretty. It was my right brain, the other, unspoken, side of me. I'd studied enough neuropsychology to understand the very act of writing with my left hand activated a part of my brain unrelated to science and mathematics and practical reasoning. In theory, it should have inhibited my ability to absorb the material properly. But in truth, I aced every aspect of organic chemistry. Pride swelled within me at the memory.

As I flipped the last page of that section, I found the next tab too irresistible to put the binder away without giving it a perusal as well. Psychology Senior Seminar. That class didn't sit with equivalent reverie. It required the writing of lengthy essays, crazy long topics that were graded on word count only, because I knew there was no way our professor took the time to read each one thoroughly. I'd gotten to the point where I'd spend one hour diving into assigned topics with fervor, writing and writing and writing, until I hit the required word count. Formal editing wasn't on the docket as mass production was the requirement, and gauging by the titles of the essays, I was taking liberties.

"Men and Toasters" was the first paper in the mix; the title alone capable of eliciting a belly laugh. Admittedly, this paper was too embarrassing to read. When I wrote it, I had acquired my first toaster oven, which I found highly functional. Being so pleased with the appliance, I deemed my traditional toaster useless, so when asked to write a paper about male and female relationships, I looked to my most recent discovery for inspiration. The outlandish parallel I drew in conclusion was one I could never forget.

I had said that, as a strong, independent female, I was akin to a toaster oven. And, newly aware of my awesomeness, I didn't need a man just like I didn't need a toaster. The conclusion made me laugh out loud because I remember having shared this essay with my college best friend seeking feedback, whose reaction to the thing was, "I find toasters useful."

The next essay was titled "Thoughts on Love and Marriage," which seemed slightly more intriguing. Nothing about that essay struck a chord, which meant it was no longer in my memory. I decided to take the time to read the whole piece.

Marriage . . . I'm not sure I can even think that word without adding an obligatory "mawwiage," which I know may paint me as possessing a sarcastic mind. But really, even William Goldman didn't believe in the institution, he's credited to having wrote one of the most romantic satires known to man, and yet, in the final pages, he reveals his irresolute disbelief. I mean, who am I to stay starry-eyed in the face of that bitter pill? Don't get me wrong, it's not like I derived my ethics on love solely based on "The Princess Bride," but marriage is not something I look fondly upon.

My perception of marriage is that naïve couples are either:

1) Succumbing to euphoric attraction, like addicts coupling up with a drug, only to fade listlessly from the operational world, or

2) Heeding intense external pressures to satisfy a religious covenant, stargazed and poised for a baptismal reality from the imminent downpour of life.

In any event, no matter what my circumstances are, I will never fall prey to something so naïve.

I mean let's be honest, is romantic love legitimate or viable? The presence or absence of it is associated with extreme highs and lows. Euphoria, then doubt. Stability, then suspicion. Essentially, all the torrent of emotions surrounding the taboos of addiction.

So, if love is addiction and its high equivalent to euphoria-inducing drugs, isn't the effect bound to wear off, or at least attenuate? Then what? Facing the reality of being tethered by a satiny leash—with one side lustrous and invigorating, and the other muted and burdensome—reality comes crashing in.

From there, many roads can be followed. Some couples evolve into muted versions of their former selves, forging a robust marriage on the firm foundation of compromise, seemingly pulling it off, but never really seeming alive.

Others stay together only in the physical sense, projecting happy facades but destructively turning to new "drugs" to cope. Others, like my parents—collapse upon themselves while destroying every last tie, leaving behind only shadows projecting to the sky.

I am a pristine end product of the distressing effects of a destructive route. The only evidence I recall signifying my parents "love" was their intense hatred for each other, an animosity so pervasive a radius of afterglow radiates from them to this day.

My parent's set a great example: any toying with romantic love will sentence me to their fate.

And, taking it one step further, let's explore my formative experience with men. First, the cruel neighborhood boy who spit on me when he passed and called me a hooker for sport. Then, my high school boyfriend who, when I tried to end our relationship, evolved into an abusive, manipulative sociopath.

Those experiences taught me something critical: boys crush girls without any hint of remorse, until all that remains are tiny bits of nothingness. But I will not succumb. I'll devise strategies to cope. I'll petrify, construct walls. Refuse to let them in. I won't repeat my parent's fate. I'll make my life my own because I'm a fighter.

The solution: push every guy that intrigues me away. Until my Pavlovian response is retreat.

Retreat? Stopping there, I went back to the beginning to re-read the entry. I'd always found freeform writing an excellent way to discover my true feelings, but as I got to the end, a nauseating wave crashed over me. How on earth did I get so jaded? Were those really my feelings? Who was I back then?

There were a lot of notions I held in college that were now haunting me. Notions I believed were moral imperatives. It was a time of defining, and for some reason, my idea of defining was to be obtusely arrogant and one-sided because I believed all other rationales were oppressive. When I stamped an opinion with my name, I believed it was in blood made ink, certain who I projected myself to be was immovable and guaranteed, like the stars and the stripes and the eventual flowers in May.

Female empowerment was my core ideal in those times. I wrote anti-marriage themed term papers citing flawed and dated religious propaganda and insisted that the institution of marriage caused more harm than good. Marriage to me was an extremist ideological notion. One that, when evaluated from our modern day societal standards, was impossible to uphold; ultimately being a destructive construct that held people captive, citing domestic rape and abuse situations condoned by religion as the extreme example.

Then there was my pro-choice stance. I fought for women's rights to control what happens to their bodies, audaciously stating that having a child before one is prepared was akin to killing their dreams and snuffing out hope of a life on their own. I didn’t ever consider the other side of this: about the cracking open of your soul and learning how to love a part of your heart wandering through the outside world. About how learning how to be an independent and strong mother-fucker of a mother can define your life too. I never had the gumption to say those critical lessons are battle scars to brag about not faults to cover with rouge.

Who did I think I was? In hindsight, it’s so obvious. I

was a child writing with my left hand, pretending to know what would only ever come with age. Taking stock of the road I traveled, a common theme unfolded. I was pro-choice and kept my child, anti-marriage and married his father. These things I thought so black and white were only ever vocalized ideals. Once I stood face to face with tangible crossroads affecting my core being, I strode down my obstinate opinions opposing road, knowing in my gut that any other path would ruin me.

After considering all of that, accepting I could no longer consider myself ambidextrous was a paltry kind of blow, the kind that made absorbing the other truth, that I once professed to espouse single minded views of delicate and fragile individual rights dogmatically, feel like a shotgun spray across my abdomen. Another donut was required.

As I rose from my chair, my eyes drifted from the old pages of my binder to the glowing computer screen. At the bottom right corner, the clock displayed 7:30 am; it felt like only minutes ago I'd sat down after my text to Leah, but thirty minutes passed in a flash. My thought train derailments were taking up too much time and energy. I decided to sit back down and forgo the pastry, the staff was due any moment, and I needed to get myself emotionally ready.

One last task needed to be tended to before doing so. It felt like a lifetime ago, but I had kicked off the morning's blast into the past by trying to read Leah's text message. To conclude the morning's extracurricular adventure, it was imperative I read her message and respond.

When I clicked on the display, I saw Leah had sent a link to a Pinterest motivational quote. With my right finger this time, I touched the link and waited. As I did, a stinging sensation hovered in my chest because, back in my earlier years, inspirational quotes were things I deemed cliché. Now, their comfort was essential, and I looked to them daily. One more thing added to the refuse pile of torn and tattered talismans of who I used to be. The only thing I could do was accept it, read the quote that lifted my spirits, and move on.

"Grief is like living two lives. One is where you pretend that everything is alright, and the other is where your heart silently screams in pain."

Damn, how does she know?

"Woman. You have laser vision into my soul. Thank you." I texted back.

I read the phrase one last time and soaked in the healing relief brought about by knowing I wasn't alone in this misery. Before exiting out of the link, I caught its site of origin, and I got stuck. "50 powerful quotes about losing a loved one," it read.

Losing a loved one?

That couldn't be right. I set my phone next to my keyboard and typed "Quotes about lost love" into a Google search. "Fifty powerful quotes about losing a loved one," populated in the first ten results, and one step deeper into the web found me staring down that same quote.

How can this be?

Sweat was condensing in my palms. I pushed them hard against the fabric of my pants covering my thighs. Maybe I should try another search?

"Love: define." I typed. The first thing that came up read:

1) Attraction that includes sexual desire.

2) A feeling of strong or constant affection for a person.

3) Sex.

I decided to explore the Urban Dictionary:

1) The most spectacular, indescribable, deep euphoric feeling for someone.

2) Giving someone the power to destroy you, and trusting them not to.

As I scrolled through and considered each one, I found they all applied. But I didn't believe in that kind of love. Starry eyed teenage girls felt that love, but not someone like me. I was smarter; I knew real love. I loved Logan for being my best friend and partner and constant companion. I loved my boys in a way I never knew love possible before them. I loved Olivia, my sister, my parents. I knew of love that was safe and whole and reciprocal and supportive.

Reckless love like loving a man because they make you feel giddy wasn't a valid emotion to me, and my read from my college essay backed this up entirely. Sure, when I was a high school girl, I once made that mistake, but I hardwired myself against any potential of that kind of love ever after. I was hardwired. But I also needed to be real. I identify with all of these things.

I haven't just lost a loved one, have I?

* * *

Some days seem to stand against you no matter how hard you try. Hope lingers and you believe the densely packed clouds blotting out the sun will dissipate if you find an angle to call fate on its hoax. But fate didn't deal you a hoax. Days like those are made exclusively for you to suffer; they are made so you stop fighting shit off and sit down to absorb what the universe is saying. On those days, the sooner you figure that out, the better. Back then, I was just learning about those days.

I made it to the workday's end, holding back tears when pop songs elicited unwanted emotions and patients divulged too much about their personal circumstances. I kept busy enough to avoid the computer and phone all day. But once all the patients and staff left, I couldn't avoid them anymore. The following morning, I was headed off to a symposium Nick and I had spoken of attending together. Preparing to go and not knowing if he would be there was like ripping a Band-Aid off a fresh wound.

In Chicago, Nick had suggested we meet up and stay together, but I emphatically shut him down, citing family to punctuate a hard no. There was no way he would show his face at that seminar after I laid that law down. But I still wished he would defy me. I was dying to feel his arms around me, dying to hear the sound of his voice.

I should have texted Leah, but in my weak and power-stripped state, crying at my cluttered desk and staring at the Google search results for "love" occupying my edified screen, I cracked. I pulled up Nick's number and shot him off a cryptic message, breaking our month-long silence.

"For what it's worth, I am very sorry for getting you involved in my existential crisis."

Idiot. I cursed myself. Seeking to end my ability to break, I deleted his number and the message. *That is the final time.*

I tossed the phone into my purse and checked over everything in my office to ensure it was shut down for a long weekend away. When I exited the front door, I did so with my head held high. Everything was going to be alright; I was going to work this out on a run. Fortunately, the weather was cooperating.

It was one of those days. May can serve up anything, and as I drove home, the intermittent cloud covering the still frozen air was brewing up a mix perfect for mulling over obscene things. Obscene like the potential that I was in love with Nick.

I burst through my mudroom and bounded up the stairs, changing into running gear in a flash. Though by May daylight lingered far longer than months prior, as I glanced out my window, the sunrays were melting into the pond. A short, hard effort was all I had time to accommodate.

Leaving from my doorstep, a vast array of routes existed, from 5K to twenty miles. Today, the 5K route was calling my name. That one was plotted for simplicity: flat and fast with only three turns, through neighborhoods and sidewalks along busy roadways. Not the kind of scenery to transport the mind, rather, the kind that forces you into your head pushing through the agony with your body.

No music was invited along. As I hit the street and started down the straight away, I shut everything out and opened my mind up to evaluate the newly acquired information from the day.

Love. What the hell? Do I love Nick? That's a ludicrous notion. Love is something that develops over time. It's something you foster, something grown and developed in a trusting fashion. Love is not something that happens in the blink of an un-searching eye.

I was so sure I was right. So sure, except, the depth of

grief I was experiencing to such a trite loss didn't align.

Could I really have passed all this time not experiencing love?

An alarm on my watch went off, indicating the first mile was complete. I looked down at the face and saw that I'd held a 7:30 pace. Apparently, I was feeling frisky, and this was no time to slow down. My lungs and legs felt fine; I needed to push the pace. Opting to take advantage of a fast first mile, I dug in deep, found the next gear, and forced my heels to quicken their turnover on the asphalt. The crisp, cold air was refreshing, and though sparse cloud cover blotted the blue sky, sunshine was still the dominant offering.

Is there a world in which everything I thought salient about me was wrong? Am I really capable of such a flippant shift in thinking? Could I possibly love Nick? And if so, what does that even mean?

It means nothing. I'm buying into propaganda. Don't be that kind of girl.

I ran harder. The cool air was a welcome relief for my burning lungs. The dense, fluffy clouds decided it was time to unleash their burden, but the frigid air kept the moisture from falling freely. Instead, droplets transformed to gargantuan flakes, which floated whimsically in swirls. Sunny snow falls are a magnificent scene to behold, and I allowed myself to get lost watching the swirls of white spindly fluff balls for the remainder of that mile. The transfixion held steady until the alarm on my watch pulled me out of the trance. Looking at the face lifted my spirits, the digging in early paid off. 7:15 min/mile pace. I was on pace for a standout 5K.

Last mile. Tuning out all the doubts and fears and pain,

I told my legs to push off with a little more force and turn over with a little more haste, focusing my eyes on the white cotton twirling haze. One last mile, and a 7:00 minute pace would be a spectacular finish to this activity. My lungs were starting to burn, but I didn't care. Running was one of the things I was born to do.

I looked up and locked my eyes on the stoplight at the end of the stretch, the three mile mark I knew so well, with the extra block after it adding the 0.1 miles required to bring this route to a proper 5K. My eyes switched from holding the flakes to holding that landmark. I was chasing that thing down.

I was smart enough to know I didn't love Nick; I was a woman who was encountering life altering shit affecting everything in her world. I could run through anything. I could conquer the worst, as long as I recognized my struggles. This was just one of those days.

I needed to run harder. The gap to the stoplight was lessening. My lungs were screaming at me to slow down. The white flakes in my peripheral were turning into streaks, and blackness was filling in where the blue saturation once held. The ground felt unwieldy.

Push harder; this is what happens when the body is reaching maximum exertion. Run through the wall.

My heart felt like it was pounding outside of my chest. "Can I still text you?" echoed in my ear, like Nick was an ephemeral figure whispering at me in surround sound. I raced toward the stoplight with renewed fervor, but as soon as I reached it, my legs and my heart and my lungs gave out. I stopped and doubled over, clasping the light pole for balance. Looking down the street at my house, the 0.1 mile was an impassable span that I would have died rather than run down. I couldn't. I just couldn't.

I pushed through the door of my house defeated and slumped into a bar stool at my kitchen island. If the run wasn't enough to send me into a heart attack, this moment surely would because, when I fished my phone from the deep pocket of my purse, the first thing I found was that Nick actually responded to my text. Gingerly, I clicked open the box to explore the content in full detail.

"Aw, I don't see it that way. I have just been avoiding talking to you because that is what you asked for, remember?"

His admission made my soul crack. A nauseating wave of realization washed over me, polluting me with the awareness that I did this to myself; his silence was the product of a dick move I pulled. I had to grip the edges of the island to hold myself up—he was *that good* of a guy.

I thought long and hard about what I should say, desperate for a means to undo my damage, and I decided to go with complete honesty.

"I know, and I wish I could take it back. I am heading to Phoenix tomorrow, and I don't even want to ask if you're going to be there because I don't want the answer to be 'no.'"

It was. And I was shattered. But we picked back up our old routine, messaging back and forth inside jokes and silly nothings, reviewing our lives and upcoming trips. And from our simple interaction—just knowing he was there—my dying spirit revitalized. Breathing suddenly felt less constricted.

But then Logan and the boys came home, and my anxiety resumed tenfold. Again, I was hiding it. I was unable to hold a proper conversation, and the vitality that surfaced when we began our exchange degenerated quickly to misery. I had to accept the harsh physical truth that our two worlds could not coincide.

I completed my packing in a fog and went to bed that night desperately pleading with the powers that be, supplicating for a revolution. There was no denying it. Nick made me feel *everything*; even the prospect of texting him hit me like a drug. I was desperate to know what that could be like in real life. Desperate to live in an honest world where I felt love for someone like that, I would have bargained my life away to any mystical figure that offered it.

CHAPTER 31

My flight to Phoenix the next morning saw me accompanied by my little man Dylan. It was strange to have a travel companion; I had grown accustomed to solitude. We took mother-son selfies at the airport, and I treated him to Snickers and M&M's and all manner of secret indulgences I partake in when I'm off traveling alone. It's funny how when Logan's not around I feel liberated to act like myself. The version of mommy he was treated to that day was one he doesn't usually see.

We rented a car, and he sat shotgun—something he never gets to do—and he mimicked the GPS voice that spoke my directions in a perfectly digitized British accent, repeatedly reminding me to "turn right on East Ray Road." We sang Birdy songs at the top of our lungs, and he proved an adorably helpful co-pilot.

He navigated me right to my sister's house in the north neighborhoods of Phoenix, and we unloaded and set up in her cozy spare room with the inside door covered in graffiti from all its previous occupants. A retreat I've been visiting so often I've come to regard it as my second home; a door decorated with scrawling by my hand. Dylan ran around wildly enthusiastic, feeding the brood of turtles livening her secret garden and acting like he owned the place. Krista and I primped in our respective bathrooms, beautifying for a night out.

That evening, she and I were meeting up with a group of her girlfriends for some much needed, uninhibited girl talk. Before heading out, we set up Dylan with the kids of the other moms in our group. He confidently took the driver's seat of a rugged Power Wheels Jeep and commenced living it up, surrounded by a playground of unfamiliar youngsters, determined to tackle the night.

Dylan has an uncanny ability to approach novel situations without fear. He genuinely wants to befriend every, single, person. He fits the standard definition of happy-go-lucky, and anyone blessed enough to meet him falls in love at first sight. Logan and I often look at him and wonder how the product of our two reclusive selves could be so unrestrained.

Our eldest is his polar opposite, and irrefutably my genomic replica—his origin will never be questioned. Cade is the most unkempt kid in the most controlled of ways. He is painfully dashing, and I fear for his future, but he is also painfully introverted, and I trust that will keep him in check.

Cade's temperament classifies best as "difficult," or, to quote his psychologist, classically diagnosed ADHD. Meeting his needs and learning how to be *his* best mother required far more edifying than learning how to be an excellent clinician. He was my greatest challenge.

Cade was a child unresponsive to reward or punishment. Every attempt we made at shaping his behavior via some parenting philosophy was an exercise in futility. We had to let him go his own way; he is one who needs the burn from the fire to appreciate the definition of hot. He challenges me on every front, and I sense all the obstacles that I have faced are imminent in his future. I would give anything for the power to intervene, to protect him from a life recreating my failures, but I know, deeper down, those lessons will be for him alone.

For years I worried about him, until recently when I realized, he is *me*, and ultimately, he too will be fine.

My boys are nearly five years apart, and at first, I was anxious about the spread. *What if they never bond as brothers*, I feared. Erroneously worried that so lengthy a gap could preclude so sacred a bond. But then they hit it off, and then they hit each other, and they became token brothers at last.

Krista and I share an eternal bond, too, and our relationship is essential to me. She is the main reason I am who I am; I would be incomplete without her. She and I are also opposites, yet not in quite the same way.

Krista is the epitome of an older sister. My earliest memories are of her chastising me, and in my scorned little sister tenacity—my I-will-never-be-what-anyone-tells-me-to-be way—I aspired to be her polar opposite. She did whatever it took to be perceived by our parents as the honorable and responsible one, so I espoused an obstinate insistence on being a problematic ass.

Krista is tall, beautiful, and perfect. In high school and college, she was obsessive about fitting in and pulling off the glamorous, fashionable appearance prescribed by exclusive brands, so I refused to don anything openly branded (except, of course, vintage Lacoste), and acquired all my clothing from thrift stores.

Krista maintained her beauty twenty-four seven and surrounded herself with people who looked like models. Together, she and her friends exemplified popular life—her photo albums could all be magazine shoots from the era—and in every picture that I ended up in, it was painfully obvious who didn't belong.

I found her restricted by her ceaseless desire to uphold traditional beauty. She skipped out on fantastically fun things like submerging in water, tent camping, or strenuous adventuring because they might flatten her hair or smudge her makeup, forcing her to look less than perfect. She always seemed to be opting out of those carefree, potentially scarring but worth the risk, beautiful moments of *life.* Upholding perfection seemed more important to her.

Being beautiful was not going to be what solely defined me. My code was to do all of the things that looked fun, regardless of appearance. I wanted to be the girl jumping in the water and ripping my clothes and tearing all the shit up. I wanted to be amazing and eye-catching and non-traditional and different. I didn't often try to look pretty, to be honest, but when I did, I made sure everyone noticed.

Krista and I had a rough go at youth; it's a miracle we didn't kill each other. We were only two years apart, almost too close for comfort, and we challenged each other to colossal heights. I assumed she despised me. I felt like I would never be beautiful and special enough to be included with her and her friends. And so, I fought, with all my might, to prove that my way of life was authentic too, just on another level.

We have lived on opposite sides of the country for the past ten years, and I doubt we are this different anymore, but that is the image of Krista branded in my mind, and memories are difficult to shed. My ceaseless drive is a product of our rivalry and has served me well throughout my life. I credit so much to her. A sibling is truly life's greatest gift, and I wouldn't have had it any other way.

For Cade to go without life's biggest gift, obstacle, and confidant, was unfathomable to me. So, along came D, a child so unique and healing, I never realized how critical he was until he was suddenly there.

On that night, I had fashioned my hair in my new favorite messy side fishbone braid while she had the perfect blowout gorgeous locks complete with salon extensions. I was feeling quite pleased with our dichotomous looks, so we snapped a selfie to post onto Facebook, expressed our love to the imaginary, make-you-believe audience, and then we delved into the harsh topic of behind-the-curtains reality.

I declared it time to update Krista on the *real* happenings in my life. All phone conversations over the last few months had resulted in a deterioration of my demeanor and ended with hysterical tantrums of alternating tears and rage.

She was not at home to see what was happening. She didn't comprehend the massive downward spiral that went down with our parents. She got away. She has the life I wanted to live. I felt angry, resentful, and slighted.

I had tried over the phone to make this real for her, but it had proved an impossible task. Some things you have to be in person for, and on this trip, I was determined to break through to her.

"They are falling apart right before my eyes," I expressed to her again. "You have no idea how hard it is to watch. And to see them decline so quickly—to see their lives come to such hasty, such definitive ends. It makes me realize their reality is not my far-off future."

In the silence that followed, she contemplated me

wordlessly, reassuring me with her striking brown eyes, mirroring mine perfectly in green. She held calm, so I carried on.

"I have never extended to my full potential—never fully achieved what I am capable of having in life—and in love. I want so much more for myself. I don't even know where to begin," I said, finishing my sentiment and internally flinching, awaiting a backhanded response.

I expected her to fight me—to tell me how I needed to accept my place and be strong. But on this matter, she shocked me.

"You see the woman in the aqua sequined top sitting at the end of our table," she said, motioning that direction with her eyes.

I looked over and nodded.

"She caught her husband cheating over Christmas, which is bad enough, but when she confronted him, he kicked her out. Blamed the whole thing on her and blasted her all over Facebook. She and her kids have been staying in her sister's guesthouse—the woman she's seated next to—for the last few months, trying to make a fresh start."

"Oh my god, that's awful! What kind of person does that?"

"The most inconspicuous kind. People can be crazy, seriously. And life isn't always as perfect as it seems."

"Amen to that," I agreed, clinking my glass to hers.

Taking advantage of the opened door, I detailed to her a truncated account of the past four months, glossing over the details and lumping the guys into one indistinct category. When I wrapped up the summary, I said in conclusion, "Being around these guys has stirred up things I've been repressing—"

"—You love being around these guys because they are *you*," she cut in. Which, poignantly enough, was the same sentiment I had expressed to Nick in the backseat of our Uber, heading into Chicago our second night. He was constantly distracted by his iPhone, intently engaged the same way I used to be, even when I was at home with family.

"You are me," I observed aloud, which earned me a sneer as he obviously thought I was an idiot. But, for me, the realization was profound. He made me feel small because he chose to pay attention to his game instead of embracing time spent alone with me. My body ached for his attention. I was actively restraining myself, fighting the urge to span the gap between us and curl up into his side because I sensed that he was annoyed by my presence. Instead, I stayed silent and insignificant in my little corner and wondered who I was hurting as I ignored them, obsessing over inanimate games.

"I have always said I would hate me if I met me," I confessed with a laugh, responding to her nail-on-the-head comment, "and I still think, in some ways, that stands true. I desperately wanted to be a part of their world, but I don't believe I could ever possess the unfaltering willpower to endure it." I spoke more softly. After this confession, I was silenced by the immense weight of the truth.

CHAPTER 32

I rose early the next morning in a tangled mess of a fiery, little man lightly snoring into my ear. He sleeps like this always, even at seven years of age, like he needs to make five points of contact to drift into sleep and has to maintain a steady five through the night to sustain an elevated body temperature required to uphold his state. It's delightfully sweet and innocently endearing, but the lucky recipient of those five points of contact sleeps in abject misery.

I unhooked myself from his hot little fingers and snuck off to the bathroom with running gear in hand, dressing as quietly as I could. I tied up the laces to my toxic-gas green Mizunos, and plugged my headphones into my iPhone, calling up my National playlist while discretely ducking out the door.

The morning's offerings were sublimely picturesque. It was the first light of dawn, and the air was thickened from suspended particles of confused desert rain. The cloud cover was varied in texture and hue, and the light that escaped illuminated the sparsely dotted wasteland in vibrant colorations that are visible only when the desert sees rain.

Heading off for the trails through the Phoenix Sonoran Desert Preserve, a hidden oasis around the bend from their house, I was enamored with my good fortune.

I ran a couple of miles up into the hills and then paused near the highest peak. I had a perfect vantage point from which to behold my surroundings for miles and miles beyond. Closing my eyes and focusing my senses, I settled in awe, breathing in the desert shower and the cleansing scent of the dampened creosote. When I opened them again, I marveled at the vertical streaks of dark blue shooting down from pockets of densely packed clouds, obscurely decorating the sky. That empyreal canvas stretching out before me mirrored all the shades of blue in my life.

I perched near the edge and pulled out my phone to capture a panorama of the extraordinarily clouded sky, and to transport back to a moment when I would need to recall peace, harboring proof that it can magnificently rain in the desert. Then I paused one brief moment more to stand quietly in that place, letting my soul soak in the peace. The quiet of my insular reflection was jolted back to harsh reality by the shrill ringing of my phone.

Krista was on the other line—her clear voice intermittently muffled by heart-crushing wails—consoling a miserable little man whom she found crying in a heap outside her bedroom door. Dylan had woken up alone and was devastated when he couldn't find me. I raced back to her place as fast as my feet would carry me, cursing myself for leaving him behind.

Back at her place, I got him some breakfast and turned his spirits around before readying myself for another day of seminar attendance.

I was attending this symposium as the final component of this stage of my educational journey. It was through a specialized group of doctors that I align with, and it tied things more into the treatment planning side, adapting it to the digital technology that I employ. This was also the class at which Steve was lecturing, the gentleman who had asked permission to use my case and saved me that week after Chicago with his kindness.

Steve frequently lectures with this group, and I was excited to have a connection that opened a door for me to meet him in person and pick his brain on the specifics of it all. My underlying intent at seminar attendance had transformed primarily to networking. Throughout my Chicago classes, the contemporaries with whom I did talk shop helped me more than all four weekends of lectures combined. I learn best by having one-on-one conversations with people, and Steve seemed like a genuine talker. I was hoping to engage him afterward for some intellectual dialog.

The day concluded with a happy hour set up for socializing; they offered bowls of popcorn and Sour Patch Kids on a florid outdoor veranda with a bar serving domestic beer and table wine. As it turned out, I didn't have any close friends in attendance, so I started conversing with a doctor from my hometown who was at least a familiar face. A quintessential upper Midwestern dentist, around whom I needed to be Proper Ruby.

I tried to keep engaged and uphold a purely academic conversational style, but I found myself lounging in introspective silence. My senses were trained on scanning the scene and watching for Steve to appear. As soon as his enormous form came into view, I bolted from our group and headed over to his crowd, trying to appear confident and self-assured. I awkwardly embraced him while stepping into their circle and then started talking fast, before my anxiety had a chance to put its foot down.

"Hey, great job today! Thanks for not calling me out as the one in need of assistance in planning that case," attempting to project that I was not intimidated at all by this guy who is a six-foot four brute of a man who looks like a mob boss and had the obvious Italian heritage to back it up.

"Thanks," he said in his boisterous manner. "I appreciate you sharing your case with me. It worked great for my topic, so you helped me out too," he said, shrugging coolly. "So, where do you practice again?" he inquired.

"Fargo, North Dakota," I started, and then I laughed emphatically and added my new favorite line to catch people before they highlight the obvious, "on purpose!"

"What's so bad about that?" he asked, like the idea people freely occupied that frozen land was nothing to bat an eye at.

"Everything!" I delved in with gusto. "Last winter we had ninety consecutive days of sub-zero temperatures; my phone was filled with photos of thermometers registering negative twenty-four degrees or more. Compound that with wind chill and you are in for a real treat!

"Not to mention a wide open expanse allowing for insatiable winds to transport incredible items with ease. A lack of mature trees and forestry to explore. All the unimaginative running routes I've killed. The manufactured neighborhoods stacked one on the other, as far as the eye can see. Countless miles of prairie grass rolling out forever and beyond."

I blathered uncontrollably, words spewing forth so fast that my intellectual processing filter didn't stand a chance. I'd never before been so carefree about admitting my unease, but right then, nothing else mattered. My tongue was loose. Elaborating the minutia of my disenchantment was the only conversation topic I could foster.

I think I have never wanted to be there in the first place, and not having felt the freedom to spread my wings and experience life outside of my home—attach authentic experiences to unfathomable worlds—had rubbed me wrong for too many years. Unsettled displeasure had taken hold of my thoughts, and its matter reigned supreme; there were no reserves left in me to conceal it. Steve stood stone-cold indifferent and took in my soliloquy with fortitude.

When I finished my "*I fucking hate where I live,*" tirade, he measured me with a fatherly frown and said, "Well, if you don't like where you practice so much, why don't you sell and get out?"

A light bulb so dazzling lit up in my brain that my face must have illuminated with bewilderment.

"People do that?" I nearly hollered in shock. To be truthful, I never even considered it an option; the whole concept seemed impossible to me.

"Sure," he bellowed back in agreement. "I'm from Nebraska. I practiced with a group there for eight years before I moved out to Washington. We picked up everything and left. Best thing I ever did. I would do it all again in a heartbeat."

My mind was swimming in that moment. A possibility existed that I could actually leave?

Everyone who practices in my town sets up their individual empire and spends the next twenty-five to thirty years investing heavily in honing their domain. When they are ready to retire, they sell and get out of the game. That is how it's done. Sure, there are parables of dentists abandoning ship, disappearing silently into the night, but those are urban myths to perpetuate fear of mismanaging your practice, not *success* stories. Normal people don't sell and leave. You stick your nose to the steel, you work yourself to the bone, and when you have nothing left in the reserves, you retire. Or you die over a patient in the chair. That is also a thing.

I possessed a heightened awareness of the possible end-product of sticking it out at all costs. Instead of chasing my dreams after graduation, I acquiesced to my mother's insistence that I join Tom's practice—we moved home, bought our forever home, and I took up a position alongside Tom and his son. Only, shit rarely works out as planned.

After a year and a half, it was obvious we were not suitably matched. When I threw up my hands and threw in the towel, I should have taken it one step further and thrown myself out of town. But then, the house market crashed. Logan and I had our front-facing, three-stall garage to uphold and it was simply not the right time.

So, instead, I accepted a position with a medical assistance clinic in a rural town twenty miles away. It was a time of exponential growth. I learned countless clinical skills and was mentored by gifted teachers who gave freely of their talents. After nine months, though, I stagnated. Around the time my discontent was surfacing, I chanced upon an opportunity with a prominent dentist in his progressive, glitzy practice, and seized it. I became part of an aggressively marketed team with the luster of a burgeoning business, and on the outside, it appeared we were the practice of everyone's dreams; only most people's dreams intertwined with nightmares, and I had aligned with the wraiths.

I had three idyllic months of honeymooner's bliss before reality sideswiped me. He became erratic and eventually stopped coming to work. Over the following year, he bounced in and out of rehab and in and out of the clinic like a yo-yo. I did my best to hold down the fort in his absence, but I did so begrudgingly at best.

His idiosyncrasies in conjunction with his rapid rise and high-profile life exposed me to the perverse side of this profession. He was the stereotypical practitioner operating a high-end practice and cracking under the pressure of it all—the demons of a chaotic life tortured his languid soul and led him to the blunt edge of death.

At the time, I did not comprehend his plight. I thought he was just unprofessional. I thought he couldn't pull himself together. I thought he had simply failed. In retrospect, I was naïve to judge. He professed to practice with flawless integrity, compassion, and skill, yet demonized me when I fell short of his impossible goals.

I didn't realize he could be suffering. All I saw was the insistence on chasing an epic rise.

I didn't realize that people work tirelessly facilitating the operations of a pristine empire and burn themselves up in the process. I didn't realize people could be agonized while watching their parents degenerate before their eyes while also being responsible for upholding a perfect lie.

I hadn't entered into my own age of suffering. I didn't know how horrible it would be, watching as the people you hold dear fade away, while everything you thought solid ran like water through cupped hands. I had yet to be brought so far.

A practice purchase opportunity surfaced right at my time of greatest need, and I snatched it up without contemplation, audaciously setting out to build my own brand—to prove everyone who thought I couldn't wrong.

Looking back on that time, I still feel like the all-powerful transformative moment whereby I became a practice owner never transpired. I mimed the actions requisite of one acquiring a business, but the enormity of it never brushed the surface. If I opened my mind to admit the immense weight of the mantle I was taking upon my shoulders, the gravity of it would have flattened me.

Instead, I did as I was advised. I moved through space a step behind the surrounding world, in an alternate slow motion universe, and held everything in perfect Scandinavian stoic disregard. I signed the papers handed to me, smiled and nodded, and kept my eyes trained on the horizon.

I had been growing and honing my practice and trying to be all of the things for three years, and I sensed tendrils of my former partner's vexing fate reaching out to me as surely as those streaks of blue in the sky. I was unclear how much longer I would last.

Steve's insightful words were precisely the thing I needed to hear, confirmation from a very normal and highly successful person that I did not have to keep moving along my path. I honestly never thought at that point in my life a transition out was viable. I believed I had to see things through, come hell or high water—or death. But he was proof. He was a legend. He pulled off what my mind until then refused to dream.

But there was one caveat—he abandoned a group enterprise. I was utterly alone. The sole proprietor of a dental practice that I was scheduled to relocate in a few short months to increase its operational capacity. A practice in which I had invested heavily since its acquisition—a place I called *home*. Could I really sell it and survive?

CHAPTER 33

When I returned from Phoenix, the idea that change was possible became an obsession. Like an amplifying seismic ripple carrying through my world, the notion was an invisible force whose din became a constant distraction. It was as though my subconscious was trying to persuade me to do *something*. Desperate to tease out the root of my unrest, I settled on a memoir project. Freeform writing had proved insightful in my early years, though writing was a muscle I hadn't exercised in a very long time. I sensed a dire need to dig in deep, so I sat down with my lap top and opened the floodgates. And this is what transpired:

My Name is Ruby Carlson. I am a wife, mother, best friend, daughter, sister, doctor, business owner, athlete, and more. I am all of the things.

I am all of the things.

I am *all* of the things.

I am tiring of being all of the things.

I carry myself to the end of each day on an energy source that refuels when I sleep; only, I chase sleep like a reckless lover and, more often than not, he escapes, so I lose myself in my work. In the moment, I rise above everything, but tendrils of black are creeping in there now too. Outwardly I smile, I nod, I exude an air of confidence befitting an amazing woman, but inwardly, a blackness has consumed my soul.

I am feigning the motions of being all of the things.

I am tiring of feigning the motions of being all of the things.

I have two amazing children, and one attentively loving husband who would do anything for me. I have the perfectly situated front-facing home with the requisite three-stall garage. I have a successful dental practice, which is my sole estate staffed by a hand-picked dream team. I am embraced by a community of supportive family and friends. I have achieved nirvana in the sense that what people say they want their perfect life to be, I have it, and more.

I have all of the things.

I have all of the things.

I want none of these things.

Having it all did not stop me from having an affair. I was willing to risk everything I had and everything I was. I was in a place so perfectly crafted that I allowed myself to be swept up in a moment and fall in love with a stranger.

Who *does* that?

Who is so vulnerable they are capable of a surge of emotional overload so vastly consuming it washes over them like a tsunami—dematerializing everything—suspending the grains of their existence and pulling them out to sea, rendering them scattered desultory among an expansive body blanketing the world? What normal, stable person is capable of that shit?

Obvious answer? I wasn't normal and stable. Let's be honest here; that's the only explanation. I had entered into a realm of instability, ergo, I opened myself up to the most destabilizing emotion of all—*passionate love.*

My affair with Nick was an act of desperation, a deafening wake-up-call siren. I yearned to connect with passionate emotion; I needed that injected into my life. And for a fleeting moment of ecstasy, everything transcended everything. To this day, if I could choose my happy place, it would be in his arms. I know no greater high. He was wild and crazy, raw and passionate. Creative, conflicted—and dark. He was the mirror of me.

When I retreat to the oasis of him in my mind, sleep is suddenly attainable. There, in that imaginary land, things are as I wish them to be.

But in reality, I retreated to my reactive mechanism and pushed him away definitively. In losing him, I lost sight of myself. It was the most horrifying thing I've ever experienced. In one weekend I spanned the entire inventory of emotions. I danced with all of the feelings. I started out euphoric at the prospect of new love and finished unhinged, a broken soul. A veritable lifespan of love and loss, stretched out over forty-eight crestfallen hours.

"It is better to have loved and lost than never to have loved at all." Credit to Alfred Lord Tennyson—*Fucking idiot.*

Anyone who is perpetuating that mantra I'd like to punch alongside the head. I do not agree at all. Having loved and lost has opened my eyes to a deep-seated vacancy that I have left unattended too long.

My encounter with Nick resulted in a conflagration. I took that fucking wall down for one second and he leaped in, deconstructed it, and taught me something critical about myself—that I was undeniably, irrevocably capable of experiencing passionate love, and not only capable, fundamentally lacking its presence in my life.

Being now acutely aware of that void, its absence is the only sensation my mind willingly concentrates on. Trying to repress this all-consuming emptiness and project a vigorously fronted persona has been the breeding grounds for a swift unraveling. Like the slackened cables of a vintage sweater, I feel myself coming apart at the seams. I am powerless to stop it. Soon, I will be nothing but a tangled mess of string in an immaterial heap on the floor. I need to halt the unraveling.

Staring down the inevitability of my demise, I contemplated my imminent future paths: I could carry on in this manner, hoping upon hope that the crimpled and coffee-stained fortune cookie fable resting on my desk held true. Time—*time* was the curative pill. Eventually, time will attenuate the disquiet. Eventually, my soul would find peace. Eventually, this will feel authentic and I will no longer be feigning the motions in the life of Ruby.

But what happens then?

To be perfectly honest, this is not the first time my soul has ached for something more; I am no stranger to this place. But previous times were less powerful and never resulted in affairs or overwhelming emotions identifiable as *love*. From the previous bouts of disquiet, I took time and healed. I recovered, and ultimately, I stayed.

My eleven years of marriage can be neatly depicted as rolling along a cyclical pattern: acceptance-settled-disquiet-breakdown-acceptance-settled-disquiet-break-down. If I simply stay here, won't I be doomed to repeat this catastrophic failure? And what if next time it gets worse—how devastating could the next breakdown be?

Can I risk that? There are people who die from trying.

The future reality I've been facing down these past two months is not one I can amiably continue. If I stay this course, I will have to resort to heavy sedatives to tame the raging sea of unrest tossing about in my soul. But life should not be a thing we have to medicate to accept. A life endured that joylessly begs the question: *why endure at all?*

Two months of enduring a clandestine life and I knew that if I stood on the edge of a cliff, I would leap. If a shiny Beretta weighed heavy and cold in my hands, I would raise it up and pull the trigger. If someone captured me and tortured me, ripped the flesh off my body then left me for dead, I would have smiled and thanked them for their kindness. If staying this path equates to death, then what are my other alternatives?

I want to be done feigning the motions of being all of the things.

I have evolved into the person I am today by taking action to please other people and meet their needs, justifying my inaction—my lack of momentum for chasing my dreams—by rationalizing that my agenda must be squandered in order to be self-sacrificing. I cannot rise to the occasion and embrace my authentic self while maintaining this submissive persona.

I am my mother's hopes and dreams; I am her dogmatic religion. I am my father's alcoholism, and I am his crippling anxieties. I am my reserved husband's subdued wife, and I am my children's ordinary mother. I am my in-laws' impeccable practicality. I am everything to everyone—*and no one to myself.* I have never felt granted the wings to soar on my own. I have never freed myself to recklessly dream.

There was a life I envisioned many years ago that was interrupted with traditional matrimony and upper Midwestern maternity, things I swore I would never, *ever* do, but then I caved, believing it was the only way to secure stability for my son. But going down that route has turned me into an eviscerated shell.

Keeping around this version of me is an obvious disservice to my kids. However, my absence would be infinitesimally more devastating. Can I evolve into who I want to be and not ruin who I need to be for them? What's the worst that would happen if I sought out another way? What's the worst that would happen if I *didn't?*

What if I just admit that the life I have been living is so incongruent with the life I dreamed of that it left me in a vulnerable state, walls down and doors open, to being blindsided by an overwhelming cacophony of emotions that I can only identify as *love*?

To continue with the course of that life invariably places me back into the cyclical pattern of acceptance-settled-disquiet-breakdown-acceptance-settled-disquiet-breakdown. Relinquished to a doomed fate. What if I insert change into the cycle at the breakdown? What if I break the pattern and carve out a new life that might not put me back in this place?

I yearn to break away from everything. To go out on my own and discover *who I am,* without the pressure of everyone else's needs and unsolicited counsel prophesizing the follies of my desire. I desperately long to clear the page, clean the slate. Plunge into the wild and force *me* out of this shell. It is way past time, the diaphanous form sheltered inside this frame is desperately trying to claw her way out. She is dying to breathe, dying for release. She will take me down if I don't give her air. To do that, I have to free myself of everything.

At one point or another along the course of life there will be a magic event, an aligning of stars and moons and space and time, and at that moment, you can alter a universe. But a person must possess a distinctive mindset willing to act on that event, and the unique inevitability it presents. You have to be unequivocally prepared to make the leap and approach whatever else comes after with abandon.

The unique mindset was present, everything aligned. I recognized the situation I was facing, and I wanted it more than I wanted a return to my former life. I wanted it more than I wanted air. I wanted it more than anything I have ever wanted in my entire life.

But I am a wife, mother, friend, doctor, business owner, athlete, caretaker, daughter, sister, and more. I am all of the things. To initiate change, I must free myself from the non-essential things, release the hold of the million things holding me here, all the while actively preserving the critical things.

"It's never too late to be what you might have been." Credit to George Eliot—*Fucking Genius.*

I want to change everything.

Careful planning and meticulous execution are essential to doing this right. Throwing my hands up and walking away is not an option. Instead, I will formulate an exit strategy and surreptitiously lay the foundation for a future path more reflective of my dreams. I will hang on in this life as best as I can until I have opened the doors to transition out with grace.

Then I will be free to take flight.
I am going to change everything . . .

End of Book One

ACKNOWLEDGEMENTS

This book was made entirely possible by the overwhelming support of my family and friends.

To Derek. For getting wildly upset with me one New Year's Eve for not taking myself seriously as a writer. For telling me I was a writer first and dentist second in your book, and re-invigorating me to pick back up this work.

To Michelle. For bringing out my very best.

To Britt. I love you. God brought us together when I needed you the most and for that I have a renewed belief in the divine.

To the team at Atmosphere. For finally taking this book off my hands and giving it to the world in this beautiful package. Thank you will never express what that means.

To Grant. I would not be here today without you. Any man who tells a woman on the brink of self-annihilation, writing about affairs and a whole host of other horrible things, "I am honored to be a part of your life at this time, as I truly believe you are doing something revolutionary," deserves a parade and a national holiday. *I love you* does not even get there.

To my boys. For snuggles, and hugs, and five points of contact. For laughter and singing and fights. For opening my heart in a way I never knew possible. For believing I am *your* best mom.

To Emma. You are my soul sister in every sense. Thank you for letting me go and reigning me in. For listening emphatically and non-judgmentally, and just generally hopping on board for all my wild adventures. For keeping up with me seamlessly. I adore you. You altered the course of my life in the most wondrous of ways.

To my Mom. A woman who, despite everything I say, has supported and loved me through this. When I returned from my self-imposed solitude and went to repair the rift, she exhibited grace, compassion, and genuine self-less love in her support for me and this project. For her to see me become a 'real writer' will likely be the thing I am most proud of achieving.

To my sister. You have always provided benchmarks for me to achieve, and I hope that throughout our lives we continue to challenge each other to take new leaps. You are my greatest gift.

To Mariah. When you looked me in the eyes and said "I believe in this book" I nearly cried. Thank you for your faith and advice and direction. Thank you for summer nights on docks and adventures in forests, and always being judgement free.

To Emily. For helping me find the right words. For being the best-friend of a bottle service girl, gifting us a legendary evening.

To Frank. You believe in nothing, but you believed in me. Your friendship has had incalculable impact.

To Eric. You sheltered me when I needed it and made me realize I was normal at a time in my life when I honestly wasn't sure that I was. I owe you big time.

To my team of amazing ladies at Motha Fuckin' Dentistry. I love you; you are my family. You supported me flawlessly through the HARDEST time in my life. When you are having a bad day, always remember, donuts help. Please know I want the best for each and every one of you.

To Michael. Your friendship and counsel have caused me to critically analyze so many aspects of myself, and I truly believe I have been spared a catastrophe, all because of your words. You held a stranger together with irrefutable strength.

To Albert. You had no idea what you were on board for that fateful day in October! I wrote this book to you, you were my audience, the first person to confirm that this was real. Your presence in my life was a gift from the universe.

To Julie. You are a woman of unfaltering strength. I strive to be like you. You are a heroine.

To Piper. Your selfless housing of my family during this time was a gift beyond measure. There is so much of this story that was written from my respite in your guest room. I am eternally grateful for our talks. Through opening up and sharing with you I realized how easy it would be for me to do the same with the world.

To Chris. For treating me like a peer. For sending me amazing photos. For encouraging me to seek the arts.

To Carrie. For tough love. You are amazing and talented and inspirational.

To Aleksandra. For being just awesome.

To Shane. For saying to me "Thank you, I do not usually receive manuscripts with such a strong voice." For saying to me "Just keep writing." For saying to me a million other things. You made me.

To Kevin #1. For showing me the worst night of my life, yet still imprinting forever on my heart.

To Kevin #2. For showing me the best night of my life, and gifting me the world's most memorable text chain.

To Mike. You and I engaged in such profound dialog through my writing process, I owe you a shit ton of gratitude. I carried on writing this story because of you. Thank you.

To Tia. For wild nights of dancing and quiet nights of talking, and ferry rides to Coronado alongside a heart beating in rhythm with mine.

To Megan. Not many women are capable of hanging with me like you do. Your keen eye for detail and artistic vision gave birth to some amazing photography. Thank you for road trips and hiking. Thank you for being my musical soul-mate.

To Tom. For making me real.

To Justin. For interacting with my page in your unique way. You almost always bring a laugh and a smile. Almost.

To Nick. To have a writer of your caliber take my work seriously was the ultimate compliment. You have an amazing gift, and I am honored to be counted among your collaborators.

To Matt. Thank you for supporting me in the publishing of this story. Your kind words had a profound effect on me.

To Both of You: Thank you to the man who starting the breaking of my heart and inspiring me to begin this work. Thank you to the man who broke it completely and compelled me to let it all go. Pain and heartbreak truly are the greatest gifts, as long as you can be attuned enough to use the depths of rock bottom as a solid foundation from which to grow. I hope more than ever that you both did.

To every Uber driver I had while writing this book. Thank you.

To all my other supporting family and friends. Everyone who missed me as I holed up to write this story. Everyone who kept me around, who did not opt to abandon me in my time of greatest need. Everyone who believed in me. I love every person who sees *me* and, in knowing how flawed I am, stays.

ABOUT ATMOSPHERE PRESS

Atmosphere Press is an independent, full-service publisher for excellent books in all genres and for all audiences. Learn more about what we do at atmospherepress.com.

We encourage you to check out some of Atmosphere's latest releases, which are available at Amazon.com and via order from your local bookstore:

Newer Testaments, a novel by Philip Brunetti
All Things in Time, a novel by Sue Buyer
Hobson's Mischief, a novel by Caitlin Decatur
The Black-Marketer's Daughter, a novel by Suman Mallick
The Farthing Quest, a novel by Casey Bruce
This Side of Babylon, a novel by James Stoia
Within the Gray, a novel by Jenna Ashlyn
Where No Man Pursueth, a novel by Micheal E. Jimerson
Here's Waldo, a novel by Nick Olson
Tales of Little Egypt, a historical novel by James Gilbert
For a Better Life, a novel by Julia Reid Galosy
The Hidden Life, a novel by Robert Castle
Big Beasts, a novel by Patrick Scott
Alvarado, a novel by John W. Horton III
Nothing to Get Nostalgic About, a novel by Eddie Brophy
GROW: A Jack and Lake Creek Book, a novel by Chris S McGee
Home is Not This Body, a novel by Karahn Washington
Whose Mary Kate, a novel by Jane Leclere Doyle